Not Art

An Imprint of HarperCollins*Publishers*

Not Art

A NOVEL

Péter Esterházy

Translated by Judith Sollosy

For information, address HarperCollins Publishers, 10 East 53rd Street, New York, NY 10022.

HarperCollins books may be purchased for educational, business, or sales promotional use. For information, please write: Special Markets Department, HarperCollins Publishers, 10 East 53rd Street, New York, NY 10022.

FIRST EDITION

Designed by Suet Yee Chong

Library of Congress Cataloging-in-Publication Data has been applied for.

ISBN: 978-0-06-179296-0

10 11 12 13 14 OV/RRD 10 9 8 7 6 5 4 3 2 1

CONTENTS

1. Poetry and Reality 1

In the hospital 1

My mother, the victim of literature 9

My mother in front of her heavenly referee (fiction) 14

"I'm glad I could help." 16

What are mothers like? 21

2. House and Father 25

Stirring 25

Situation 27

The world according to my mother 33

My father's angels 34

Secret police étude 43

Wound 49

A little milk, a nail 51

3. Love, Love, Love 55

The babbling brook 55

The eternal plane tree 63

4. Factory and Mother 64

Landing a job 64
My mother and sex 67
A piece of cherry (sour) 69
A word (grandmother detour) 70
My mother and soaring 74
1956 75
The soaring, continued 81
The beginning of a beautiful friendship 85
Cont. 89
The time of relics comes to an end 93
A Péter Balassa sentence 96

5. Puskás 97

The visit, 1952 97
My mother pulls down her panties, no,
her stockings, for Bozsik and Puskás 100
The visit, continued 107
On fear (Aunt Emma) 110
Cont. 113
Plus one spieler 117

6. It Comes to Light 119

Lunch, detour: boulevard 119
So it goes 123
The one 124
So it goes, continued 124
Interpolation on eternity 126

Lunch, detour: the Transylvanian auntie 126
My mother dishes it out (aria) 135
Cont. 137

7. Love, Love, Love 140

Adalbert Tóth rings my bell, 2007 140
Adalbert Tóth has his say (aria) 142
The ringing, continued 144
My mother, the soccer fan 145
Cont. 146
Józsi Kaszás, Junior, inspects the field 152
Cont. 155

8. Would You Like to Be a Great Soccer Player, Son? 156

You bet 156
The Ragweed ordeal 159
The field 163
Distaff 166

9. My Mother's Congenial Time Passes 168

10. Love, Love, Love 174

Five seconds 174
This is definitely not true, son 175
The first meeting, detour: Dr. Gruber 175
A Péter Balassa sentence (repetition) 178

Body 179
On remembering 181
That blessed serenity 182
Body, continued 184

11. Farewell to the Characters and Other Linguistic Units 187

Sentences 187
Uncle Lajos pays a visit 193
Hungary's orography and hydrography 199
Dreaming of my mother 200
Paragraphs 203
One more dream 207
On target 207

12. Miki Görög. Epilogue, Or: Another Mother 210

Pascal 210
Ballroom 217

To die is a sin.

—MIHÁLY BABITS

Love is a dung hill, Betty, and I am but a cock that climbs upon it to crow.

—ROB ROY

. . . the essence of my rather confused maneuvers to fence in the approaching reality is to exhaust it the way we exhaust an olive, let's say, before sticking it on the fork . . .

—JEAN-PHILIPPE TOUSSAINT: *CAMERA*

Not Art

1.

Poetry and Reality

IN THE HOSPITAL

In the name of the mother and the son!* This is not what woke me, because I wasn't sleeping, this sentence startled me out of my stupor, this scream, this shriek which sounded triumphant and resigned at the same time, demanding, but certainly head-strong, yet self-effacing, too, like a prayer. I knew the voice well.

I lay in bed, between pillows, as the poet says,† and yet martial-like, as if with a gunshot wound. I've often wondered why in so-called contemporary Hungarian fiction it should be so difficult to imagine someone getting shot. And if they are, it's never the narrator! Though come to think of it, he could subsequently recover and go on narrating to his heart's content, couldn't he?

* A take on the first sentence of Esterházy's novel *Helping Verbs of the Heart* (*A szív segédigéi*, 1985), "In the name of the Father and the Son . . ."

† A reference to a patriotic poem by Hungary's national poet Sándor Petőfi (1822–1849), who wanted to die on the battlefield and not between pillows. (His wish was granted during the anti-Habsburg war of independence in 1849. His grave has never been found.)

He'd be lying in a hospital, like me, and he'd be in a daze about where he was and why, like me, the painkillers and tranquilizers not having worn off yet, the only fixed point of reference being the police detective standing (talking? arguing?) by the door.

Whereas we're gradually gaining familiarity with shootouts ourselves. In the nineties, the Ukrainian and the Albanian mafia, they say, were battling it out in Budapest. Or for Budapest. I heard shooting myself near my house on Szentendre Road. It wasn't until next morning's papers that I learned that that's what it was; at the time, it being evening, I assumed it was another one of those parvenu neighborhood shindigs, a privately financed fireworks. Exasperated, I kept my eye peeled to the dark sky, but to no avail; there was nothing there but the dark sky, a fact I noted with glee. Later things settled down. The Albanians won. I think. Which means that now we have Albanian mafiosi. I also can't understand why we need an import mafia. What do the Albanians have over us? Or the Ukrainians? Because, provided that we consider the Ukrainians Russians and the Russians communists, it's a cinch to think of them as the bad guys. Still, the people of Bartók and Puskás,* that they shouldn't be able to whip up a piddling mafia of their own, I find that curious. Or else we already have one, except they're modest and have integrated themselves into the European community. Though come to think of it, why didn't the Albanians integrate themselves into us? Puskás with a great big Magnum, that's not so hard to imagine. My mother was the only one, I think, who called him

* Béla Bartók (1881–1945) was one of the preeminent composers of the twentieth century. Ferenc Puskás (1927–2006), the legendary Hungarian footballer, is considered one of the greatest football players of all time.

Ferenc (and not Junior). Admittedly, Bartók is a tougher case. Still, even if at first it may seem the obvious thing to do, it would be a slipup, putting a delicate lady's gun in his hand. We'd have to do some research and find out whether, despite their delicacy, there isn't a big hulking specimen among them, or, better still, barbarous*—it looks for all the world like a piece of fine jewelry, but the police inspector could tell you a thing or two about the smashed skulls and penetrated chests. A locomotive could pass through it, what pass?, dash full speed, gentlemen, a veritable tunnel through the chest!

I don't see why a gifted nation like ours shouldn't have a mafia all its own. The requisite passion is there, and so is the requisite suffering, and also the requisite corruption. Because, the Finns may be resourceful, with a high GDP, but they're not sufficiently corrupt. By the way, at one time I used to stop my car by the traffic light at the foot of Rózsadomb where that bigwig businessman was shot while waiting for the light to turn. On February 11, 1998, at 5:44 p.m., an old Mitsubishi Lancer stopped next to his car, a young man sitting next to the driver got out, his every gesture calm and resolute, like a plumber, twentyish, by trade a hired assassin, he slammed the door shut, skirted the Mitsubishi, and with his Agram 2000 submachine gun equipped with a silencer, he let loose, discharging thirty bullets, if one, into the victim's head and neck, who, like always, had a gun on him, but this time it didn't do him much good—which, come to think of it, could be the cue for my favorite .38-caliber Smith & Wesson

* An indirect reference to Bartók's *Allegro Barbaro for Solo Piano*, 1911, one of his most frequently performed compositions. Emerson, Lake and Palmer played it in rock style with organ, bass, and drums.

to make an appearance—in short, he didn't even have time to shield his face with his hands, and though they say he was on his guard every moment of every day, they say, and knew his mortal enemies (this was part and parcel of the business he was in), he must've felt safe in the afternoon rush hour, because he didn't take his bodyguards with him. Meanwhile, the Mitsubishi took off, not yet on the green, yet just barely on the red, and the young man disappeared among the late-afternoon crowd in the direction of the bookstore where I've been known to make an occasional appearance myself.

Our Hungarian book offerings beyond the country's borders are impressive. For instance, Hungarian writers in the former Yugoslavia know a lot more about killing than we do from the motherland; they had the NATO bombings, don't forget, not to mention the Balkan war as such. I'm a child of peacetime. Which is ridiculous; probably a lot more people get killed in peacetime than in war, for private reasons, anyway. Or take *Pulp Fiction*. Or films as such. Brains go flying, squirting, splattering blood with such matter-of-fact gusto, anyone would think they were in one of those countless gastro-turistico shows on TV (motto: *Travel and enjoy, or the World as antipasto*).

I closed my eyes again, I reclosed them. The operation, the fact that they had sliced into my flesh, that they had carved me up—the miraculous life of a carved-up turkey*—that they had cut into me, this wore me out; or perhaps I should say it wore my body out. For instance, I felt that if I were to make just one bad move, my leg would immediately cramp up. I was especially wary

* A reference to the author's book *The Miraculous Life of a Little Fish* (A Halacska csodálatos élete, 1991).

of my left calf, as if that were the weak point, the inferior dam over which the frothy waves of pain would crash, though I had bestowed this flattering role on my calf only because of my recollections, because it's my calf that used to cramp up on me. One bad move—this preyed on my mind more than the foreseeable "sudden, convulsive, involuntary contraction" of the muscles; in short, I had no idea what form this bad would take, and so I had to regard everything as bad, every possible move. And so, I didn't. I lay rigid and frightened, which I knew was a mistake (bad).

This mistake, this guilt-ridden Catholic angst that comes from living in a perpetual state of wrongdoing, hung over me like a storm cloud. On the other hand, the fact that the fatigue was so unequivocally bound up with the body filled me with hardly justifiable good cheer. Grinning, I opened my eyes. I had my own room, which was good, though it isolated me from the rest of humanity. Now and then mysterious sounds filtered in from the corridor. Plus the unmistakable lighthearted laughter of a woman, as if that woman, the one with the laugh, were standing by my side. This was the most disturbing, the most unsettling thing of all. My mother was standing in the door, neither in nor out, with nurse Emma, and they seemed to be deep in conversation. Nurse Emma was aloof and severe, and I trusted her implicitly. For some reason she seemed to have a poor opinion of me, but—from a sense of professionalism—she, too, kept it under wraps.

We're taking those stitches out today, she announced one morning. It was snowing outside, the flakes as big as in a fairy tale.

When?

Curiosity killed the cat, she replied, looking at me as if her words had surprised her. Years ago, waiters used to ask how many slices of bread you had with your meal. At which my father, when he could still talk, always, like a mean-spirited joke, said, curiosity killed the cat. I wrote this down somewhere already, but never mind, it's what this curiosity killed the cat brought to mind, and I was grateful to nurse Emma for it.

Is it going to hurt?

No more than sex. Her deadpan expression told me that if I were to allow myself the luxury of anything double-barreled now, she'd slap me. Or shoot me. But definitely, she would demand satisfaction. There would be hell to pay.

My mother allowed herself—still, and from then on—to wear her yellow turban, the headgear that clearly indicated her status as a so-called gentlewoman. To sport it. Not that she was playing at being a gentlewoman, she was—I think—past playing, she's not playing at anything, she's a very old lady now, almost ninety; and yet, she was not just an old lady with formidable energies and an outrageous yellow hat, she made sure to indicate that by all odds this old woman had at one time been a gentlewoman. Perhaps, at times, even a fine lady. That there had been a time—a secret time, I know—when she was inventoried as a fine lady. . . . Though that's just it, who did the inventory? In Eastern Europe, the second half of the twentieth century did not favor fine ladies, not that my mother minded very much. Still—in that secret, nonofficial time—she'd always let on that, among other things, she's that, too, a fine lady, that's how she inventoried—herself.

The terra firma for the flippant finery (sorry for the alliteration, it just slipped out) was a contraption made of felt (a potty, the insensitive Hungarian male would say), and the turbanity was worked over that. Mother bought it in Kígyó utca, in the

Inner City, at Bozsik's.* When he ended his career (or as my mother likes to say, or, rather, impatiently corrects me: he didn't end it, son, and they didn't make him end it, it just did, it was absorbed by the fetid dreariness of the sixties), the second brightest light (or as my mother says, or, rather, corrects me, screeching, the third!) of the Mighty Magyars opened a hat shop. Or was it a knit shop?

Cucukám—the only one my mother called by his affectionate nickname—look at me. This won't do. I look like a worn-out Catholic mother of four.

Oh, Aunt Lilike.

Look, son, I'm fifty years old. So don't Aunt Lilike me. Uncle Bozsik. Bozsik blushed. I need something outlandish in a moderate price range, Cucukám. And then the legendary player, capped a hundred times for the national team, came up with this turbanoid relic for my mother. If the Catholic Church hadn't crossed swords, or, rather, paths with Saint Stephen,† instead of her favorite steed, we'd probably be burying her with her faithful turban.

My mother couldn't have cared less about mother clichés, and so at times she used them in full earnest, without irony or ridicule, hanging on to them for dear life; at other times she mocked them as if she were above them, and at such times, she was. She and nurse Emma seemed to be arguing about some-

* József "Cucu" Bozsik played right halfback for the legendary Mighty Magyars, the national select football team of the 1950s. Like so many of his teammates, he was known nationwide by his nickname.

† King Saint Stephen (c. 975–1038) was the first king of Hungary. During his reign he united the pagan Magyar tribes of the Carpathian Basin to create a Hungarian Christian state.

thing, two serious faces in the half-open door shooting glances my way. A commonplace, but commonplaces are true—another commonplace; and this, too; and so on: and perhaps *in the end*, i.e., *just after* a semicolon, the *n*th in an infinite series of semicolons, the assertion will *suddenly* say something new: this is how I imagine the world, as a sooner or later world, where the black holes do not swallow up information after all—in the presence of his mother, a man will revert back to being a child; even though he's fifty-eight, let's say, his status is that of a child once again, though admittedly, the difference between one child and another can boggle the mind. Besides, on a hospital bed you have no age, you're an object lacking a date, and you can't hope to confront the unknown threat that is—clearly—lying in wait for you here with the exuberance of youth, nor can you console yourself by slipping inside the protective cocoon of old age, hoping that only what *can* happen will happen; there is nothing, just the bed, the bedpan, nurse Emma, stuff like that. And my mother.

Sluggish with the aroma of split peas, the northwestern breeze wafted sentence fragments my way. Lunch was good: the soup of indeterminate nature, it tasted like vegetable soup, if anything, the split pea purée, as if we were back in the sixties, the first edible split pea of my life!, and the minced meat patty prepared the crudest possible way: coarse, chunky and too spicy, but in the direction I'm partial to—I was chewing and spitting out bits of black pepper and garlic. It felt good.

Because, my dear, a mother is always a mother. And her child is always her child. Such is the fate of the mother and the son.

But the professor is not a . . . a . . . a child anymore.

Good Lord! You're calling my son professor? What's the world coming to?

It was his idea, because we didn't know what to call him. Initially he said he doesn't care, as long as it's not Feri. Which we didn't understand. That's when he made the suggestion, adding that in Italy everyone calls him professor anyway.

My mother waved it off. I closed my eyes. An electric shock. I thought I could hear the twang of the muscle snapping in the back of my left thigh, my body went rigid, and I broke out in a cold sweat. If this isn't like being shot (underhandedly), then I don't know what is. There's even been a shooting in the Inner City over a parking spot. The bullet holes are still there in the public garage, like the pockmarks from '56 on the walls of buildings, except the latter have a loftier aura; they've been there a longer time, and they have been visible for a longer time, whereas nobody wanted to remember them, neither we, nor they.

MY MOTHER, THE VICTIM OF LITERATURE

In my last book, meaning the one before the last, because in the meantime *Rubens** had come out, there's a scene where I'm explaining the offside rule to my mother, who is lying on her deathbed. Perhaps I am not exaggerating when I say that this scene is *highly* effective. Let's fix in the mind's eye the "self-sacrificing and much suffering" mother, my mother, tubes sticking out of her, "a curious, remote object with tubes coming out of it in complex configurations and wind whistling through the

* *Rubens and the Non-Euclidian Women* (Rubens és a nemeuklideszi asszonyok, 2006). The book the author is referring to as his "last" is *Journey to the Depths of the Eighteen-Yard Line* (Utazás a tizenhatos mélyére, 2006), his tribute to soccer and to his father, a great soccer fan.

sunken lips," her eyes are closed, but you can tell she's not sleeping, and she's not dead, you can tell that, too, her soul is still intact (more than a breath but less than a proof of God), and yet something has irrevocably changed—don't say irrevocably when referring to me—has irrevocably changed, my mother is on her way, it's not that she's lost weight as we'd naturally conclude seeing her sunken cheeks, the flabby sagging of the skin and that white that could hardly be called white, which gives off light in reverse, absorbing the light, the light of the eyes, sucking in the whole world, annihilating everything; it does not feel good looking at her, and it is impossible not to. It's the proportions that had shifted. *Everything was distorted.*

I hate to say this, but she grew a face like a horse (in those books of mine in which she lay on her deathbed). Before the alterations set in, she looked remarkably like Queen Elizabeth, they were the spitting image of each other, or if not spitting, which might be construed as filial partiality, yet image just the same. (My sister and brothers even discovered our mother's beauty in Éva Ruttkai's own;* our lack of objectivity was based on the similarity of their hairstyle, I guess; at one time they wore their hair in an almost identical fashion; the way they wore it, there was something of a true gentlewoman in it, though by true gentlewoman we had in mind mostly the smell—scent, son, scent—scent. Concretely, perfume. Though we didn't call every woman who used perfume a gentlewoman, every gentlewoman used perfume. As for Ruttkai, we didn't even have reliable infor-

* Éva Ruttkai (1927–1986) was a popular Hungarian stage and movie actress known for her beauty, her sex appeal, and the crown of reddish hair that she wore with exceptional flair.

mation about the way she smelled. Years later I stood next to her onstage. That's when I saw what a thespian bow entails, the intricate system of interconnected motions, and though the routine is there, you must pay very close attention. I told her that she looked like my mother. She smiled as if she hadn't heard. But at the end of the night, she called over to me just the same that I should give her regards to my dear mother. I don't remember if I conveyed it or not.) In short, she bore a close resemblance to the British queen, because when I asked anybody, does she look like her?, or more to the point, she looks like her, doesn't she?, they all said, without exception (practically snapping their fingers), now that you mention it or, more to the point, a remarkable semblance!, even though in Hungary we rarely think (on our own initiative) of the queen of England; the sixties and the seventies of the previous century were not spent in conjuring up the surprisingly unaristocratic, refined yet not overdelicate features of the queen of all the Brits. From time to time she would appear on the news between two guards in bearskins, I just called them beehives, and then mostly to myself, though sometimes I would actually cry out, just like Mommy! I had a color postcard of her, again between two beehives. I still have it, I use it as a bookmark, and I look at it as if, for some reason, my mother were a queen. Got elected, if unexpectedly and only with a slight majority, yet to general acclaim, on the icy Thames.* Queen Lilike! To your knees, dogs! Her chin grew longer on the

* King Matthias Corvinus (1443–1490), the legendary Renaissance monarch, humanist, and hero of many folktales in which he goes among his subjects in disguise, was elected on the frozen ice of the river Danube on January 24, 1458, by 40,000 Hungarian noblemen.

hospital bed, her eyes the size of walnuts. The shifting proportions were most evident in the nose, her younger brother's nose looking out of my mother's countenance, a fleshy, robust, oafish nose out of the pinched, scrubbed, weathered face. A Falstaffian protrusion on a gothic base.

This is what we should see with the mind's eye.

There's a translucent veil of sweat shifting on her brow with its leaden weight as if she had just finished some hard menial task, as if to bring news of the hardship of decades of drudgery, her damp locks hanging over her forehead, hanging limp (like in a Mándy novella),* while on the sides, in the back, and on the top it's disheveled, like the ruffled feathers of a bird. It's shorter than usual. And then, in that book, I sat on the side of her bed, her thighs on fire even through the blanket. Let's not forget, she was dying. At first I didn't want to say anything, because I had nothing to say. In that cheap silence, amid the slurping of the machines keeping my mother, my mother's body alive, I recalled her laughter, my mother's rarer than rare laughter. Smiling, yes—she's smiling like a barley loaf on the oven peel: this rather less often—a cheerful glance, yes, but laughter, that was rare. Bubbling with laughter, that was rare. Screaming with laughter. "And then my mother screamed with laughter": no such sentence exists, I thought sitting on the side of her bed.

From time to time my sister and I (meaning my younger brother, specifically, one of my two younger brothers, the one I generally turn into a younger sister in my books, I make a younger sister of him, my reasons owing less to in-depth psychology than

* Iván Mándy (1918–1995) is known for his minimalist style and sharp eye for detail. Numerous of his characters have hair hanging over their foreheads.

to practical considerations, a concern with dramatic structure: I don't need all four of us, three directions will usually suffice), we used mother to test the macho preconception whereby a woman's brain is constitutionally incapable of comprehending the offside rule. We tried to ram it into her, but to no avail. At such times she would laugh (I can't rule out the possibility that this is why we kept up this infantile joke), or rather giggle, she giggled merrily, practically chortled, that she doesn't get it, no, no, no. I don't get it!, she announced triumphantly, glancing at us as if we were her good children, and at such times we felt that that's what we were.

I stroked the blanket. So then, this now is my last chance, even if, in a sense, every moment is the last, given that it's unique. Which is enough to make one reflect. People who reflect to begin with look at life, to begin with, from the vantage point of death, or so I've read. The last chance to make her understand—in what was *de facto* the last moment—that darned offside rule. I knew no shame, I began murmuring to her, like a prayer addressed to a supposedly empty sky, first keeping strictly to the definition—how it always made her laugh: the mo-ho-ho-ho-ment of ke-he-heeck-off!, I know!, and tears of laughter rolled down her cheeks!—followed by the fundamental problems, the familiar traps, rarities, specialties, followed by the story of the offside, its history and ontology, its psychology and mystery, miracle and wonder, the brilliance behind the apparent simplicity, these were the last words I addressed to my mother, which, I felt, had at last not fallen on barren soil; her lashes stirred and she squeezed my hand, just like in the movies. I wouldn't have wanted her to stand in front of her heavenly referee unprepared.

MY MOTHER IN FRONT OF HER HEAVENLY REFEREE (FICTION)

My mother would be standing there, between two curlicue clouds, like the English queen between her beehives, shifting her ground, glancing about her, and there'd be a light friendly in progress between the angels and the novelists, let's say. Which smells to me like the game's been fixed, of course, because we know that the vanguard of novelists will end up in hell (or who knows, it all depends on who makes the decisions; it's Saint Peter, they say, he's the one standing at the pearly gates—why beat about the bush, a simple doorman, even if celestial, except with less [more?] power, in which case, let's face it, only Cervantes might get off, but only because of a misunderstanding; on the other hand, the Lord's no bureaucrat, and also—we may as well face it—He's all-knowing, so He'd know, and He'd feel, too, that in the final analysis, and who'd be more interested in finality than the Lord, all those dubious, questionable characters are in fact busy singing the praises of Creation, helping to finish the work of Creation, and even though it may appear that (a saint?) I am pointing a finger at myself, the situation is more complicated, alas, because what's the situation if, plainly speaking, the novel was conceived in love, but not so the writer's life?; for instance, it is often said, I've heard it said, that a certain writer is identical with his work, but in that case, where is his life?, the Lord raises the work aloft like a boulder, and the writer's pale, frightened life, his life remnants, having never seen the light of day, come scurrying out from under it like so many half-blind, frightened bugs); in short, there's my mother, freshly recruited into heaven, standing by the handle of the Big Dipper, at the eighteen-yard line, with the archangel Michael chasing a through ball at right flank, from next to the cumbersome Chesterton (the *seemingly* cumbersome Chesterton, because the next instant he bounds up to the archangel and kicks him in the shin like nobody's business, like only Gabi Tóth could, who tried to teach me—in my novels—how to commit a foul without the referee being any the wiser, but it was like water off a duck's back, even if, speaking from personal experience, certain individuals, mostly gifted Hungarian writers, claim the opposite); in short, at that juncture the Lord, they haven't even been formally introduced, they haven't even exchanged greetings yet, shoots my mother a questioning look, the Lord's a pro at this, this questioning look, in short, was that an offside or my backside, *nagyságos asszonyom*? (Which audaciously assumes that the Lord is Hungarian. But why couldn't the Lord be Hungarian when *all* the atomic physicists are? Or else He's not Hungarian just speaks Hungarian? Good heavens, that was a quote, but maybe we shouldn't drag the Lord into this. It's possible that He spoke Hungarian only with my mother, as a sign of His respect.) My mother standing there like Baalam's ass, I wouldn't have wanted that, then she'd start giggling like a schoolgirl, meanwhile Chesterton has made mincemeat of the archangel, dear Lord, my mother would say to the Lord, who doesn't always have a sense of humor, and in this case He'd be right, the offside is no joke, it's not something to be taken lightly (*offside or not offside*, Lucifer had jested, and though he was right, look where it got him; they wouldn't put up with frivolity of this kind with respect to the subject), dear Lord, couldn't we talk about something else? The universe is so vast. I wouldn't have wanted that.

"I'M GLAD I COULD HELP."

The killing off (not a stylistic *faux pas*!—from time to time such things must be pointed out, because language forges ahead like a wild boar, it goes after its own head, and, well, who can *really and truly* see into that?), I didn't ask permission, but I did tell mother about it. The expression "killing off" is hers, too, which is not surprising; after all, I'm writing in my mother tongue. She said the same to nurse Emma, you know, dear, from time to time my son evidences great delight in killing me off. Nurse Emma's face remained a blank. She caught only the tail end of the previous regime, yet retained an old-fashioned regard for the arts, especially literature, a sort of antiquated, touching solemnity, respect, as if she were the land of avid readers all rolled into one, as if today's writers were all veritable Petőfis and Mikszáths,* and as such I was also the object of this awe, all the while that she went about her business not rudely, yet with unpleasant objectivity. She didn't make an exception of me, she just went about her business. She thought of my books with awe, not concretely, just in general, not *Fancsikó és Pinta*,† but my being a writer, which for her must have been like some enchanted castle hover-

* Sándor Petőfi's "National Song" was said to have been the rallying cry that inspired the 1848 Hungarian uprising against the Habsburgs. Kálmán Mikszáth (1847–1910), the son of lesser nobles, was a leading novelist much admired for the compassion he showed for the ordinary folk and for the satiric tone with which he treated the bourgeoisie and the aristocracy. He, like Petőfi, is still widely read.

† *Fancsikó és Pinta* (1976) was Esterházy's first foray into literature. An instant success, it described the escapades of a young boy's two imaginary friends.

ing in colorful glory between earth and sky (in the background palm trees, plus Kazinczy* or, better yet, Goethe), but she didn't think of me with awe. She could've been, but was not, a snob. Not in the least.

My mother's death has come in handy, if I may use this possibly impertinent expression, whereas it's not, it's just objective, it really has come in handy; it was clever of me to think of it, cunning, with helping verbs† (plus lots of Handke quotes, because his mother really died, which shows on the sentences of his book *A Sorrow Beyond Dreams*) nearly thirty years now! I remember that day in August as if it were yesterday. A bitter cold descended on the city, and though there was no snow and the cars had their summer tires and the clocks daylight saving time, everything seemed cold as ice, inside and out. Death, or, to revert (with undying gratitude!) to my mother's expression, the killing off, turned out to be a fruitful authorial conceit. Pow (or varoom!), it was like instantly plunging into a deep, dark, very deep, very dark well, and I was able to imagine myself in the situation in no time; I haven't got much of an imagination, but even with the little that I have I was able to make it appear (to me, at any rate) as if it had really happened, as if my mother had really died, which, from the point of view of the psychology of art (whose autobiographical, self-analytical, self-resigned

* The writer and poet Ferenc Kazinczy (1759–1831), who hailed from the nobility, was the foremost agent in the regeneration of the Hungarian language and literature. His name is connected today to the extensive Language Reform of the nineteenth century, when thousands of words were coined or revived.

† A reference to the author's *Helping Verbs of the Heart* (A szív segédigéi, 1985), about the death of his mother.

and self-pitying motifs, i.e., its bellyaches I'd rather not bore the reader with, nor excite him either, for that matter); in short, this state is highly serviceable, for the painful words come of their own accord, if come they must, if that is what is called for; no, not of their own accord, just naturally, and possibly it's not even the pain that imbues the words with content, but that certain something between orphanhood and fear, let's say no more than that, it's this that brings on the pain, or whose icy grip on the heart is mercifully mitigated by the pain.

In short, on the one hand I experienced the intricate stirrings of the presence of pain and the lack of pain in an authentic and creative manner, while on the other, and possibly not independently of the former, this book of mine, written twenty years ago, was the first to break out, as we Finno-Ugrians like to say, of the jailhouse of our language. To this day, my mother talks about its success with amusing fanfaronade, it wouldn't have made quite such a splash without me, son, isn't that right? I'm glad that with my so-called death I could help further your cahreer. With an *ah*, as in tahxi. And I just stared at her enchanting hazel eyes. She got them from grandfather, whom I never knew, and extrapolating from those eyes, I am truly sorry. I was glad that she was glad; still, when I read that the book was a memorial to my mother, or that a very private pain had taken spectacular literary shape in it, I couldn't help pulling a face.

What mother?!, what pain?!, I bristled.

What do you mean what mother?! How many mothers have you got, she laughed. Again, I couldn't help looking at her eyes. See this? They say that you've finally grown up, that I give your book depth, and that you're not just clowning now, you don't just have words, you have a mother, too. And kindly finish your meal.

I don't wanna.

Want to.

What's the difference. Besides, you're just a bunch of words yourself!

I wouldn't go into that, son, if I were you.

Fine.

The family tried not to have an opinion about my working hypothesis. Families that get caught up in literature don't have an easy time of it; for one thing, they resent being caught up to begin with, then they resent it if what's on the page accords with the facts, what they consider the facts, and also, if they don't accord with the facts. Surprisingly, Uncle Sárli was the first to raise his voice against the family's self-imposed forbearance, Uncle Sárli, my mother's younger sister's husband, who never had an opinion about anything, the world's too quick for him, my mischief-minded brothers and I used to say. He never, ever harmed anyone; he was *sweet* in his commerce with the world, polite to the point of parody. I think it was these empty forms that lent him his bearing. He was exceptionally handsome; when they were resettled in the countryside, a woman from the ÁVÓ* had the hots for him, but didn't get from *a* to *b*. On the other

* The ÁVÓ (Államrendőrség Államvédelmi Osztálya—State Security Department of the State Police), the main arm of the ÁVH (Államvédelmi Hatóság—State Security Authority), was the much-feared Hungarian political police active between 1946 and 1957. Following the Soviet model, its official function was the persecution of the enemies of communism and the protection of its leaders.

hand, this information comes courtesy of my aunt. The secret police woman is supposed to have ordered him up to her office in Hatvan, she sent a car for him, my aunt, my always elegant and aloof aunt (she was as elegant as if the dictatorship of the proletariat weren't even around), dropped to the ground, flung her arms around the driver's legs and begged, screaming, that they shouldn't take her husband away, please, Comrade driver, I beg you, have mercy on us. The driver was not from the secret police, he was working for the city council at Hatvan as an odd jobs man, he may have even known that the husband of this hysterical woman was on his way to a tryst and not an interrogation, possibly even my aunt knew; be that as it may, the driver held her in contempt for her histrionics, and though he was constitutionally a gentle, even-tempered soul, with time he came to feel his unofficial power, certainly that people were afraid of him, which at first embarrassed him, then it didn't; he freed his legs from my aunt's dramatic clutches, fuck off, he growled, and as for you, damn you, get in, and he shoved Uncle Sárli into the car as if he were with the secret police after all; the secret police woman made Uncle Sárli an offer as clear as the sun at high noon, whereupon he was supposed to have said, madam, I am living in holy matrimony, wherein my hands and feet and other bodily parts are bound. He liked old texts. The secret police woman gave him a backhanded slap; she must've known her business, because for the rest of his life, at the most unexpected and embarrassing moments, at lunch, at a concert, at Mass, his nose would start bleeding. The blood came flowing from my uncle in buckets, the blood of East European history. In no time at all his dress handkerchief was soaked through because, and this goes without saying, it was always peeking out gallantly, or maybe, I don't know, more like meticulously, I don't know where dress handkerchiefs peek out of gallantly. Excuse the nuisance, he'd say, apologizing, when this happened. As children, we looked down on him, because we could tell that he was weak, which meant we could do it, and we did. But as we grew older, we came to like him more and more. And also, we discovered the strength behind the weakness. And the courage.

The novel describing his sister-in-law's death shocked him, it was the first time I saw him go unsmiling for any length of time, and it was the first time he wouldn't look me in the eye, whereas before he'd always do so, steadily, openly, innocently—and in a thoroughly misleading way, because the duration and intensity of his gaze seemed to suggest that he wanted something, whereas Uncle Sárli, I believe, never wanted anything as such, his life just happened to him, and he drifted along. Had he been disillusioned, he'd have turned into a dandy of sorts, ironic, resigned, cynical. But that was not in his nature. He had no illusions, so he had no illusions to lose. He lived on the surface—the two-dimensional man, one might jest. He looked into space in front of him and said: This won't do. He said the same thing about daylight saving time. It is either eight o'clock or it is nine o'clock, it can't be eight o'clock and then we say, from now on it's nine o'clock. That just won't do.

Mother liked the book.

WHAT ARE MOTHERS LIKE?

It may sound frivolous, and so it is, frivolous, fickle and foolhardy, careless, reckless, whimsically inappropriate to its subject, but not irresponsible, because it is true: as far as I'm concerned, my mother's absurdity is like the concentration camp for Imre Kertész,* it is natural, because that's how I came to know, how we came to know the world. I took for granted, I learned to take for granted that my mother would always (day and night, night and day, year in, year out [*habitually*], constantly, without exception [*invariably*], continually [*always*], regularly, regular [*chiefly dial.*], always and evermore [*arch.*], ever and anon, forever, forever and a day [*coll.*], *ora e sempre* [*It.*], endlessly, incessantly [*constantly*], invariably and habitually, hourly, daily [*perpetually*], nonstop, around the clock, persistently, customarily and without exception [*by force of habit*], this is getting out of hand [and will], without a break, in one stretch, in one go—*Roget's Thesaurus*) talk about soccer, comparing everything to it, always coming round to it in the end. My mother was the first mother in my life, little wonder that I thought all mothers were like this. The world is like this, that mothers are like this. We call them mommy, they have warm necks and warm shoulders where we bury our head, and they smell nice. Mothers are always (day and night, night and day, year in and year out, etc.) busy looking after us, always keeping an eye on us, and this obviously fills them with joy. They're bursting with joy. The color of their eye, it's like the overcast sky on a sunny day. In the depths of their laughing eyes we—later—discover the sadness, too, the nagging, inexhaustible and persistent fountain of pain whose object remains a mystery to us, unless it's the laughter itself. They feed us, they dress us,

* A reference to *Fateless* (Sorstalanság, 1975), the semiautobiographical novel by Nobel Prize laureate Imre Kertész (b. 1929), in which he describes his experiences in the concentration camps of Auschwitz, Buchenwald, and Zeits through the innocent eyes of a young Jewish boy.

they kiss us. This is how our day begins, they kiss us, that's what wakes us. Or we wake to the sight of them sitting on the side of our bed, holding our hand. Or they lay their feather-light palm on our chest, on top of our beating hearts, and that's what wakes us. In any case, when we open our eye, their face fills up the entire visible world. The world. Later there will come a brief period when we won't like it (it will drive us up the wall) when they touch us. We won't have to tell them, they'll know and they will feel it, too, and they will stop short in the doorway, but we don't see this yet, nor do we see them standing there at leisure, feasting their eyes on us, if we did, this too would drive us up the wall, these lyrical maternal cameo appearances, nor do we know yet about the fleeting, satisfied smile, though we know of course that in secret they look proudly our way, veritably smacking their lips, but only when we're fast asleep do they lose their self-control and sense of proportion to such an extent that they actually believe that what they are looking at (for the record: us!) is a source of solace to them; they see a universal solace in the not so terribly acned adolescent whom they know better than to address; we are still floating in a haze of dreams when gentle and shimmering, as if we were hearing the voice of an angel, resplendent, soft, fleeting, yes, our name, tremulous, we hear an angel whisper our name, in response to the stirring that ushers in our first stretch the mothers stir as well, lapsing back into that other life where we cannot follow, a place of shadows that never really interested us in the first place; we hear our name from the skies and so we do not understand, just accept as a logical *development* that the good that takes its start as we gently slip back into the world is in some way connected to our mother. Our fathers are in far-off rooms conversing with angels of their own. Also, in the evening mothers tell us stories, that's what they're like. A story is a beautiful, cheerful and edifying narrative, our mothers told us (which instructs and entertains), and is true, yes?, that's one way of putting it, son, and is furthermore exclusively about soccer. Plus anything related to it. The goal post, for instance. Goal posts are made of pine—these days it's aluminum, and the ball doesn't bounce like it should!, a couple of congenital twins, Néró Gál and Hektor Gál from Sopron, supply the entire country, not much of a business, but steady. I know them well, son, I knitted them sweaters, two green turtlenecks. It's a bit much, these congenital goal post makers in their turtlenecks. Most of the stories are about a soccer player called Puskás, who came from a poor family, went to see the world, and then became its king.*

* Ferenc Puskás (1927–2006) was a legendary Hungarian footballer and manager who is regarded as one of the greatest soccer players of all time, and the best shooter in football history. During the 1950s he was captain of the legendary Hungarian national team, alternately known as the Golden Team, the Magical Magyars, the Magnificent Magyars, and the Mighty Magyars. The team, which included Ferenc Puskás, József Bozsik, László Budai, Jenő Buzánszky, Zoltán Czibor, Gyula Grosics, Nándor Hidegkuti, Sándor Kocsis, Mihály Lantos, Gyula Lóránt, and József Zakariás, went unbeaten for thirty-three consecutive games, a record that still stands today. In 1953 they beat the English 6–3 at Wembley, where the English team had not lost a match for ninety years. Thanks to his likable and forthright character, Puskás was not only a national hero but a much-loved sportsman, hence his affectionate nickname of Junior. One would be hard put to find anyone in Hungary even today who has not heard of him. When he died, he was buried in the crypt of Budapest's Saint Stephen's Basilica, and the day of his burial was declared a national day of mourning.

2.

House and Father

STIRRING

When I made up my mind to write my mother's story, her amazing but certainly highly unconventional relationship to soccer, I had no idea that I would have a story of my own that would merge into this (that like a babbling brook to a mountain stream I would hasten to my mother's bosom—but let's not exaggerate). I had already indicated my intention in my football book, though at the time I thought I'd keep it a man's story ("the story of a man whose whole life is about football," "who tells story after story, is past his prime, a brandy-blossom on his nose, and knows all the great soccer players in the world," *Journey to the Depths of the Eighteen-Yard Line,** 2006, p. 146), I thought I'd have an easier time of it this way; basically, I was hoping to steer clear of my mother, the conflict with her, because I took it for granted that there was bound to be conflict. Not because I was getting her involved in yet another book, she's used to that; in fact, though

* *Utazás a tizenhatos mélyére,* 2006, the author's book about his father, his family, life, and football.

she makes a show of protest, she enjoys it; but no, that's not fair, what she enjoys is being able to help me, and so she grumbles, but her face is radiant. Every time I discover in it the face of the young girl I could never know, this is the sense of yearning every boy feels (and tries hard to deny).

The sensitive butterfly of chaos theories—there's no butterfly without nettles!, she screeched at me out of the blue, this transpired a long time ago, a woman by the name of Karola pierced me with her eye, histrionically and meaningfully and like someone expecting an all-important answer, and I had no idea what she wanted, or whether she wanted anything at all, and that, in this not wanting, whether I was the nettle or the butterfly; the thing was less complicated, though, because sometime after the Great Depression the chaos butterfly stirred its innocent wings, thereby bringing about, a decade and a half later, a dramatic shift in my mother's story, my mother's, I say, whereas it changed my father's directly, and with the brutality of a wild beast, and thus, as a matter of course, my own as well, but let's not go into that, because in that case I would also have to consider as the forger of my fate a quite ordinary horseshoe that the saddle horse Star—a thoroughbred!—had left behind on one of the upward slopes of the Zemplén hills around the turbulent turn of the seventeenth century, plus it had rained heavily just before, as a consequence of which its rider, the younger of two brothers, reached the Thököly castle later, what I mean is, the castle didn't belong to the Thökölys, not *von Haus aus*, it's just that Imre had married into the family, if I got this right, as a consequence of which the blood of one of the two daughters of the house and not the other is flowing (gurgling!) through my veins, stirring God only knows what stormy passions and stormy lethargies in me centuries later, and I as innocent of the cause as a newborn babe.

The stirring of the butterfly wings materialized in the shape of Dr. Aurél Bognár's impatience. The good doctor built the house where I live now in 1929, and my neighbor is his grandson, but nobody in the neighborhood knows his first name, so we just call him Bognár. Or Bognár the millionaire. On the other hand, his wife is known only by her pet name Bogi that, or so the local community believes, is derived not from Bognár, but presumably from her first name, Boglárka.

SITUATION

It would have been quite a challenge to draw conclusions about the psychology of the builder based on his house, a barely comprehensible, incoherent if touching mixture of refinement and bad taste or, to put it more kindly, of the theatrical. As a whole the house lacks character, the details cancel each other out while, taken on their own, sometimes they're one way, sometimes another, absurd, meek, unwieldy.

I should say it the other way around, still, I say it like this: to me, the street where the house is situated, the main road leading down to the Danube in this village-like suburb of Budapest, looked just like a *boulevard* in a László Végel novel,* and that's just a hop, skip and a jump away from a promenade, not a haute bourgeois promenade with top hats, poodles, and operettas,

* László Végel (b. 1941 in Szenttamás—Srbobran, Serbia) is a Hungarian writer, essayist, and playwright.

mind you, but young girls strolling arm in arm, stepping out like sailors, loud and silly, foolish amazons, while the boys whistle after them with yearning in their eye. Also, they're selling fancy ice cream cones and white pálinka somewhere. My own boulevard is more sober, a daytime boulevard. I walked along it every day to school, to buy groceries, or a short distance to the ice cream vendor; I walked along it every Sunday to church, and for a while in the opposite direction to football practice, twice weekly, then three times, and once to a game, or twice if, instead of one of our workouts, we played a friendly practice match on Wednesday.

The middle section of the house that was by all odds its most outlandish feature, frustrating any sober expectation or logical flight of fancy, jutted out like a tower; this contains my study now, a fact I am almost reluctant to mention, it's so embarrassingly metaphorical, the poet in his ivory tower, and if I were to add that this tower is situated along the outer reaches of Pannonia, the former frontier of the great Roman Empire and, in fact, as I have already mentioned in my football book, even one commuter train stop beyond, it would be impossible to untangle the sentence from the seaweed of symbols, with nothing left for me to fall back on except for the silent arrogance of "I be a plus one stop barbarian." The tower is as hefty as if it had been built in the sixteenth century by a robber baron with a creative bent grown tired of the constant, tedious character of wrongdoing, who would have thought that with time it would leave him quite so depleted?; the tower had an antiquated ruggedness about it, it appeared serene and combative at the same time, I might even venture to say masculine. Naturally, an expert eye could see right off that it was a cheap imitation, the bluffing posture inherent in the playful pseudo-crenellations on the flat roof, so even if it were masculine, it would take a biased, coldhearted Amazon who thinks of a male as that whining, helpless creature with the huge ego whose superfluous thingamajig hangs limp God only knows where to see it that way. Something like this: as if.

An iron staircase led from my circular study up to the flat roof encircled by a breastwork carelessly sprayed over with rough mortar, thanks to which the tower really did take on the character of a bastion; your eye went in search of the crenellations and you anxiously began making plans for what you hoped would be the most advantageous positioning of the gun-howitzers. Always anxiously, and always gun-howitzers. How big is a gun-howitzer? The size of a cow, I bet. Though it probably gives less milk. Besides, how would I haul it up here? If cows could fly, it would clearly be a cinch. I wouldn't call it a hill, more like an incline, a random mound—to repeat the old joke: in Hungary anything higher than a hole is considered a mountain—the house was situated on top of this, thereby enhancing the bastion-like character of the unlikely bastion. Up there, the slightly unhinged captain of the fort presently turned into a slightly unhinged philosopher; he wasn't just worried about the gun-howitzers now (there were the tortuous misgivings, could a gun-howitzer be the same as a plain howitzer?), he was also tied up in knots over what might be called the structure of the world: if this is the bastion, then where, oh where—yet another uncertainty!—are the others, the king, the queen, my faithful subjects? Among the crags of the nearby Pilis Mountains, in that mysterious Magyar past and Magyar sacrality, no doubt.* The bishops at Solymár, at the foot of the Pilis. The question is: how big is the field? And who is playing the game? This is all-important. And so, whoever climbed up on the roof—me—quite soon, basically in no time, ended up thinking of God. The Nimzo-Indian conception of God, this is what usually and invariably came to mind, although I don't as a rule like to talk about God lightly, because He may then end up talking lightly about me. To me. It's been a while since He last talked to me.

I don't know whether there are still people, whether in today's Hungary there are men and women, who think about the *situation* of a house, a room. In the late nineteen twenties, Dr. Aurél Bognár certainly must have, because I can't very well consider the sophisticated placement of the windows of my study accidental. To his great good luck, the doctor invested his money (a part of it, anyway) in the house before the Great Depression could nibble away at it, and so I cannot very well place the blame for the above-mentioned fatal impatience on the shoulders of inhuman capitalist structures. (I have already mentioned elsewhere that ever since I was a child, I've had the ability to take, or have been the victim of the ability of taking, all metaphorical linguistic structures literally; I can just see the wide shoulders of the capitalist structures and am wondering about the similarity between these and the greasy, creased,

* According to some patriotic Hungarian scholars and amateur researchers, the Pilis Mountains just north of Budapest are the geological and transcendental "heart of the world" and contain the so far undiscovered bones of some of the chieftains who led the Magyar tribes into the area of present-day Hungary.

sausage-like, glaringly realistic neck of the Russian officer on the 1989 *"tovarishi koniec"* poster*—because, what can I say, that's what they looked like!)

A couple of years ago a woman rang our doorbell, she was visiting back home from Australia, she used to live here, and could she take a look at the favorite venue of her childhood, and she immediately stalked off, with me walking behind her like a group of Japanese tourists. She kept stopping short, regarding a wall or a door trim for some time, shaking her head in disapproval, because of the heaps of books, magazines and letters, I thought, that were not in their place—if they had their appointed place at all!, but that's just the crux (one crux) of the problem. I was under a cloud just then (the morning sun caught me under a cloud), and at such times I "amplify the chaos," meaning that I don't do anything, I don't increase, I don't decrease, I don't do the nothing that I do at other times, and this increases the chaos, which is far worse than a simple mess, because I am part of it. The visitor, an obese lady with an amicable face, was decked out in such an inconceivable ugliness of cascades of pinks, sudden flounces, false frills, sleeves and accessories and silk shawls and silk panties, also pink, that from time to time afforded a glimpse of themselves from under her skirt, and a hat, that I couldn't think of it as real, as perfect in its imperfection, and so it appeared as perfect, after all (tone deafness as an instance of per-

* *"Tovarishi koniec"*—Comrades, the end—are the words on the famous poster by István Orosz celebrating the departure of the Soviet troops. The poster was also the campaign vehicle for the Hungarian Democratic Forum in the first free elections held in Hungary after World War II. It also exists in a version that reads, *"Tovarishi adieu."*

fect hearing), a sort of ingenious sleight of hand with just one aim in mind, to cheekily force itself, its triumphant, victorious existence on us—this would have been the effect had I not been familiar with these panty-, Trabant-, knitted-sweater post-'89 proli-market colors from my window, in short, the sky, the bottom of the sky. Is nature endowed with bad taste, the unhinged philosopher might ask up on the flat roof. Is Trabant green God's creation? Because that was this sort of pink.

I had a window for dawn in purple mantle clad, the dullness of a somnolent sky, the whitish languor of the break of day, this improbable, indolent oscillation of distant whites and reds, one for a rainy morning, the reflected light, while at the next window the yellowish curtain of undisciplined woodbine tendrils that the purple autumn painted in the unlikely colors that I saw on the woman curbed the roaring noonday sun, and finally, the evening window, the scandal-free kitsch parade of the light of the setting sun ricocheting off the clouds. Sitting in my room, I had familiarized myself with the beauty of nature's ugliness, this feebleness masquerading as a mistake, which generally leaves us perplexed, embarrassed, we giggle, could it be that reality legitimizes itself esthetically as well, as if we suddenly learned that the Good Lord loved third-rate vulgarity, X's novels, is passionately fond of kittens playing with spools of thread, dancing Gypsy girls with bare midriffs and huge bosoms (though let me add . . . , but never mind), and last but not least, sunsets bathed in tomato blood; and naturally, we are in no position to indulge ourselves in our squeamishness; on the contrary, more and more it would seem that we'd do best to look inside ourselves and ask whether our own lives as such are not a mistake.

I was looking at the stranger from behind, her colors and

her ample, one might say amicable, leisurely wobbling behind—in Australia she became Jennifer, from Jutka Jennifer (why not Judy?) Smith, that's her husband's name, who is groundsman at the Hungarian soccer club in Sydney, they're not divorced, but it's as if they were—the woman, for whom my home was more of a home than it was for me, suddenly spun around and screamed in my face: It can't be this small, it can't! She glared at me as if I were the most infamous shrinker in Hungarian history. Proportions shift in a dictatorship, I said to myself, but thought better than to spring this on an Australian, even if she's Hungarian. Then she burst out laughing.

THE WORLD ACCORDING TO MY MOTHER

My mother had the rare ability, which lost hardly any of its luster with age, of repeatedly revealing, at times abruptly, pulling the veil off it, as it were, at other times gradually, with quiet persistence—the richness of things. But she didn't allow you to see the inexhaustible richness of the world with the soft yearning of self-indulgence, her motives were more earnest, even frivolous: earnest, as if she were qualifying the created universe (positively), and frivolous, as if in this way she could deflect responsibility. As if, with her habitual giggle she were saying: Even I consider what I am positing something of an exaggeration. And yet, time and again she made it adequately clear that neither the world as a whole nor any part of it (its subset, I used to cry self-importantly) can be fully fathomed, that there is no aspect of the universe, however infinitesimal, no event, however inconsequential, no person, however humble, no object, country, town, mountain, lake, or famous person, so that it shouldn't be inconceivably *much*, and though she was by all odds motivated by the need to know, and this need is first cousin to yearning, still, her fundamental stance was essentially one of surprise; again and again she was surprised that the things of the world are the way she had intuited them to be. Though possibly she didn't intuit anything, just that—surprisingly, even for her—she kept rediscovering this *much*, this fullness, this richness, this mystery.

In mother's eyes, everything was a mystery. Me included. She'd have liked me to become a great soccer player. It follows from the above that she was not prejudiced in my favor, she eyed (followed, nursed) my budding talent with cold objectivity, and was not the least surprised when on my fifteenth birthday, on April 14th "on the dot," "I hanged up the ball" and have not touched one with my foot since.

MY FATHER'S ANGELS

At home, a lot of things happened the other way around. We attended the games with my mother, while father would often lie in the darkened back room nursing a splitting headache. As far as he was concerned, tennis was the only legitimate ball game, he played it himself, tolerably well, as he liked to say. He had a thing for these, what shall we call them, English-style expressions which rely so blatantly on the false modesty inherent in understatement, are so obvious about it, so heavy-handed, that we have ample reason to suspect the presence of real modesty behind it, some reserve, certainly, a certain *humility*. I saw him around the boathouse many times—after 1956 he was made odd jobs man in a boathouse by the Danube, sometimes he even slept there, it's not true that he disappeared, or as grandmother wailed, that mother of yours chased him away, it's just that he slipped further down the boulevard in the direction of the Danube—behind the boathouse by the pools, in his working clothes: long white slacks, they're not slacks, son, they're *pantaloons!*, a soft, white cotton top, a light, thin sweater with a light blue trim around its V-neck, and the same trim around the sleeves. And sometimes that white knitted vest! Every time he wore it, he hastened to apologize for "what might reasonably be construed as a lack of taste," the small logo, the tiny purplish red embroidered airplane, a *doppeldecker* flying above his much-suffering heart which, had he not made a point of it, no one would have noticed in the first place (save for my mother).

Something happened to our father sometime after the war, but what it was we didn't know, nor did we particularly care; our father was all too transparent (unlike our mother). We knew about his drinking, what I mean is, we never saw him drink, but he was always under the influence, not very, not outrageously, just that his eyes always had a gleam to them, but this didn't bother us either, the smell of booze hovering around him, ditto; *mutatis mutandis*, for us, this must've been like dear daddy's familiar tobacco smell had been for Stalin's daughter. When he looked at me, and he was always looking for a chance to buttonhole one of us, veritably hunting us down, I could feel that he wanted something of me, as if he were the child, and I the grownup. Indeed, I acted like a grownup, serious, with a sense of responsibility. A quiet child. Which my mother noted with apprehension. It's like you're always just catching a cold. *If at least you had a proper fever, noodle.* How I hated this, this noodle! I had no idea what it meant, or maybe I did, just that I didn't want to acknowledge that my mother would talk like that. When, in the flower of my young manhood I mentioned this aversion to my first wife, who—a cliché—resembled my mother in more ways than one, shrugged, what do you expect?, you want she should have called you a little prick, little prick? Well, what can I say? My first wife had boobs like a smallish watermelon or a largish honeydew. What made me think of that? It doesn't even belong here. A good thing I didn't say winter squash. That, too, is spherical in shape.

My father always seemed to be crying, crying and smiling, crying and smiling and begging a boon. This didn't faze me either, he was the only father we knew (*cf.* mother), he suited us just fine. And it didn't bother me either that I couldn't understand what he was after, what he wanted, and consequently, I couldn't give it to him. I didn't (I don't) have a guilty conscience. Which meant that I didn't try to get out of his way, I didn't go looking for excuses. During those boathouse days I enjoyed going to see him; my mother would also send me, the way she sent me to the grocer's. She'd give my shoulder a shove, as if she doubted whether I could take the first step on my own. Compared to my mother everyone is short on alacrity.

Our father would often sit for hours smiling by the window in the room where I now sit by my desk every day, looking outside. Or God knows where, maybe inside, symbolically. Sometimes he wouldn't get up for days, even weeks; he lay in bed, there was no talking to him, we weren't even allowed to go to his room. I will not have him in a hospital, mother, I can take care of him, and I will! You're killing my son. Me, mother dear?! Can't you see, you silly old woman, he'd been killed a long time ago?! The Lord will punish you for talking like that! I'm glad you brought Him up, mother. Why don't you ask Him about what He did to your son? You're worried about me harming him? Worry about your horse's arse!

There was a great deal we didn't understand, but we saw no mystery in things. For instance, grandmother would have nothing but bad things to say about our mother, warning us about her as it were, and yet it was clear as day, we knew for a fact, that she loved her. Well, what were we supposed to make of that? When we were very small, we could talk with father practically any time, but later, the "communicative periods" grew shorter. On the other hand, earlier there were the outbursts: from one moment to the next, father would start crying, not simply crying, but shrieking, howling. Wailing. That's the right word. Nobody knew what brought it on, it wasn't fatigue, or chagrin, or people, or the dark, or the light, it issued from within, from some deep and distant place, some difficult, unfamiliar terrain. At which my grandmother would also burst into tears; she buried her face in her hands, she didn't want to see. We glanced at our mother. (If we had guests, they also tried to make themselves invisible.) Our mother would sit tight up against the heaving body, gently stroking and caressing it like a child. It was a touching sight. If only it had not been so difficult to put up with the contrast between the silence of her movements and the shrillness of his wails. We were scared, too, but none of us ever buried our face like grandmother. You've got more courage than I. You got it from your mother. And she nodded. And she also said: I'm happy my son is still alive, tell your mother that, tell her I'm happy. But we didn't say anything, we saw no point in getting caught up in grown-up affairs. When we stopped being afraid, which transpired quickly, we also went to stand by father's side gently to stroke him, like a child. But then we were always afraid again, every time. That loudness and that trembling! More like convulsions and writhing! For me, the worst thing was seeing into my father's open mouth. My eyes were riveted to it. It was as if they'd dug a great big hole, a great dark cavern inside my father. A cavern full of teeth. The scales, the yellow, nicotine-stained teeth, these are the most vivid memories of my father. You'd think his mouth was adorned with amber, and I knew that amber is precious. Rare, uncommon, ancient. And that it has old times trapped inside it. I respected him (my father) very much for these things.

Toward the end, his life quieted down, comatose weeks taking the place of weeks that were hardly more lively. But he picked up a fresh new habit: he wouldn't stop talking. For weeks he wouldn't say anything, then he wouldn't stop talking. To everything he appended—not an explanation, not an explication or opinion, but a word. He smeared everything, the room, the garden, us, with words. He plastered everything with words. Like a raging bull in springtime, he was possessed by the rage for naming things, sprinkling things waiting to be named full of synonyms. He never shut up. He even added words to words, which goes without saying. This was a lot more embarrassing than his previous outbursts; what I mean is they didn't embarrass us, just grandmother and strangers, they didn't know what to make of my father's inhuman suffering, people generally don't like to think about other people's suffering. It's impolite. It's uncivil. *Gehört sich nicht*, our mother's younger sister used to say. In the meanwhile, Uncle Sárli hanged his head in shame. I think he'd have liked to join us strokers, but was loath to get on the wrong side of his wife (his esteemed wife, as he liked to say, and for years we didn't know what esteemed was, so we said steamed up instead, my steamed-up wife, gentlemen, and just so there's no mistaking, Uncle Sárli's steamed-up wife). The suffering remained, because this suffering was our father; more than anything, suffering was part of him. And I also knew that the amber, that, too, is him.

According to grandmother, our father had become a Swedenborgian, and though this didn't happen in secret, yet it happened without warning, in the blinking of an eye. And he a Catholic! (My grandmother must have misunderstood something.) I think he's the only Catholic Swedenborgian in the world! I've seen worse, mother dear. In public places, in the park, on the shores of the Danube, the commuter train, the tram, in front of the church (this less frequently), father lost no time in collaring a victim, who was forced to listen to a learned disquisition on the age of the angels. But only a few would let him, most people must have seen it as a provocation and—mostly—advised him to take his angels elsewhere. Concrete places were also mentioned, and not just a warmer clime, or hell (if it's going to be hot, it might as well be scorching hot!), but also back to his wife, or back inside the church. Or better still, have them join the farmers' co-op!* Everyone was afraid of everyone else. It saddened my father that people should speak so rudely about celestial beings, but he refused to beat a retreat.

And are you aware that Swedenborg has a number of important learned tomes to his credit? Imagine the crowded commuter train, the students, the navies from the nearby shipyard!

* Farmers' cooperatives, introduced to Hungary on the basis of the Soviet model during the Rákosi era, were highly unpopular with farmers, who were forced to relinquish their land and produce.

You don't say, old man!

Oh, but I do, gentlemen. He intuited the Nebular hypothesis light-years ahead of Laplace. What do you say to that?!

We're not saying a thing, Comrade, and you should thank your lucky stars that we're not.

Fine, gentlemen, you're right, let's talk serious. My father was afraid of nothing and no one, that was the most embarrassing. Still, I am sure we can agree, gentlemen, and not just by way of a hypothesis, I wish to make this very clear, not by way of a hypothesis!, that the Bible is the word of God. The word of the Catholic God, let this much restriction and generalization suffice, and I hope you don't think that the Old Testament went clear out of my head. By the way, I am firmly convinced that all men, whether yellow, white, or black, pray to the same God. This is my sacred conviction. But let's not chew more than we can swallow. I'd rather not describe the types of laughter that greeted such a sentence, and the body parts my father was advised to grip. The signs are there in the Bible, friends, they just need to be read with an open mind. An open mind and an open heart. Because zeal alone—lots of people think so, but they are mistaken—will not suffice, it takes erudition, if you'll excuse the expression. Let us not forget, we are reading a text, the words of God, but words just the same. He is using our words, our grammar, which we cannot write off as incidental. And as for the signs, I'm not saying that the Greeks didn't concern themselves with such things, especially the great Plato. Look about you, gentlemen, and think of what you see, the here and now, the *hic et nunc*, as the manifestation of the kingdom of God. Its indistinct double. And the other way around: the world of the spirit for which it is our sacred duty to strive, the reality of that other existence—and the

Holy Writ points this out—is every bit as much of a given as the *hic et nunc* I've just mentioned. Gentlemen, Without the renewal of Christianity the future of mankind is bleak, indeed.

What about communism, old man? By then my father did not shave every day, the stubble covered his face in tufts of grayish red, like a winter forest floor, like that. This faded rusty color carried the element of surprise, it did not follow at all from the once bluish-black raven hair, now tamed the color of poppy seeds, which still—until his death—fell over his legendary forehead and temples, blazing, like Alain Delon's in the sixties; there was always something boyish about him, in his straight posture, his youthful slenderness and sprightly gait, or, more to the point, the sprightliness that faithfully preserved the characteristic stiffness, the typical soft bounce of his steps.

It may surprise you, sir, but all forces must join hands. All well-intentioned powers. A principle, sir, and I'd like to emphasize this, a principle that has pinned the noble dream of the equality of men on its banner, what else could it be if not well intentioned? At this juncture, the public usually balked. It's one thing for the old man to conduct PR for the angels, but trying to force the commies down our throats?! No one was paying him attention by then, people even turned their backs so they wouldn't have to see his face, that weary feline face, while he, mindful of the balance of his lecture's motifs, briefly returned to Swedenborg's scientific discoveries, gentlemen, he expressed his ingenious views in what today we'd call *abstracts*, elegant page-and-a-half writings. And that by page, though there's probably no need for him to even bring it up, he means 30 x 60 characters as opposed to the small, 20 x 50 character page, of course, and if the gentlemen are interested, it'd cost him nothing, it would be no bother giving them the differential. One large page adds up to . . . come on, Simple Simon, even you can figure that out. Double-spaced. Mortification, it seems, knows no bounds, I thought, and saw by the reflection of the train window that I, too, had turned my head.

It's been nearly ten years since he died, that's when we bought our mother this apartment at the end of the boulevard nearest the Danube, there are more mosquitoes than we had bargained for, my father's difficult, unfortunate life ended easily and fortunately, he carried a heavy weight all his life so that later he should die weightless, without illness, without pain, without the humiliation of the body and the stinging solitude of the soul; it took but a moment, and he slept himself into eternity; he knew they were waiting for him, he had something to eat, but took his time, though he came to eat less and less and also turned paler with time, translucent, he drank a small glass of wine, toward the end he liked only the red, a certain red from Tuscany, a reliable if not distinguished wine, Rosso di Montalcino, Castello Banfi, it was complicated (circuitous) to obtain it in Pest, but still, he insisted, our considerations of principle or the practical outcome of our fortuitous, so-called *random* trains of thought (adjective courtesy of Péter Nádas*) left him unimpressed (and not because it was generally someone else who bore the brunt), he covered himself with a red knitted comforter, now I use it for my "afternoon nap," as I get older I like taking half-hour

* Péter Nádas (b. 1942) is a Hungarian writer, playwright, and essayist who has dealt eloquently with the obligations and moral conundrums of memory. He is best known in England and America for *A Book of Memories* (*Egy családregény vége*), published in Hungarian in 1977 and in English in 1997.

naps in the afternoon before I go back to work, even less than half an hour, but it refreshes me or, at the very least, it keeps me going, lying on his side, he pulled up his knees like a child and fell fast asleep (an ability, a great gift, that I must have inherited from him), so that barely an hour later—though by then time had come to a standstill!—he should wake up in the circle of his angels, whom he knew well, and they him, after all, he'd spent the last fifteen years of his life in their company, in peace and celestial harmony (how my pen slipped into this of its own accord!*), closer and closer to the Lord—this is how I imagine my poor father's fate.

SECRET POLICE ÉTUDE

By way of counterpoint, because it would feel good, I would like to embroider the way the ÁVÓ beat my father to within an inch of his life around the time of my birth, though independently of it, I should think, methodically, from the bottom up, not that they stuck to their chosen method at all cost, no, at times they threw caution to the wind, and the way we sometimes describe a friendly brawl in the local pub: don't spare him, he ain't your old man (yes he is!), they lashed out, without rhyme or reason, it seems, but in tune with the personal feelings that tend to surface at such times, which in turn legitimized their actions; they felt they were right even if while striking their victim they did not reflect on the social and historical interrelationships that, though these did not furnish concrete proof of the necessity of

* A reference to the author's novel *Celestial Harmonies* (Harmonia caelestis), published in Hungarian in 2001 and in English in 2003.

their concrete actions, yet an action of some sort was evidently called for, and so this could be regarded as an initial warm-up of sorts, the first if tentative step on the path to social justice that nobody said would be an easy ride. The thugs doing the beating were young, and the young need an ideology. It wasn't always the thugs who did the beating, though, but whoever was on hand, sometimes even the driver of the police car charged with the delivery (conveyance), despite the fact that he was not on the secret police payroll; after the war he joined the police force because he had to make a living, and before long was promoted to sergeant, the older ones, because this is what I was getting at, didn't bother thinking this much while beating their victim, they didn't think at all, they just lashed out, they were already tired when they got up in the early morning, they'd grown tired carrying around the burden of their lives, and they had to carry it even at night, and even in their sleep; by the time they went to work in the morning their face was ashen gray, their eye red with fatigue, their body bent under the indeterminate weight of their lives, and it is even conceivable—a flimsy psychological explanation—that they were simply getting this, this helplessness off their chest, and so they beat whoever was on hand—the same hand as above, I should think—it could have been their wives, their children, their buddies, they themselves, but my father happened to be on hand, so they beat him, from the bottom up, methodically. The naked soles of his feet with a rubber stick, a classical standard, the kicks to the ankles I will revert to later, but to get back to the rubber stick: the next station is the terrain of the calves, which at first may bear with no significance, but then years later the varicose veins swell, the impressive, three-dimensional map of the hydrography of a strange country, they throb, smart, burn, they present a thousand petty variations on pain, thus forcing one to continually rekindle one's memories, one glance is enough, pulling up one's socks in the morning while the pinky practically gets caught on a protruding vein (whose line is reminiscent of a babbling brook hastening toward a mountain stream, etc.—in which case the country outlined on the calf is no stranger to us after all), or a gentle stroke, the loving yet apprehensive stirring of a strange hand suffices for the question to arise, again and again and again, in the morning, at noon, in the evening, at night, any time, in wind and in rain, in the scorching sun, on a rail, on water and in the air (I wrote this somewhere already): but why? The kidneys, the stomach, the entire soft area down below, and then the rib cage, these are habitually kicked, though beating the latter with some object is also popular and serves the same purpose; once on the floor, kicking the head offers itself as a matter of course, but this really pertains to an emotion-laden, hot-tempered, chaotic beating, while in a standing position—this is the most personal, most critical moment—a macho slap in the face is the natural gesture. But back to the ankles: just like the beating of the soles of the feet with a rubber stick, so may we regard the kicking of the ankles with short lace-up boots as both commonplace and logical. Lace-ups are preferable to plain boots, though boots will do as well, except they're sluggish to set in motion, not fast enough, not suited to quick and thus surprising transitions, though once they're set in motion—there is plenty of space and time, experience and sober-headed patience will see to it—the momentum is anything if not impressive. Street shoes are hardly suitable, they lag behind boots. The lace-up, on the other hand, unites the advantages of the street shoe and the long boot, while the innocent status of street shoes, their past, presumably peaceful record, in short, their civilian character, might awaken hopes in the person being beaten, he prognosticates the next instant as pleasantly normal, yes, he prognosticates it as normal, so that the person being beaten or the person about to be beaten will fling all caution to the wind, accommodating himself to the shoe's polished leather, obviously shined with loving care; in short, he forgets, first and foremost, that once already—during the course of the cold and dreary dawn—he'd known that the norms had changed, and what's normal is the fact that (to follow Imre Kertész's scandalously simple line of thought once again) he, the beaten, the one being beaten, as well as the one who will be beaten: *should* be beaten. The street shoes were being worn by the driver of the police car, he sincerely hated what he was doing, but didn't wish to call attention to himself by his passivity. It was bad enough that the people in the neighborhood remembered his family as churchgoing and religious. Needless to say, he'd left all that behind by now, which made him feel bad; still, as a cautionary measure he didn't even pray in silence, murmuring to himself, though he spoke to his God all the same, without words; they were not pleasant chats, he felt he had to make excuses for himself, offer explanations, while for His part, God kept mum. He could've shown a little understanding, damn it! He must see what's going on, what animals these people are! On the other hand, who the fuck is omniscient anyway? Sorry about that. But still. In 1956 he defected, went to Australia, and played in the Hungarian Sydney soccer club, a solid man in midfield; it's like a bad joke, a truly third-rate joke concocted by nature, language, and history; his kicking technique was first-rate, he passed the ball through space effortlessly, with a full instep; the Australian soccer fans back then may not have been the most sensitive and astute audience in the world of soccer, still, they knew how to appreciate these dead-on, cannoning passes, this Hungarian knows the ropes; they revered him as if he'd brought a message directly from the great Puskás to the Australian people, though possibly the fans, recruited from relatives and friends, forty at best, did not go quite so far on that cinder track in Sydney, and while Japanese fans acknowledge the height of a ball kicked into the air with laughter and cheer and a storm of applause—the Japanese laugh in a stadium, which in Europe is inconceivable—in this particular case, the length of the kick must have caught people's eye. The Magyar, this is what people called him, was an odd jobs man at the parsonage, where he had a room, looked after the garden, attended to the chores around the house, could fix anything from the eaves to the water taps, went to the farmers' market, did the shopping, cooked for his priest, my priest, or my priestie, this is how he called him, he learned English quickly, round of beef, he knew that, too, a small round of beef for my priestie, and what are you eating, Magyar?, there's plenty to go around, the sergeant said quietly; sometimes he even got to drive the small Ford; his teammates called him Tootie because they couldn't pronounce Tyutyi, for a while the sergeant made them practice it, go tootie your toots toots tootie goodbye!, but then he gave up, so Tootie it is; he was a hardworking, conscientious player, after a meal never, after a friendly never, but after a championship bout he'd get drunk as a skunk, a couple of beers with whisky, I'm the real pro, because for me this is stress!, and then he'd push his bike home, and then the moment would always come and the bicycle would get out of hand and like an unruly colt would kick out its hind legs while up front it seemed to be biting, fine, if that's how you want it, go on home on your own, go pray with my priestie, the two of you, and he gave it a shove and lay down by the ditch, he joined his hands as if in prayer and turning to the side, placed them under his head, his cheek, for a pillow; after every championship game the priest would stay awake from worry, the sergeant wouldn't let him come and see him home, *nem érted?!*, he shouted, *hogy tegyem abba a kemény ausztrál koponyádba!*, can't you get it through your thick skull?, I need to be alone a bit, just a bit, and the priest really didn't understand as he listened to his sergeant with a mixture of joy and incomprehension.

And then they stuck a board up my father's ass. With time, all the objects in the room found their appointed role. As if he'd been drawn on a stake. Your father could never say the sentence about what they did to him back then, he almost managed it, but then he couldn't, his expression changed, the muscles around his lips hardened, his body on the verge of tears, but then nothing, after all. The board . . . with that board . . . , that's all he said. He couldn't even say up. And as for me, I didn't dare to ask my mother, and I still can't, how thick that board was, how thick a board *like that* is, and whether it's got splinters, or whether in the long run it makes no difference. That a lot of splinters might be a sign of ill will, and less that of mercy. Acacia and oak. What sort of wood is a stake used for drawing at the stake made of? Which is greater, the pain or the humiliation? Or is everything great? Or nothing?

It could have happened like this, the way it happened to so many people, my father's chances for it to happen to him were good "both as a human being and artistically." But (actually) this is not how it happened, this is not what derailed my father's life.

WOUND

Four handsome lads, this is what we were in our mother's eye, an honor guard standing by our father's deathbed. He was still warm. One after the other, in order of seniority, we each of us planted a kiss on his cheek. Kiss your father good-bye. His stubble pricked, his fox-colored stubble, but apart from that, because the stubble seemed recklessly alive, he looked properly dead, in keeping with the unwritten rules, the cheeks sunken in the pale face, the jaw sagging, the hands lying next to the body. That certain red knitted comforter was still covering him. We recited the Lord's Prayer. A maybeetle was crawling on the floor. Some people are afraid of them, or have an aversion to them, I like to make them crawl on the back of my hand, and I also like the scratching of their feet. Recite the Lord's Prayer. Our mother acted a bit as if we'd brought home bad marks from school, she looked hurt and surprised, she had expected better of us.

Péter, she rasped, the way the severe but fair biology teachers (women) turn on you to wring out of you your most cherished, personal thoughts about the lives of the dicotyledons, and I couldn't say to her what I'd read from Péter Balassa* not long ago (whom I miss more and more with the passing of time;

* Péter Balassa (1947–2003) was a highly respected critic and professor of esthetics and literature, the author of several books, including *Thoughts and Forms* (Észjárás és forma, 1985) and *Spectacles and Words* (A Látvány és a szavak, 1987). He wrote extensively on both Péter Nádas and Péter Esterházy.

there's nothing I can say about his death, in this bad helplessness there is nothing of the loftiness that this silence would be meant to express, namely, that I have no words, that I couldn't find words for this—whereas, oh God, for so many things, yes!—it's as if we'd landed in a world devoid of words, among majestic, wordless *peaks*, whereas there are no peaks, no, and certainly nothing of the beyond; on the contrary, it's from this side, he from this side, and me, too, from this side, except he died, his lungs drowned, and I don't know how to handle this, and of course there's no handling *this* ever, which generally doesn't bother me, but now it does), I couldn't answer my mother with the aged Verdi's words: The mere mention of my name turns my stomach (oh, mother).

While reciting the Lord's Prayer, it occurred to me, for the first time, that maybe it's our father who art in heaven, and it is his name that is hallowed, his kingdom come, his will be done—though he didn't seem to have a will, and things just happened: palaces, the secret police, sons, wife, angels, and he swept along before us? behind us? instead of us?—in earth as in heaven, he gave us our daily bread, working all his life like a dumb beast of burden, as if it were the most natural thing in the world, forgive us, father, our sins, as we forgive yours, and lead us not into temptation, but deliver us from evil. *Libera nos a malo,* liberahnose amenoh!, back then, this is what it sounded like to me. Amen, mother repeated, because back then Amen was still compulsory, whereas now it's not. Then she leaned over the dead body, I thought she was going to kiss it, look, and she smoothed father's hair back from his brow. It was not death but this that turned his face into a stranger's, this *uncovering,* this is when we realized that we'd never seen him like this, only with the Alain Delon locks. We were unprepared for what we saw, a secret wound that blackened our father's left temple like some revolting, throbbing creature oozing pus. The last time I had seen such a terrifying *void*, best suited to a horror film, was on György Petri's cancerous neck.* Like there, here, too, I averted my eyes, practically in unison with my brothers (just like a dance troupe from the boondocks, *practically* in unison), but I saw. Kindly take a proper look, our mother ordered. The wound was not sizable—though compared to what? What's the yardstick *here*?—it was bounded by a reddish ring, the light inflammation of the skin, followed by a lighter ring with small scab remnants, debris from stitches and pus marks, and all the way inside, a dark inner core or maybe a hole, like a pin. Right away, mechanically, I thought of what Kafka had said of a wound, that he could not help letting out a low whistle of surprise, and nor could I. Mother headed for the door with us, her ducklings, in tow.

A LITTLE MILK, A NAIL

My mother didn't know and I couldn't begin to guess what made Dr. Aurél Bognár lose his patience (possibly the bankruptcy of the Viennese Credit Anstalt or the abdication and flight of Alfonso XIII of Spain?), possibly it needed no special reason, what happened sufficed: twice in a row, his black cashmere sweater

* Like Péter Balassa, György Petri (1943–2000), poet, translator, and journalist, was at the center of Hungarian literary life. He was much read, revered, and respected by the public and his fellow writers alike. As a member of the Hungarian democratic opposition, between 1975 and 1988 he was under a publishing ban, but his works were circulated in samizdat editions.

("which I bought at such great expense, and whose fatal virtue it is that it is as befitting a woman as a man," Giuseppe Tomasi di Lampedusa) got caught in a nail that had been inadroitly hammered into the handle of the tool shed to fix it in place, or maybe to make it work—by being pushed down?—in the first place. Got caught in the head of the nail. At which, outraged, Dr. Bognár took a pair of pliers and nipped off the head, all the while bemoaning his beloved sweater. This shed stood there for a long time, we used it to store coal, it had to be hauled inside every morning in two buckets, coke and fuel cake, this is where that certain noteworthy (noteworthy because I have noted it) summit meeting between my father, myself, my younger brother and Aunt Eta, the cleaning lady, took place with respect to that certain cat that we had discovered one morning among the coal heaps; it was obviously sick, or was on its last legs, a repulsive, wet secretion covered not only its eyes and the whole eye area, but all the way down to the cheeks. It looked like it was carrying some horrible infectious disease. The plague. Cholera. Malaria. Dropsy. The summit meeting took place in two parts. In part one the three of us men discussed the various ways of doing away with the cat—call out the People's Health Service, poison it, or what we, after brief consideration, unanimously agreed upon: to clobber it to death with the coal shovel, the heart shovel! Today it seems brutal, but then, I remember, it seemed no more than the practical solution to a practical problem. That's when Aunt Eta appeared on the scene, whose husband, I might add, had served as a paratrooper, and during one August 20th celebration he had to jump into the Danube—for some reason, Hungarians love it when, come Constitution Day, which is celebrated in honor of Saint Stephen, whom, to be on the safe side, we used to call Stephen the First even though we all knew he's really a saint,* their valiant sons make them, the people, happy by jumping into the waters of the Danube—but miscalculated, or else the northeastern wind proved too tricky, be that as it may, he landed on the dome of Parliament, on top of the red star. He got his ass caught on the red star! Aunt Eta loved to tell this tale, because—independently of the jump—they'd been separated for years. The paratrooper was a great drinker. It's not his fault, poor man, he was unhappy living with me. In short, Aunt Eta may have actually still loved him. We looked down our nose at her, I don't remember why. She joined us during the second half of the cat symposium, she brought the wash out to dry, and we let her in on the situation, because we were still just a wee bit uncertain about the three possible solutions. Try as we might, we couldn't come up with anything better. Aunt Eta, who was hanging out the wash, had her back to us, that's how she asked: Have you tried a little milk?

Mother led us to the empty spot where the shed had stood. We were standing in the middle of this void, and she began waving her arm in the middle of this void, like a mime busily engaged in creating the world with her movements. And recounting the life of a man, the mystery of his life. In short, that the handle is more or less right here, and that this nail, by now headless but as pointed as an assassin's dagger, this nail gradually began slipping farther and farther out, without, however, dislodging itself of the handle, in short, it went unnoticed, if a cashmere

* King Saint Stephen I (1001–1038) was canonized by Pope Gregory VII on August 20, 1083. During communist times, however, this particular merit of Stephen I was swept under the carpet.

sweater had got caught in it, it would've been, of course, but it didn't. Get to the point. Once your father—it was around the time Aunt Eta's husband landed on the star—was bending over, shoveling coal, when a draft or the wind . . . —the wind that blew this way from the direction of the Parliament?—or maybe your father slipped, in short, the door at him, he at the door, and the nail veritably exploded inside his temple. Here. Like that. A bit farther back, she pointed. That the nail sticking out of the door handle pinned his brain up like a butterfly. This butterfly was not the previously mentioned chaos butterfly. The professor said the chances of him dying were a hundred times greater than the chances of him not dying, and he didn't die. He lay in a coma for a year. Meanwhile, I came into the world. It was bad, seeing our mother pointing at the thin air. She's talking about a shed, and the shed is gone, a lethal door handle, and the door handle is gone, a nail sticking out of it, and the nail, too, is gone, and about our father's pierced brain, and our father, and he, too, is gone, he's gone.

3.

Love, Love, Love

THE BABBLING BROOK

Don't turn around, Count, or your goose is cooked. The sentence came from up close, as if someone were breathing cold, stale, musty cellar air down my neck, and from a distance, from a far-off time; this is how my football pals called me when I was a child, not before, not after; at the time, my solitude on the pitch (otherwise complex, but from a psychological point of view a simple rectangle) looked for all the world like colossal affectation and arrogance—this may have been where the count came from. But it functioned like a pet name, Tyutyi, Socks, Lungs, Rat, Pepe, Colt. Sometimes I was Pepe, maybe because in the blinking of an eye my bad mood, the result of my solitude, would turn into good cheer (the result of my solitude). When you're a Pepe, you're a Pepe all the way, are you not? The sentence was uttered seriously, whereas it is difficult to take a sentence like this seriously, it's so obviously made up, and yet I took it seriously, and was frightened. "Stop or I shoot!" is also a made-up sentence, yet people have been known to die from it.

Needless to say, I turned around. If they threaten you by

saying don't turn around, you're so frightened, you turn around before you know what hit you. The startled features of an older and a younger man stared back at me. There is—there came to be—a new kind of man in recent years, we take them for security guards or criminals or soccer fans or bodybuilders, that's what the younger of the two looked like; his jacket could hardly contain his bulging muscles, his shoulders were straining to get out, out, while the sleeves around his upper arms were as tight as a T-shirt. The older man's eyebrows looked familiar. Czeslaw Milosz has eyebrows like this. We said not to turn around. They spoke in unison, in a chorus, the way the Kessler sisters raise their legs—or used to; they had reverted to the formal mode of address. Walk straight ahead and don't look anymore, the younger of the two barked. At us, the older one added.

I turned back round, I continued walking. We were heading along the section of the boulevard lined with plane trees. This turning back and forth, this whole business, in fact, was ridiculous, but that was no comfort to me. I tried to find my way back to the world I knew. I stopped. What do you want? They gave a coarse laugh, and this time I didn't turn around (just almost). What's so funny, I asked the deserted street in front of me. You're just like the rest of them. You either walk or you talk. I stood in place, they guffawed, then there was silence, then the younger of the two turned on me, but with so much anger and contempt, I didn't know where I was again.

They switched to the informal mode of address again, but they didn't say count anymore, as if with this count they'd let slip more than they'd intended. They kept talking until we reached the post office; you'd think they were musicians, the way they reiterated motifs, performed solos, duets, switched voices, and though they worked with humble musical material, they made no concessions in the direction of the anecdotal style of representation; they clearly favored a strictly modernist approach. Consequently, I had no idea what they were getting at. A shame, because it would have been in my interest. That I shouldn't bother asking questions, they're gonna tell me all I need to know, and they know perfectly well what these questions, these cross-questions are for, to confuse things, that's what, but they're not about to get confused, even if I got higher learning, they heard on the radio how I'm a member of the Academy, something that they, for their part, consider a slight exaggeration, concretely, ridiculous, a silk purse from a sow's ear?, in short, I should shut my trap, 'cause they're gonna say only what they're gonna say, in short, what needs to be said, in short, as much as'll do the trick.

This transpired just before I went to hospital, my mother had been telling me for some time to use my muscles consciously, to watch the symmetry because, let's face it, it has come undone, she wouldn't like to be constantly telling a grown man what to do, like don't hold yourself lopsided, son, what's more, don't limp, son, because I might as well not go hide my head in the sand, I'm lopsided, and I limp. She recommended some simple exercises like when I'm sitting and standing, I should flex my butt muscles, first one side, then the other, then suddenly pull them both in, flex, hold, relax, and while walking I should watch my walk, meta-walk, son, roll on the balls of the feet, start with the tip of the toes, it flexes the muscles. It was strange listening to the two associates talking about the fact that they're talking. Well I'll be darned, what postmodernity!, fascinating how my thoughts are not in sync with my fear, I'm scared, yet my thoughts run free. It's not the first time I've noticed it.

In short, I better lay off—who?—and I better not play innocent and ask who, because he's gonna slap me down like a taximeter. The younger of the two was talking. It's been ages since there were taximeters to be slapped down, but I knew that this would not protect me from anything. Still, I thought, how interesting, this blockhead using an expression that has no correspondence in the real world. So much abstraction! If I were to tell him this, he'd slap me down like a taximeter, I thought. We'd been circling around this for some time; the cantata did not progress further; I should lay off, who?, and get out of the picture. Since Hungarian lacks the distinguishing pronouns he and she, I couldn't even tell if it was a man or a woman I was supposed to lay off of. A woman, most probably. And it's a rotten deal, taking advantage of a person's solitude. A rotten deal. A person's life-solitude. Because I shouldn't go thinking for a second that this solitude ever let up. The old man spoke meekly. What do I know about real solitude? It's like living in a glass house, under a bell jar, you call people to you, then you try luring them, and they come, and then bang, up against the glass, bewildered, they stop, you even hear the bang, then watch them walk away, fuming mad. And it's no use calling to them again. Then after a while you don't even call. Fuck them! You feel like you're a leper, your body covered with tiny pussy sores, the filthy yellow pus oozing out, stinking little sulfurous puffs of cloud rising from you, or as if there were a sign on you, beware, infectious! Or second class. And if you happen to meet another man with a sign, you act like you're not like that, and he acts like you. A solitary man has been deserted by the Lord, sonny.

Shit, Uncle Lajos, will you stop, shit, the little rat needs a good scare is what he needs, I told you not to come and let me handle this, you see what a little prick he is, shitting in his pants, look at his ass, him clenching his muscles, oh, *excusez-moi*, Uncle Lajos, I near forgot, he's an Academic, an Academic *and* a shithead, a moron, a living oxymoron. You can see for yourself. At which point a black Volga rounded the corner from the post office street, and slowly, silently, as if it were still one of those old Party-state Volgas,* nosed toward us. My companions stopped behind me, I did, too, and squeezed my butt muscles together. Flex, relax. It's Karesz, Uncle Lajos, time to go, I'll just summarize our say, Uncle Lajos, he'll catch on just fine, it's as easy as shitting between the sheets.

Right away my ears slipped inside my skull; they're going to wring my neck, I thought, literally wring it, like a chicken, his lower arm gripped me like a vise, his paddle hands clenched on top of my head, then he twisted my head to the side, I was so surprised that luckily I forgot to tense my neck muscles (my mother would have approved), he leaned forward, right into my face, and as if in keeping with the rough-and-tumble etiquette of a soccer pitch on the outskirts of town he was about to head me, I squeezed my eyes shut, then opened them again, I glared at him, his warm breath trickled down by cheeks, down into my mouth, down my neck, and under my shirt collar. The mentholated chewing gum made it feel fresh, too. There's no seeing a face closer than this, so why all the fuss over me not turning around? He didn't even look forty, someone like that I consider

* Curtained-off black Volgas were used by the communist secret police to cart people off for interrogation and imprisonment, preferably at night, and without any previous warning. They thus became objects of fear and symbols of state repression.

young without a second thought; funny that I should still think this fact is worth mentioning. His dark complexion was gleaming, as if it had been smoothed over with oil, smoothed with ceremony, a designer job, but it wasn't the extravagant and, need we add, ill-begotten wealth that showed, nor the taste that was not wholly independent of it but, simply put, nature: the way nature arranged for the hazel eyes to go with the bright, raven-black hair (all raven-black hair reminds me of my father), and also black eyebrows, as if lined with black pencil, a hint of bluish stubble, faultless skin, in short, nature's bounty, its dispassionate beauty hung over me in that strange face, and so aggressively and mysteriously close that I could no longer think of it as a stranger's. And whoever orchestrated all this, the picture, the distances, the movements and the pounding of the heart, also took pains that everything should not seem unaccountably perfect: what in his body, in that *much* was above reproach as muscle now seemed like an odd, gentle chubbiness, enervation or defenselessness, while the body, threatening still, was the source of threatening misunderstandings, and though the premature oedemic pouches under the eyes indicated the approach of the fourth X, this innocent accretion of the cheeks seemed, on the contrary, to bring news of a preadolescent Eden, as if on purpose to give added emphasis to the pink carnality of the lips. It's been a long time since a man's lips have been this close to me, to my own.

Let him go, the old man said quietly, and shoved us, both of us at the same time, like a sculpture group. Meanwhile, the car came to a halt beside us. Luckily, this reminded me of my fear again, otherwise I'd have begun to feel like the hero of a novel, and this hero-of-a-novel feeling outside of a novel is not without its risks, because you can't resist the smug temptation to think that you are also the author. I remember, it was at least forty years ago, I was heading right here, to the corner, next to the post office to buy groceries, I walked into the grocery store immersed in my mother's usual brief list, 4 pds. bread, 2 quarts milk, 1 bunch soup greens (but only if they're nice!), when is a bunch of soup greens nice?, I asked myself, oblivious to the unnatural silence that greeted me, with everyone looking in the same direction, me, too; a young man was standing by the cashier, brandishing a knife. Without thinking, in sync with the soup greens, as it were, I kicked the knife out of his hand, he gave me a look of surprise, disgruntled, shook his head, and before anyone could do anything beat a retreat. The shoppers became animated once again, they congratulated me and thanked me. The shop manager even hugged me. I forgot the shopping, I said good-bye to the cashier, keep it up, son, she said distracted, trying to shorten the swelling line of shoppers, she didn't even look up, I walked out the door, and when I reached the first plane tree, I hugged it, sobbing. I'm sorry, I'm sorry, I kept repeating.

You stop shoving, Uncle Lajos, you mind, stop shoving me around, at which another silence ensued; I didn't know what game we were playing, and as for them, they kept slipping out of their roles. The old man looked at me differently now, the tears welling up in his eye. Look, Count, don't do it, I know you didn't start it but that's neither here nor there, the person in question, for them it's serious, while you're just playing, Count, having your bit of fun, he breathed softly, without a trace of emotion, so fuck off and stop your little game.

That's it, Lajos old pal, good for you, go tell the little shit go fuck his Academic oxymoron whore of a mother, that's who!

Shut up. The younger man shrugged, strolled over to the car, opened the front door, leaned in, kissed the driver on both cheeks, strengthened up again and, like a hotel porter, opened wide the back door, then sat up front, but to the side, his legs hanging out, like on a bench. The old man stepped over to me, I backed away, but the pleasant cloud of his perfume reached me just the same. No need to be scared, Petikém. I'm not scared, I lied as quickly as when I kicked the knife out of that guy's hand. He took me by the shoulder, but then didn't know what to do with the gesture and released me. This slight hesitation made me draw a false conclusion regarding my own strength and predicament, and I resorted to the old rough-and-tumble soccer pitch style.

What the fuck's up, old man?

The younger of the two attempted to rise, banged his head, smothered a curse, plumped back down, and stroked where it hurt.

The fuck that's up, Count, is that I love the individual in question. As the old man said the word "love," his features hardened, all the while that the tears kept streaming down his cheeks, down on the sides of his nose into the sharply defined grooves that seemed to have been created expressly to channel these rare tears, though when dry (in dry season), they're the banal embodiment of manhood. Consider, Count, we're talking about an old man, the idiot waxes nostalgic, you understand, don't you?!, let 'em go, I beg you, toss 'em away from you, say, go away, say, go back to your Uncle Lajos. He took one step toward me, then immediately another one back, as if practicing a dance step. But then he touched me just the same and gently placed his huge hand on my chest. I thought I could hear the beating of my heart. I know you will understand me, son.

Which was too much for the other guy, he leaped out of the car, will you come on, Uncle Lajos, we're not about to beg the little prick on bended knees, and with that he shoved the old man in the back, slipped in beside him, and with a playful movement of the hips pushed him, shoved him farther in, slammed the door, said something to me in parting, but I didn't catch what, then just as slowly as it had come, the car started up the boulevard in the direction of the main road; the indicator light was left on, it was blinking from afar as they gained distance, yellow and weak, like a recently discovered old and remote star.

THE ETERNAL PLANE TREE

I threw my arms around the plane tree. I can't be sobbing and hugging a plane tree all the time.

4. FACTORY AND MOTHER

LANDING A JOB

Like my father in the darkened room, so my mother in the factory; I want to talk about this first, and only afterward about the fabulous changes in our lives brought about by Puskás's meditation. After which my mother landed a job at the Farkasvölgy Spinning Works, or, as the locals called it, the Works. I didn't land that job, son, I took the place by storm. You'd think I was not a simple fan, but a player myself, some important person from center field, what can I say, a veritable Dodó Stefanek who, as everyone knows, played halfback for the Opticals. It patronizes, this is how they always put it, and never supports, the Works patronizes the football team, the whole sports club in fact, which consisted of the football team. We later learned that the Works was patronizing us as well, except we weren't clear about what this involved. Don't ask anybody to patronize you, son, or you'll live to regret it.* We

* In case there should be any doubt about the political implications of being "patronized," the Works, like any other large company, was an unofficial arm of the government and state security, so when it "patronized" or sponsored a club or organization, it was also spying on them.

also heard something about a base of operations,* and the reality of it was just as vague as the words themselves. The majority of the players from the grownup team (with the possible exception of a certain Ivan Miatoff) had a job at the Works, mostly alibi jobs; prior to '56 they actually had to be there full-time, but after '56 they just had to show up for their pay, though sometimes they miscalculated the so-called payday, which became a bone of contention between operations and the operationees, during which the expression *socialist morale* would also come up. No need for the crap, Chief. Then after a long and meaningful silence: Oh, yes, there is! After another long and meaningful silence: Well, if there's a need, Chief, then there's a need. The two of them, each in his own way, were just reflecting on the practical and cynical nature of the new, nascent dictatorship.

On that May morning when, freshly rouged, in a rustling, bustling cotton skirt, my mother elbowed her merry way past little Kas's grandmother, the porter, she was no longer in the first blush of youth. There are such May mornings (and there are such sentences). People said that little Kas had a bright future ahead of him, even though at the time the ball reached up to his knees, if that, but then nothing became of him except Kas, Ferenc Kas, mechanic; he didn't even attend the games, why should he, nobody keeps tags on a has-been. Although . . . there are always witnesses. In short, my mother was no longer in the first blush of youth; on the other hand, she had just shed ten pounds; how she managed it was a mystery, she never made a strong commit-

* If a company acting as a "patron" or sponsor was big enough, it would act as a base of operations for both the Party and the secret police, the ÁVÓ. Thus, just like the concept of "patronizing," the term "base of operations" was also thoroughly politicized and took on a highly sinister coloring.

ment or anything—she put her conscience at ease by resorting to petty discipline: from now on I eat only and exclusively when I eat, and not in between—still, she managed to "work off" ten pounds without a real decision. As a result, her arms—the most elegant arms in the world!—regained their original thinness, her belly, too, was smaller, if far from ideal, it remained what it was, a fat belly, but thanks to the ten pounds she'd lost, when looking at my mother, no one thought that her belly was fat, whereas her belly was fat, they thought that her belly had become smaller, in short, that she is almost not even fat anymore. She also changed her hair color; she started turning gray early, and so she had it tinted as a matter of course; back then women had a collective fear of graying hair; my mother, too, had only recently made up her mind to try and see if gray hair might suit her, and it's like I always said, a silver diadem shooting sparks on her head; it doesn't make her look older, just more dignified. Though who knows? When you're young, maybe it's the dignity that adds years to your age. Be that as it may, my mother lost no time in having it tinted brown (she chose her older sister's hair color), it's this that she had now changed to a lighter shade to go with the minus ten pounds. Her beautician was called Ernő, Ernőke. Ernőke, the wizard of the hydrogen bottle. YourexcellencywhatImeaniscomrade, this is how he addressed his customers, all in one breath. Oh, Ernőke, the dictatorship of the proletariat can't get the better of you! But it did. In '56 a Russian tank rolled over him. At first it looked like the angels were holding his hand then, too, because he'd gone around the corner for a poppy seed roll; Ernőke had a reputation for being passionate about poppy seed rolls, a veritable poppy seed fanatic; the only thing he loved more than poppy seed rolls was (possibly) Aunt Rózsi, his mother; like everybody else, he also called her Aunt Rózsi, who, ever since her fortunate return from Theresienstadt, refused to open her mouth to speak even though her son pleaded with her, don't be contrary, dear Aunt Rózsi, I know you could if you wanted to; but after a brief period of shouting and threatening, he acquiesced to the silence that awaited him every day when he walked through the door, and conducted nice, long one-sided conversations with his mother about all sorts of things, his day-to-day business, the secret of making preserves, the arts, politics, love. Is dear Rózsika talking yet, Ernőke? You could say that yourexcellencywhatImeaniscomrade, you could say that, good, kindly hold your head just so, thank you. Before he reached the bakery he saw that his shoelaces had come undone, and while he was tying them a Russian tank behind him aimed a direct hit at the bakery, with not as much as a single poppy seed role remaining, if that. When he got back to the beauty parlor, he was just thinking about how he would color the story of his miraculous escape for the benefit of Aunt Rózsi, when the same tank appeared before him through the shop window, it couldn't negotiate a turn and slowly, with its breaks on, it rolled into the beauty parlor. That's where the small take-out place is now. That woman makes the best tripes! When Ernőke was crushed underneath the tank, that very instant Aunt Rózsika opened her mouth to speak, and from then on, through every moment of her life, she cursed God incessantly, hardly pausing for breath; she even slept less, so she shouldn't waste time.

MY MOTHER AND SEX

Take it easy, son, my mother's fat belly, I can just see your hand shake as you write it, my mother's fat belly. And then we haven't even gone farther south. I understand that you're doing your best to forget I'm a woman. Tomes have been written on the subject. Or that I was. Of course, it's more complicated than this I am I was thing, but I wouldn't want to shock you. You'd rather hear me say that my body hasn't got a gender anymore, just pain, after a certain age every day inevitably brings its own pain, I recently read this in a book by some Italian or other. (Not some Italian, but Giuseppi Tomasi di Lampedusa, she knows, and I know.) I have nothing to look forward to except death, you like being scandalized by stuff like that. Death and the Champions League. I didn't like her talking about death as if it were some insipid TV series or a banal invitation to dinner. Of the two of us I was (and am) more of a prude, which she considered hypocritical. No matter how congenial our conversations, and these conversations light up my life, my days with my mother are lighter, more radiant than my days without her, there will always be a wall between us, but I know that this is not the consequence of us being on our guard, and that it can't be demolished through the raw, or just consistent application of honesty, saying what's on your mind; it's not even a wall, it's worse, because it is less distinct, less palpable, a veil, or, rather, two hanging veils, and between them the distance of which there is no knowing the size. It lacks dimension. It's not even a distance but a haze, it's as if a haze had settled between us, between our separate times. The way she talks about things and the way I talk about things, between that. That I don't fully understand what she is telling me. Look, son, I obviously have no problem with prudery. Oh, yes, you do! Bona fide prudery is not tendentious, it's not there to guarantee that you behave as you should, it's of no use, it should be wiped off the books, you either have it in you or you don't. And if you ask me, you don't, that's why you accuse me of it. Assuredly, it has occurred to you, and let me put this delicately, that you have been in my lap. Assuredly. There we were, trying to reinvent Freudism with nothing to fall back on but our own resources. It has even occurred to me that I'd been where my father had been. Could it be that this haze, this affection-filled helplessness, could it not be that this, that this, too, has its explanation there, between my mother's and my father's legs? My relationship to the space between these legs is like no one else's (bar my siblings). And their relationship to me. And to each other. Never in my life have I been closer to a human being, and yet I can't get close enough. My mother says that when I was born, when she was bringing me into the world, that at the moment of my birth, she laughed. That I came into the world to the sound of her joyous laughter. And that at times she thinks, at times she can tell just by looking at me—subconsciously, of course, of course!—that I remember it.

A PIECE OF CHERRY (SOUR)

I saw my father closest to my mother when—the beauty of the scene frightened me so that I can still hear my heart pounding—my father dropped a cherry or sour cherry between my mother's lips, who panted, wheezed, and grunted, like an animal. A thin sliver of saliva dribbled down the corner of her lips. Are you very lonely, son?

A WORD (GRANDMOTHER DETOUR)

My grandmother spent every moment of her life praying for my father. In what *remained*, she spent haranguing my mother. My mother had these jumping to her feet things. You just go on eating, don't mind me, mother would say jumping to her feet—any time, at dinner, at lunch, less often at breakfast, at which my grandmother would pipe, as if reciting a folk song: Oh, dear heart, if only you knew how *little* we mind. My mother functioned like a classical mother almost exclusively at breakfast, or when she was really worn out. She insisted on breakfast, which the busy lifestyle of European mornings has done away with as a genre, but she wouldn't have it, munching on the run, that's the non plus ultra of ill breeding (she loved this expression, I used it before I could understand it), but there's a solution, son, we get up half an hour earlier, this way there's plenty of time for everything, and I do mean everything, the day must be given time, it must be given its due, it must be sanctified! I always felt like a young man by my mother's side, then, as now, at the age of five, and at the age of fifty-eight.

Don't you make light of that word! Grandmother did not take breakfast with us; a space less than a chamber but more than a recess opened from the inner room, basically taken up with grandmother's bed with no space left on the side, her bed reached to the walls, so she had to climb up from the foot of the bed, holding on, and the same thing getting off. Quite a feat, either way. Grandmother knelt on the bed, then tried to negotiate her center of gravity toward the middle; if she managed this too quickly, she fell face-first on the bed, otherwise she rested in the middle of the maneuver, balancing on her hands and knees. Halftime, mother dear! The cotton nightdress lay taut on her, you got a nice ass on you still, mother dear, and do tell, is this chemise *that certain* chemise?; grandmother, I could hear, groaned and moaned like my mother with that cherry, God will punish you, child! They generally ended with God, sometimes addressing each other in the familiar, sometimes in the formal, without rhyme or reason.

But when it's got to be sanctified! Besides, why shouldn't I use it, mother dear?

Need you ask?

Are you trying to bring God into this, mother dear? My mother laughed, offended, my grandmother kept mum, like a child. She was fat, fleshy, but her flesh belied her age, and her skin, too, was free of wrinkles. You think the Lord is a philistine like you?

Don't say that.

Alright, for once you're right. She smoothed down her coral-red skirt. Or poppy red? Your mother doesn't know where to draw the line. Do you know what you are, mother dear?

Grandmother was incapable of not answering a question. A question must be answered, "I don't know," that's an answer, too; because only where there's an answer is there a question, she preached. I later read something of the sort in Wittgenstein. Every question must be properly considered, the Good Lord didn't create the question mark for nothing. Oh, please, mother dear! On the other hand, she refused to consider questions related to mathematics, whether properly or improperly. The truth is, the minute she heard a number, she tuned out, as if she'd fainted. Quick! The smelling salts! But when out of the blue I began reciting from the credo, oh, Tancredi, what shall become of us and our unhappy homeland?!,* she'd stop hulling the peas, I had picked them from the garden, sighed, or rather the air forced itself out of her, let me see now, it might be advisable to divide the question into two parts thus: *a*: what will become of us, what shall, grandmother, what shall become of us, and *b*: what shall become of our homeland? Which is unhappy, grandmother. Don't interrupt, and who is this Tancredi anyway? Music to my ears. Grandmother clapped her hands together. You're thinking of your father again! But she was wrong, I never thought of my father *in secret*. Grandmother always said it like this: your father, my poor, hapless son, as if we were inside a traditional play where it's still important to know who is who. Our father, as you surely know, was a corn merchant.

What am I, is that the question? Grandmother took the bait again, let's call it the Wittgenstein bait. My mother was getting ready to leave; as opposed to the jumpings up from the table, there were these leisurely leavings; mother was mostly getting ready to leave, preparing herself to leave, fixing her hair or applying her lipstick; this is the picture that has remained with me, her standing in front of the mirror, and while she's reciting the forwards of a team, Laci Csordás, Szűcs, Hermann, Birkás I, Birkás II, as if counting her rosaries, she's trying a variety of lip colors. Women used more lipstick in the old days, it seems to me. I think. (This was one of my father's jokes: I'm unsure of myself. I think.) For this once, dear, I'd rather not be wanting to answer your question, lest I be tempted to say what you are, dear, a great big you know what, dear, and unless I'm sadly mistaken, your reaction would be temperate at best. My father

* A line from Gioacchino Rossini's patriotic opera *Tancredi* (1813).

took to using the word "temperate" from her, and I from him; so it goes.

Come, come, mother dear, and, laughing heartily, she clasped her mother-in-law in an extravagant embrace, who was at a loss to protect herself from both the embrace and the kisses assailing her cheeks.

At least think of your lipstick, grandmother said, fuming quietly.

My mother suddenly left, not so much grandmother as her kisses and the embrace, she laughed and danced, skipping toward the door like a schoolgirl, out, out and away; when she reached the door, she turned around. Don't hold yourself back, mother, don't be afraid to say it; though she had stopped laughing by then, she said it in high spirits. She invariably spoke in high spirits and she invariably listened in low. She was prompting her mother-in-law like a child, go on, dear, say it; grandmother listened, sulking, truly like a child, keeping her tears in check, her lips compressed. Would you like a little help? It's just a word, mother, come on, don't be shy. . . . Would you like me to give you the first letter?

I was familiar with the word in question, sometimes I felt like shouting it out already, this thing always lasted too long, with both of them caught up in the helpless ruffling of each other's feathers. If my mother had a small glass or two beforehand, a liqueur glass, son, a liqueur glass, I must hand it to them, those monks knew something besides their prayers!, then she took less time saying the word. You see, mother dear, it didn't kill you. And it didn't kill me either, she said quietly, solemnly. Grandmother waited for the door to close. Nobody dies of anything, these days it's not fashionable to die of anything, especially not of shame.

She turned to me. She didn't die from it, but my poor son, your poor hapless father, did. She peered at me, then she lowered her head, then she shook her head. Let's not be unreasonable, that's not what killed him.

How come he died, when he's alive? I never asked. As for that word, whatever the context, even if it's a traffic sign saying thru traffic, it makes me think of my mother. And so, I have a friendly relationship with that word. Concretely, I love it.

MY MOTHER AND SOARING

We might safely say that my mother's career at the Works took off in tune with the flight of socialism. We soared, son, you couldn't find a better word if you tried, we soared. When this so-called socialist regime finally understood, when it acknowledged, however reluctantly, that there's such a thing as money, money as such, it also acknowledged, reluctantly, that there's a world outside the Camp; whether life was possible there it would not say, it kept as equivocally tight-lipped on the subject—if not encouraging, yet tolerating the various kinds of silences—as on the subject of the possibility of life after death. The awkward complexity of the sentence faithfully reflects the circumstances at the time, a certain one might say new adjustment to the facts that for all intents and purposes appeared to be facts, as well as the ideologically tainted stage fright (fear) that was its consequence.

The Works also discovered the West, concretely France, for the simple reason that Laci Vizi, who was playing left-winger back then and who, exceptionally, really worked at the plant as a locksmith—laugh all you want, I like working, when I'm not working, my heart aches, oh, sure, Laci Vizi and his heart!, so then, as I was saying, Laci Vizi's older brother, Feri Vizi, who was supposed to have a God-given talent for playing center-half, which is interesting, son, because in Hungary no one ever says of a defense that he's talented, no man living says that Lóránt or Buzánszky is talented, tough yes, reliable yes, good, indispensable, but talented?, on the other hand that's what they said about Feri Vizi, except he got so fat from some thyroid problem that by thirty he was as obese as an American capitalist on one of those contemporary caricatures, and in '55 he nearly became manager of the Works because he joined the Party, Imre Nagy wing and so on,* details that would be boring to detail here; he was a clever man, he veritably skipped up the rungs of the hierarchy, but before ambition, ability, cunning and surely no more than the absolute requisite slyness (on the far side of aspiration yet possibly just on this side of baseness) could help him reach his epiphany, and like an ode to joy place him in the factory manager's chair, there came

· 1956

the revolution broke out, and carried away by the discreet charm of liberty, Feri Vizi turned revolutionary like nobody's business; he intuited that he wouldn't have many more opportunities in

* Prior to the Hungarian Revolution of 1956, the reform communist Imre Nagy (1896–1958) was for a short time prime minister of Hungary, but fell out of favor with the Soviet Politburo when he promoted a "new course" in socialism. He surfaced again as prime minister by popular demand during the anti-Soviet uprising of 1956, when he made his famous appeal on radio, vainly asking the West for help. Two years after the revolution was crushed by Soviet troops, Nagy was secretly tried and executed on charges of high treason. His trial and execution were made public only after the sentence had been carried out.

his life to be a revolutionary, when there are no routine every-days, when eternal brightness sheds its light on us, then we find that despite the odds we are still alive, and it no longer makes sense to draw distinctions between good and bad, because everything that concerns us is good, there is no need for the routine, fastidious, energy-draining effort of weighing who is like what among us, because we are the good, we are the nation, we are Sándor Petőfi, except that Feri is fat, a fact, if a negligible fact, because it's the twinkle in the eye that counts, we feel like one big, brilliant football team where, granted, you are you, but you are you through *us*, only through the team can you be you, and the team is the way it is because you are you, and there is nothing jarring in this give-and-take, nothing is swept under the big national carpet; true, the nation requires that you give it your all now, but nothing that you wouldn't give of your own accord, you're not sacrificing yourself, you are simply living, but you're living on a higher plane—except, in keeping with the local tradition of lost causes, this too was a lost cause, in that bleak November drabness deceptively pierced by the sunny rays of hope, yes, as if the sky were always blue behind the clouds, the usual future was approaching with the usual weighty tedium of fact, with the appeals to the nation or in the name of the nation, among which it will be impossible to differentiate, it will even ask things that Feri Vizi will not want to give, but no, it's not going to ask, it's going to demand, but no, it's not even going to demand, there will be no need for demands because there will be the rule of law, but no, there will only be order, but not law, the homeland will issue hysterical dictates, and for a while yet you can bristle, grumbling that you are the homeland and those others the state, at best, but then, alone, by yourself, you can't be a homeland, and when you walked along the long inner courtyard of the Works like before, nobody looked you in the eye, the makeshift podium assembled from crates was still standing by the wall in the loom chamber, now just crates again, nailed together awkwardly and in haste, awkwardly and without much thought, and how unnecessarily!, it'd be best not even to remember it, have it disassembled in the night, so that by morning there should be no reminder left of the chaos in which the by no means appropriate use of the crates may have seemed—for certain parties!—natural, and in fact, by the next day, Karesz Hazai, the Party secretary, had it disassembled, and if, like a hunting dog thrown off the scent, anyone should have come sniffing around the empty spot where the crates had been, looking for what is gone, gone, gone, and yet as if it had once been, he'd have heard nothing but the clatter of the spinning looms and the laughter of the women and girls, because working by the spinning machines—why?—even she, the wife of Birkás I, who suspected that it was just a matter of days before her husband would be taken to police headquarters, even she could laugh, true, it was only for two days, but they beat him within an inch of his life, and there was no knowing why; they asked him questions, Birkás I answered honestly, to the best of his ability, then they beat him, then more questions, a nice, coherent answer, then they beat him, and even those laughed who hadn't seen their boyfriend for two days, nor their boyfriend's friend; on the other hand, his friend Sasha Kertész was very much in evidence, as if he were orchestrating this brave new world all on his own, he had an explosive kick, son, especially from place, a free kick by Sasha was half a goal, they said appreciatively nodding in the stands, but old man Gruber always corrected this in line with the latest concrete statistics, he wore a black linen jacket like theater directors do these days, black takes pounds off you, with a dizzying number of pockets, though you could count them, four on the outside, but the lower two had a secret pocket of sorts applied to them, divided secret pockets, in fact, and inside on top the usual, and at the bottom, too, plus two more, and regardless of what Uncle Gruber was looking for, he fumbled through all those pockets, then brought the slip up close to his eye, pushed his glasses up on his forehead and leaned into the slip of paper as if he were hard of seeing, just like my math teacher in high school, except Uncle Gruber didn't bring an icy fear to my heart; still, everyone fell silent now, too, the bench fell silent as the old man deciphered the truth from the slip of paper, gentlemen, your excellency, of the women milling around, the players' girlfriends, wives, younger sisters, older sisters, mothers (!), only my mother counted—to use a quaint expression—as a human being, it is with regret if not unmixed with satisfaction at the factuality of the facts, and despite the correction, it behooves me to announce, with the highest esteem, that Mr. Lajos Kertész's free kick (no one knows how Lajos had turned into Sasha, but Uncle Gruber never used his nickname, a circumstance which in some eyes might have made the highest esteem he never neglected to emphasize suspect; Gruber, son, is a man of integrity) is not a half, meaning a 0.5 goal, but a 0.37 goal, which is a leading score in the team, still, allow me to comment at this point, without the slightest hint of insinuation, that the unofficial championship table which it is my duty to register is headed by Ferenc Vizi with a 0.46 goal average; Sasha had promised the women that there would be no trouble, and there was almost none, nearly all of them made it home without incident, yet there was less laughter in the spinning room, Birkás I would not talk to Birkás II, and as for Feri Vizi—after he walked along the empty factory yard, empty because although people came toward him, nobody stopped to chat, their greeting an uneasy version of a mumble whose nature could be gainsaid at any time, the factory yard is empty, everything is empty, the country is empty, he thought, whereas he'd never thought of the country before, he thought mostly of the eighteen-yard line, because he was always kicking free kicks in his head, making the exercises more and more difficult, then *he'd* give *it a go* at practice, son, ten times out of ten Feri would hit the upper goal post from the eighteen-yard line, and what momentum!, like Göröcs and his team later on; there's this video with Ronaldinho now, but if you ask me, it's trick photography—anyway, Feri Vizi went looking for Sasha Kertész, who as usual was loafing around the women, he made them laugh and they laughed (which is what I meant just now, when I said that there was less laughter), in short, Feri Vizi went and stood by him, an old story, but it's safer to tell stories around the soccer field, where they even know about Sándor Szűcs being murdered, whereas that was highly classified, I think it may still be classified, the Hollywood story of the football player and the popular singer spruced up with the East European bestiality of the early fifties; later it was mostly Laci Gál who brought it up, and Gruber just shook his head, and there was no knowing what he found offensive, the story or the way it was told, what're you, Uncle Gruber, a nodding machine?, stop shaking your head like that, what's become of your sense of humor?; they set a trap for them, a man from the ÁVÓ, don't shit in your pants, Uncle Gruber, it's okay to say the word now, it's okay to come down on Rákosi,[*] we haven't even taken full advantage of it yet, Uncle Gruber, we haven't taken full advantage of Rákosi, the man from the ÁVÓ said he'd help them leave the country, but they were waiting for them at the frontier, the question being, old man, why, what was the use, the profit in sentencing him to death, because Szűcs was executed, while that sweet singer got put behind bars for four years, they didn't even serve as a deterrent, because the story was kept top secret, or was it just for their amusement?, or is it like this?, that it just happens?, that you don't even have to want what's bad?; I didn't realize you had a philosophical streak in you, Lacikám, at which there was silence, Feri Vizi went up to Sasha, the first KISZ[†] secretary of the plant, with the clear and avowed intention of slugging him, but then he didn't, though according to one version he spit on the ground at his feet, but this version sprouted two other versions, the more interesting of the two purports to know about the yellowish green, angry color of the phlegmy spit, the white foam encircling the mound like a crown, the jelly-like quiver of its consistency, thanks to which the

* Mátyás Rákosi (1892–1971) was the de facto head of Hungary from 1945 to 1956. As general secretary of the Hungarian communist party who described himself as "Stalin's best Hungarian disciple," he continued to be a hard-line communist even after Stalin's death in 1953. In June 1956, under pressure from the Soviet Politburo, he was stripped of his office and forced to move to a remote region of the Soviet Union, officially to "seek medical attention." Accordingly, by the sixties it was okay "to come down on Rákosi."

† Acronym of the Magyar Kommunista Ifjúsági Szövetség—the Young Communist League of Hungary, the official youth organization of the Party founded in 1957 to indoctrinate and keep the youth of the nation in line after the failed revolution of '56.

phlegm didn't just look like a piece of art but a living creature, a pulsating, unpredictable creature which in its trembling and vomitous strength said practically everything about the putrid future in which it would be possible to live after all, you can always live, son, because you must, while according to the second version, Feri Vizi did nothing and turned right around as if he'd come in only by mistake, leaving behind Sasha, the man of the new times, the empty factory yard, emptier than empty, everything, his family, the country, and defected.

THE SOARING, CONTINUED

To France. And did very well by himself. He was practically an industrialist, Laci Vizi used to say, by which he meant that he was an industrialist, and he can hardly believe it; my brother the magnate, it can't be. But it was.

And as for Lajos Kertész, seeing how things were shaping up at home, he didn't elbow Károly Hazai out of his post as Party secretary but became his right hand, meaning—and this is already part of the joke, possibly the wittiest joke of the Party organization at the plant—his left!, the left is the right hand!, hey, Comrades, let's not get caught up in the words of the new times!, and there was great rejoicing, for Karcsi Hazai was blessed with a cheerful temperament by, well, there's another question for you, because by whom indeed?, because it could easily be that it was the Lord Himself who blessed him, because granted that the commies did not concern themselves with God *von Haus aus*, yet there are instances of God concerning Himself with them; for instance, He loves them, or (and) blesses them with a cheerful temperament; nonetheless, district headquarters frowned on Karesz's unrelenting good cheer, that's no way to build socialism, a minor big shot from the Party was supposed to have said, but for his part, Karesz didn't want a career, he loved the plant and wanted to secure advantages and to safeguard the ones they already enjoyed, to protect his own, as it were, though we can't rule out the possibility that his unrelenting and unwarranted good cheer was due less to having found his calling at the plant than to finding a woman; his wife, Ica, was a veritable Brigitte Bardot, except she wasn't a flirt, she lived a chaste and quiet life and held my mother in contempt with all her heart, with all her heart, son, and that's something I can respect, because of her bright red skirt and, let's put it this way, her enthusiastic style of cheering; they attended Sunday night Mass together, where Ica confessed her contempt of my mother, and after Mass personally asked for her forgiveness, too, she didn't give concrete reasons, just mentioned her human frailty as such; nodding, my mother pretended sympathy, we weren't born to be perfect, Ica dear, and looking about her, desperately sought an escape route and was immediately found out; nothing was lost on Mrs. Károly Hazai, so by the time they parted, there was again enough accumulated contempt to last until the next confession, until the next championship, son; everything about Ica was mediocre except her body, she was a mediocre believer, she tried to please the Lord and in return humbly expected Him to assist her in everyday life, for instance, that she should not gain weight but should be able to find a round of beef, and that they should leave Karesz alone, etc.; basically, her relationship to the Lord was like her husband's to the district Party organization, with the one exception that her opinion of her superior was better than Karesz's was of his, but even though she was generally known to be a regular, and in fact, because of her husband's position, what we may safely call an intrepid churchgoer, she couldn't dress plainly and unassumingly enough so that her hills and dales shouldn't become the metaphysical center during Mass, this is what I meant by Brigitte Bardot, this light, this radiance, this apotheosis of flesh, don't get yourself worked up, son!, and this is what the choir of Virgin Marys in church called indecent, while the Saint Josephs kept as quiet as the big bells on Good Friday, meaning like slithering snakes in the grass; they called her a slut unfairly and without any basis in fact, but the nasty injustice never came to light, because, as if on purpose, to corroborate the truth of the rumors about her, Ica up and left her husband, she packed her belongings and left him because, as luck would have it, on the way to church she met an engineer from Pécs who had just bought flowers at Ibi's, gladioli, and when he saw those hills and dales undulating toward him, that geokinetic wonder, he dropped to his knees in front of her and gave her the gladioli meant for someone else; Ica went to Mass, the engineer waited impatiently outside the church, my one true love, I believe in nothing but you, in response to which it wasn't what you'd expect with Karesz Hazai seeking cure by taking the hair of the dog that bit him and finding another woman a.s.a.p., charming her out of her pants with his assuredly winning smile or his assuredly very real political power, or both; one of the spinners at the plant would have been the logical choice (especially the wife of Birkás I), but he didn't charm anyone either short distance or long, the smile did not wither from his face, he did not tip the bottle on the sly and so did not neglect his daily shower and shave, he did not cause a scandal at the Party meeting by comparing Lenin's whatnot to

Stalin's, a pink bum or a hairy ass, that's the question, Comrades, because life sometimes depends on that, on a good ass; in short, he did not mention the two leaders out of disrespect; on the contrary, with this question he placed them in the mainstream of life or, rather, Comrade Stalin, or rather not comrade, because, and he's the first to admit it, he's getting things a bit muddled, the Workers' Movement has such a lot of twists and turns in the road, good turns, important turns, there's so much purification that if your attention lags for just an instant, you end up saying Rákosi, whereas you meant Kádár,* or the other way around, the devil take this fucking life and stick it up where it hurts; this is not what happened, what happened is that when the following Monday Sárika the cleaning lady (whom, if *Production Novel* were not a novel,† we'd know in the flesh—laughter from the peanut gallery) found Karesz Hazai hanging from a rope, there they hung, dear hearts, all four of them, Comrade Marx, Comrade Engels, Comrade Lenin, and Comrade Hazai, the first three on the wall behind the desk, a veritable Trinity, and Karesz on the handle of the swinging window; that's all that was left, it seems, because the wrought iron chandelier lay in pieces on the floor; whether the comrades live or die, it's always me having to pick up the pieces; and so in the

* János Kádár (1912–1989) was made head of the Hungarian communist party after he called in the Russian troops to crush the 1956 uprising. Having declared that "he who is not against us is with us," his rule brought a modicum of freedom into people's lives for which he is fondly remembered by some and affectionately called Uncle Kádár by others. Still, his regime exercised absolute control over the government, in which it resembled the Rákosi years.

† The author's third novel, *Termelési-regény*, 1979.

end Sasha Kertész was made Party secretary after all, with the proviso that he hang up his soccer shoes, and he hanged them up right away, but before that, when he became the Party secretary's right hand, it's called an eager beaver, son!, then, in that capacity, he nice and slow got wind of everything, everything that transpired in and around the plant; Sasha didn't like the stool-pigeon expression, it's not to the point, there's an aim, the future of the country, that's what we're all aiming for, some embracing one means and method, some another, the path is one, the trails are myriad, etcetera, etcetera; he had concrete people working for him, Uncle Ádi for one, though basically just to be on the safe side, to keep to form, because he also knew that as it makes the rounds, information is inevitably warped, altered, deformed, it doesn't take malicious intent or intention, and yet, whether the shit hits the fan or the fan hits the shit, it's not the same, it doesn't call for the implementation of equal measures.

THE BEGINNING OF A BEAUTIFUL FRIENDSHIP

Tóth was called to the Party office. He was a latter-day commie who joined the Party so that not having joined the Party shouldn't stand in his way at least. We'd like to ask you something, Comrade Tóth, the Party secretary said absently, for by then he'd grown tired—it would be hard to say of what. Possibly the standing in place. Whereas any other option would have been worse. Because if things got worse, then they got worse, but if things got better the well-trodden paths changed and there was real danger of upsetting the highly delicate balance of mutually stipulated unspoken agreements, and then, as a consequence of the positive changes—by now no longer unexpectedly—

everything would get worse. They appreciated his cynicism at the plant because cynicism is rational, it's something you can count on. He asked Tóth to keep an eye on the soccer players. Bagatelle, Tóth thought to himself, still, he played hard to get, is it imperative, Comrade Secretary? What do you mean is it imperative? Everything is imperative. What's imperative is imperative. Tóth made a mental note of Kertész's circuitous reasoning. It was past noon, Kertész had been into his cups. I'll keep the problem under control, Tóth assured the district comrade. As you know, Tóth, we got a bunch of Swabs, the entire defense in fact is Swab to the last man,* which is no problem, Steigerwald coordinates them in the center, while Salzmann, a.k.a. Szőllő,† he's like a brick wall, there's no getting past him. In which case, what's the problem, Tóth?

Among other things, keeping the problem under control meant playing for time, gaining time, for what purpose was unclear. Mostly, to find the thread. Find out where we stand, who we are, and why. Clearly, Kertész was preoccupied with the same fundamental questions of existence as Kant.

The problem, Tóth, is the West German relatives, or rather whether the problem is a problem, that's the problem, Tóth, be-

* Hungarians refer to those of their countrymen whose German ancestors were invited to settle in a depopulated Hungary after the Turkish occupation as Swabs or Swabians, and therefore not *quite* Hungarians. Thus, during Hungary's hard-line communist regime, they would fall under suspicion as possible subversives.

† Since they were meant to raise the prestige of the Hungarian communist state, sportsmen were generally asked to adopt easily recognizable Hungarian names. This is how Ferenc Purczeld came down in football history as Ferenc Puskás and Nándor Breier as Nándor Bányai.

cause on the other hand!, the country needs the hard currency, Comrade Lenin neglected to think of that, though Comrade Marx did, I bet, Tóth thought but didn't wish to interrupt, in short, we need hard currency relatives, and yet, Tóth, there's no making a silk purse out of a sow's ear, which should suffice by way of an explanation.

It more than suffices, Comrade Secretary. He overshot the mark, he either didn't recognize or else underestimated the sudden soberness of the alcoholic, they sober up when you least expect it, the way certainty strikes the nonbeliever and doubt the believer, even if many may not share this symmetry-based opinion, neither believer nor nonbeliever. Hold your horses, Tóth, and there was a sudden silence while Adalbert Tóth cheerfully waited to see into what murky waters Kertész would venture next, caution had become second nature to him, like to us all, son, the life-preserving, routine knowledge of "how much and how far," so that he didn't even know he was afraid, constant fear can be ignored, he experienced his animal knowledge of his environment as freedom—for lack of counterproof. Are you being impertinent, Tóth? Tóth seemed to have transgressed against some unspoken agreement, but it was not to either man's advantage to acknowledge it. Who do you think you are?, Kertész said, raising his voice and scratching the inside of his thigh. He had asked fundamental questions but was hoping that Tóth would not take them seriously. Do you really think you have nothing to lose? Though stressing the nature of the threat as threat did not mean that the threat was more serious than before, yet it would be foolhardy to assume that it didn't mean *something*. Do you think we don't know everything there is to know about you?

Tóth had already made his peace with, and in fact he saw nothing objectionable in snooping on others in the first place. They were just running their cooling-down laps. He was immersed in scrutinizing Kertész's handsome, regular features, which betrayed no traces of drink, neither the texture of the skin nor the brush handling of the lines. Still, nobody knows everything, he said warmly.

Which landed them in yet another awkward silence. In a dictatorship the simplest things can be infinitely complex, and our situation isn't made any easier when—as if it were a gift of history, the universal spirit, Party headquarters, but it is not—the most complex things are alarmingly simple. Kertész had to decide whether this was a threat in answer to his threat, perhaps he's being misled by these rounded shapes, while Tóth misconstrued the silence, he thought he had really committed a blunder. Only he knows everything, he said quickly, pointing toward the ceiling, and by extension, because he felt that the situation called for a touch of the figurative, also at the sky. The Party secretary gave a relieved laugh, oh, sure, the Lord and the department heads, *they* know everything.

He said Lord, the atheists prefer to use the less committed god (with a small *g*), but this is how Sasha Kertész heard it from his mother, and words brought from home, especially if it's past noon, in spite of and as a consequence of the problem brought under control, are stronger than those learned with a particular purpose in mind. Alright, Tóth, that's enough, don't be a wise guy, we know as much as we need to. And he really knew this, just as he knew that just then, under the circumstances, in short, what later, when it was over, people would call a dictatorship, there was no need to know anything, it was as good as knowing everything. Or nearly. We know enough, and to himself (or just very quietly) he added: sweetheart. And also: Shall we be on a first-name basis, what do you say?

CONT.

Having heard everything, and thus also hearing that Laci Vizi's older brother was practically an industrialist in Lyon, Sasha picked up this thread, you'd think the Kádár regime was created especially for him, but by whom, son, by whom?, he had a secure knowledge of the limits that could not be known, he was not brave, because this word will be needed elsewhere, when I'll be writing about Imrus Thököly, though "foolhardy" will do better service there, but he knew himself, and he knew the most that could be known at the time: he was only as scared as the situation warranted, and so the French connection matured in safety for the good of all, the brand-new French capitalist was happy because they were able to treat his thyroid over there and he lost weight and came home in such dazzling suits, people didn't recognize him, the plant management was happy, freebies to Lyon, the plant was happy, because even if at a slower pace than the freebies, but business, too, started to pick up, without having to spend hard currency, Comrades!; and once the initial scruples were put to rest, in part by answering the question, "Would one of the comrades kindly tell us why we're not building a better future through reliance on the trustworthy communist engineering expertise of the Soviet comrades?," and partly by providing adequate technical and ethical answers to the query, "I hope you don't expect me to fall for this third-rate garbage?," Feri Vizi brought power looms (wide Picanolos), and he bought linen. That's when my mother also started to soar. Actually, she'd been soaring up till then as well, though not through work but . . . My mother played *ulti*[*] like Géza Ottlik[†] played bridge, except, when it comes to describing it, there's a hitch—I have no idea how Ottlik played bridge. I am a card game illiterate, and although someone had promised to enlighten me, she then (temporarily) beat a retreat. And so there's a scene missing, a scene in May as my mother, pushing past the gatekeeper, little Kas's grandmother, (she couldn't hiss between her teeth yet, snooping gatekeeper country, because the expression didn't exist yet, though she was thinking something like it, granted that without words it is difficult to think what you'd be thinking if the words were at your disposal [in a pleading voice] but let's not go into that now!) in order to see the personnel director (who made a rare exception, she wasn't out to harm anyone, her successor after '57 was Aunt Rózsi, the hairdresser Ernőke's mother, what a fucking b . . . !, always looking for trouble and finding it, and taking it out on the first person that walked into her office; a clever, spiteful, mean-spirited white folk, lord of life and death—I wonder what became of her), got the floor wrong and touched base in the Party office, just like a ship in a heavy, spell-bound ocean mist, like that, because that's how the thick ciga-

* A popular Hungarian card game played with a pack of special Hungarian cards.

† The renowned author Géza Ottlik (1912–1990) and one of Péter Esterházy's favorite writers—he once copied out the manuscript of Ottlik's classic novel *School at the Frontier* (Iskola a határon, 1959) by hand—in 1989 coauthored a bridge handbook with Hugh Kelsey, *Adventures in Card Play*. One critic called it "the most advanced book on bridge ever written."

rette smoke eddied in that room; a bunch of men were playing cards, the factory foursome, let's see, who were they?, the Party representative, the union representative, the KISZ representative, plus someone else, they didn't even see my mother in that veil of smoke, unless it was her shimmering red skirt sending flashes of color across the room as if the sun were already setting in its full kitschy splendor. My mother went and stood behind them to kibitz, and when she gently touched Karesz Hazai's shoulder, no, you'd better wait with that forty-hundred *ultimó** (that's not what she said, I'm just indicating and miming the words, as it were), then these men—obese, sweating, pálinka-swilling, shirtsleeves rolled up—and with stubbles, son, I'm a great one for stubble envy—thought that an angel had descended among them, and in what followed, my mother continued to enjoy this status, even though she was working in the most humdrum administrative job otherwise. Also, she regularly milked them dry twice a week, and so she was bestowed the one honor that for a long time these hulking, sweating, pálinka-swilling men with rolled-up sleeves were able to bestow on a woman in Hungary: Lilike, consider yourself a man!

My mother took them at their word. Which the other women regarded with suspicion, whereas my mother, though I'm not saying she was an Alice Schwarzer or dear little Simon Beauvoir, was fully aware of the importance of women's solidarity and made wholehearted attempts to use her privileged position in the interest of the others—even if no one could play *ulti* like she could—but thinking that they smelled a rat, the women beat back her efforts with derision. Without doubt, there was some-

* Last trick.

thing suspicious in my mother's principled actions, but still, she liked being friends with men, a gut reaction, son, a gut reaction. A Hungarian woman does not make friends with men, she either hates them with a passion, or worships them, or tames them, or all three at the same time.

The new, nascent French connection propelled mother upward as well. My mother spoke French like my father did in my novels (if he happened to be speaking French), in short, like a native. No, son, no Frenchman speaks their mother tongue like a native, they're so overfastidious, so arrogant and stuck-up, not so much with respect to learning the language, but with respect to the French language as such, that even they don't speak their mother tongue like a native, you'd think the French didn't even have mothers. Sasha Kertész was the chief by then, and along with soccer Sasha too wore off of him and he became Lajos, then Uncle Lajos, first in jest, but then it stuck. My mother was assigned to him, which became the source of further juicy rumors. When Feri Vizi's men came from Lyon my mother was the interpreter, the negotiations took place through her, as it were, she translated the contracts, inscriptions, transcriptions, notes, minutes and memorandums, when hell freezes over, stop, *je vous prie d'agréer, Monsieur, l'expression de mes sentiments les plus respectueux, Feri,* letters, you name it. Metaphorically speaking, Lilike, you are the heart of the factory. *Aber,* Uncle Lajos, German in the original. My mother spent the sixties and seventies speaking French. In French, son, even comrade has a certain *je ne sais quoi* to it. She hid inside the French language as if it were a bunker. But no, a bunker is too German, a shelter made of cement, language is lighter, in case of danger it wouldn't protect you from anything, a comforting hideout, a protective pair of wings, but it's not something you can slip into. Whenever she emerged from the French language, she slipped into soccer. Another way of putting it is that throughout her life, my mother was fleeing. And another way of putting it is that she was always happy.

THE TIME OF RELICS COMES TO AN END

Anyone entering the Party office (did not abandon all hope, nor was overwhelmed with hope—that would have taken different doors) found himself face-to-face with sacred images that suffered discrete changes with the changing times; Lenin, I believe, held out the longest, while due to the vicissitudes of fortune Engels' performance suffered the most ups and downs (whereas, as football reporters would say, we could do with some Engels just now), and well, in the last stretch Kádár, so unremarkable for so long (only to change the unremarkable into the unremarkable in an unremarkable way) also produced a terrific finish in the last stretch; as you entered, this is what met your eye, eye riveted to eye, and even afterward, not the person sitting under them (whom we've come to see, or who, how shall we put it, had asked to see us), because everyone, my mother included, first shot a furtive glance up to the right, looking for the fabled handle of the swinging window, while the man sitting under it, the present, current, actual, factual man of the moment tactfully allowed them time for the ritual inspection. Under the dictatorship, the window handle could simultaneously serve as the holy depository of the most legitimate feelings of spiteful pleasure (every commie will bite the dust!), as well as the object of a real sense of shock, and not only of compassionate mourning (a decent man like Karesz Hazai, and see where it got him?) but, and this followed from the former, of self-discovery; one look at the fatal window handle, and for a moment everyone began to reflect about their own fate and would inspect the bad aluminum thingamajig with a sense of unease. Whether any of this continued after 1990 and in what shape or form is impossible to say; the privatized plant was bought up by a French company, not Feri Vizi's, though, but they didn't do anything, just let it go to the dogs, production came to a halt, but people (those who still believed in anything) believed that thanks to the well-established French connections, the French privatization was not only advantageous and logical, but a downright intelligent, well-considered, and fortuitous move. Except, they weren't familiar with the bestial nature of capital, alas. Capital knows no mercy, Lajos Kertész, who took an active part in the privatization (took part, meaning that the part he took was now his), explained. Because, ladies and gentlemen, in that—and let's not mince words, dunghill of a socialism, worse than a dunghill, there was always a morsel of humanity present, no thanks to the regime, but rather in spite of it, and not because we put up a fight, but because the old tradition, the *shlamperei** having joined forces with the new, namely, the cynicism of the Kádár era, couldn't take anything really seriously, neither itself nor the regime, wherewithal, again and again, some human gesture

* A certain devil-may-care attitude, a permissive slovenliness that was typical of the bourgeoisie in the Austro-Hungarian empire and which continued into the communist era in Hungary. In both regimes, the life of extreme regimentation and too many strict rules would have been unlivable without the *shlamperei* that helped people survive and keep their sanity.

would slip through the apertures in its wobbly workings, not for its own sake, but so some progress should be made even when there was no progress, in short, ladies and gentlemen, it was not the implacable laws of the regime that came into play, but the all too human, unpredictable rules of corruption, cowardice, and personal ambition so easily subject to manipulation. But what the point of this lecture may have been we shall never know; all we know is that Sasha Kertész became filthy rich, though how rich in comparison to his millionaire neighbor I'd be loath to say. When life in the factory ceased and the factory yard was overgrown with weed, especially where long ago, a very long time ago, the hastily assembled crates had stood, they tore down the buildings, the spinning hall, the warehouses, the "administration," and the dumpers, like so many ants, carted off the debris, God only knows where. The hair-raising void thus created was parceled out, small streets sprang up, mostly villas with turrets, painted in harsh colors, and a condo. Apparently, everything was secured with payola beforehand. I walked that way with mother the other day, though I don't like walking with her too often, what I mean is I don't like spending time with her in the open, she appears more vigorous inside the house; time has hardly made inroads with her, but in natural light she's more bent, smaller, weaker, frail. I didn't need to support her, we walked hand in hand, like always. Don't slouch, son, she said as always, step out. We turned the corner toward the factory, this is where the factory used to stand, she said, beating me to it. Where was the Party office? She counted the steps from Ibi's flower shop. The porter's cubicle stood here. It's hard to take your bearings. That's the only part of the complex they dynamited. Some of the fittings, the furniture, the heating pipes had been stolen by then, but the pictures remained on the wall, though there was already a market for them, dead lions are highly amusing, they look good in discos and bedrooms. During the blast, all those serious men with those serious faces went flying through the air, out the window, some got hoisted up by the wind and sailed along merrily instead of plunging to the ground, one of the picture frames fell apart, puff!, the splintered wooden frame came bouncing back, Lenin or Marx or Kádár or Engels was hurling curses, anyone who happened to be standing around just then might have thought. Then all found peace in a little heap of livid dust. Let's go, son, I can't find it. Give me your hand.

♣ A PÉTER BALASSA SENTENCE

"'Give me your hand.' So then is this Zerlina or the Commendatore?"*

* A line from an essay by the professor of literature Péter Balassa, about whose death the author has written in an earlier chapter. Zerlina and the Commendatore are characters from the opera *Don Juan*.

5.

PUSKÁS

THE VISIT, 1952

The same age as my eldest grandchild is now, whose resemblance to Philippe Noiret could be the source of a drama about jealousy in a middling yet well-written French farce, that's how old I must have been when: No practice today!, Today is the day!, my mother screamed, as if someone were after her hide. At other times she always started by throwing on my clothes, quickly, skillfully, absently, sensibly, with only the characteristics of the continental weather indigenous to these parts on her mind, routinely varying the little that was there to be varied. But this time, after that scream she made straight for the bathroom, not even bothering to close the door behind her, and so I was able to watch the abracadabra of her metamorphosis. I remember her lipstick pout best, I've described it many times, because she seemed to belong to a different world then, maybe the world of actresses?, and also there was the sound of her lips popping against each other, like the popping of an elegant champagne. And the coral skirt. And the hat. Hat off, I keep forgetting about the dictatorship of the proletariat. Hat on, but I'm going to see a man, after all. Hat off, still, he's an officer of the Hungarian People's Republic. Hat on, but so what, it's just a hat, and I might as well look my best. This is what has remained with me from those early times, her beauty, concretely, one: her sprightly gait, her stirring skirt and her long, elegant legs flashing from under it, two: the curves, these shady hats, just like in a film. Even now I sometimes look at her legs in secret, she pretends she doesn't see, and I pretend I don't see her pretending, her legs are still beautiful, only the skin drier, with scales. As for my father, the way he lay in bed during the day in his ubiquitous Harris tweed jacket, as if it were a sweater, on his side, this is what has remained with me, his knees pulled up like a child, but I've mentioned this already a number of times. (The fact of the matter—not to say the truth of the matter—is that this picture has me in thrall.) Moths love tweed, my father wore it even after they'd been at it and it looked like a sieve. It was a loosely knit material, but nearly as sturdy as a blanket, and when my mother threw that unwearable jacket out (when she could throw it out at last), my father, at the price of not a little cunning, cut a piece out of it, a sample, and mailed it to the homeland of all tweeds; he kept up a correspondence with them for years, but they had stopped manufacturing that particular material, the world is changing, the haughty English wrote politely, but not so my father, and when the time came, he was buried in tweed.

Lilike, is that really you?!, Ferenc Puskás shouted as he came bounding down the staircase, the brightest star of the Mighty Magyars, by which, son, no irony is intended, that's when the team was set up, that's when Uncle Guszti Sebes finished setting it up, he had the guts to leave out Sándor and find a place for Nándi Hidegkuti, its brightest star, and that's a fact, though not its only genius!, I'm not saying that, and I can back it up with names, besides, a genius is like infinity, at that point differences disappear, let's not go into that, mother, it is not only possible but imperative that we differentiate between infinites, I learned it in school, oh! well that settles it then, son, they teach all sorts of things these days, I can also back it up with examples, but let's drop it, the wide staircase of city headquarters, tugging at the jacket of his uniform. He spoke like a grand seigneur, attending only to himself, you need a slip for everything here, to enter, to leave, to go next door or to the john, and he waved an arm toward the young soldier standing guard by the porter's box, staring straight ahead, it's hopeless, Lilike, a good thing I can make out as many slips as I want. Anyone playing for the Honvéd team* was made into an army man, he wasn't turned into a real soldier, he was merely regarded as one. At the time Puskás had only made it to first lieutenant, it wasn't until later that the newspaper headlines promoted him to "the dashing major." He was stationed at the Kilián barracks, the army's City Headquarters, where MPs brought soldiers accused of disorderly conduct. As for Junior, he helped where he could. Hey, don't shit in your pants, son, he said to the private standing at the bottom of the staircase, and gave him a couple of friendly pats on the cheek. That's when Czibor reached the bottom of the stairs, see? Dummy's here, too, introduce yourself to the auntie, Dummy,† sorry, Lilike, that's not what I meant, feast your eyes, Dummy, this is what a lady looks like, you don't see the likes of her down the left

* The venerable Honvéd Football Club, established in 1901, was run by the Honvédség, the Hungarian Armed Forces.

† Zoltán Czibor's nickname. Czibor played left forward on the Honvéd and Mighty Magyar teams.

flank; Czibor seemed to be under a cloud, he'd gotten plastered the night before at the Emke, he couldn't remember a thing, by the looks of him you'd think he got beaten up, whereas according to an informant, he took the place apart. Shut up, Swab, and he kissed mother's hand and made himself scarce so quickly, the defense would've never had a chance, son, if they tried. That Czibor had at least four dimensions, he kept disappearing in the fourth, and the backs kept whirling around, where's he gone to this time? They were tied up in knots. You can see for yourself, Lilike, he's a real nutcase and drives everybody else nuts, too. I know, my mother said more in sorrow than in anger, I know, Ferenc. Puskás blushed to the roots of his hair.

MY MOTHER PULLS DOWN HER PANTIES, NO, HER STOCKINGS, FOR BOZSIK AND PUSKÁS

He knew mother from when he was a child, through Uncle Sárli, who played for Fervas* at the time, but more to the point, the family owned and operated a soda water plant in Kispest, the "Lehner." We thought it only natural that Uncle Sárli should come from a family that made bubbles! Mind on mischief, we kept asking our uncle about the essence of bubbles, their pith, quintessence, and substance, and whether you can make something from nothing, and Uncle Sárli willingly launched into a painstaking description of the technical processes involved. When we laughed, and we laughed, he really and truly thought that it was the functioning of their soda water plant that was

* Short for the Ferencváros Railroad Workers football team. (Ferencváros is part of greater Budapest.)

humorous. When we caught on to this, each time, every time, shamefaced, we stopped laughing. Uncle Sárli—this is always the first thing that comes to mind with respect to him—was a lovable man and we loved him, but with no more feeling (passion) than a cactus. Try as we might, we just couldn't, though we tried, because he was a lovable man. My mother was more than ten years Puskás's senior; they first "met" on a makeshift football pitch in Kispest, my mother was on her way to her future brother-in-law at the bubble factory located behind the Hoffer (later the Red Star) tractor factory, when her feet were literally rooted to the ground: a group of young adolescents were playing ball, Puskás and Bozsik among them, and that instant, my mother knew that she was witnessing one of the wonders of the world, because even back then they weren't just playing the game, they were creating it. Then suddenly Bozsik stopped the ball with his instep, suspending it in midair as it were, for a second holding it up for the others, here, behold my beloved ball, in whom I am well pleased, impatient, Puskás made a face, this ain't no circus, keep that ball moving (the ball is always faster than you, this was one of my mother's major recurrent parental motifs), Bozsik flipped the ball into the air, caught it with both hands, and like the dramatic operatic hero at the end of act two, when everything is at its darkest, everyone is a villain, and poor Mimi, too, has just lost her voice, he made the following announcement: This here is soft. They were playing with a rag ball, a ball made from stockings, actually, you can imagine, son, how Cucu and the others used to laugh at this, that's where the saying don't kick the ball in the cunt, it might bite back comes from, in the evening, after a game, my mother would always check me for traces of a bite; the round essence, the pith and quintessence of the ball was dependent on the worn-out, torn, cheap stockings of the boys' sisters, this is how they prolonged their titillating lives; rolled up tight, they were for the ball what bubbles were for soda, bread for the body, etcetera, son, etcetera, and then I haven't said half. Hold on, gentlemen, my mother said, the first time anyone had addressed Bozsik and company in this formal manner, and they stared at this decked-out, perfumed woman, my mother, dressed in a classical Catholic mid-gentry garb, the unity of form and content, they stared wide eyed, and inexplicably they made no nasty remarks; hold on, but first, turn your back. What? Us?, Puskás and Bozsik barked in unison. No what, just do it. They all turned their backs. And then, having first hoisted up her skirt, my mother snapped loose the hooks of her garters, rolled down the silk stocking from her already much lauded legs, gentlemen, please. No peeking. When it was all right for them to turn back round, they turned back round, my mother held out her stockings to Bozsik, if you add this, maybe it won't be soft. My mother's thighs were instantly covered with goose bumps. She rubbed them through her skirt.

My mother's story (one of her stories) began here, with the two silk stockings that landed in Puskás and company's rag ball; nothing awakened as much passion in her as soccer, neither her husband, nor her children, not even the Lord God, with whom she had a comfortable, I might say pre-Nietzschean relationship much akin to friendship; she believed in God the way a thirsty man drinks water, without thinking, without doubt, without feeling particularly grateful; correction, she did, but in an absentminded way, she took great gulps from the water jug, then with the unshakable good cheer of the believer she looked around to see if the reserves were warming up, because it was high time that they did. This richness of the world that she enjoyed seeing and pointing out to others (without any hidden didactic intention; for her, the Lord's might was so self-evident, in fact, tangible, that she didn't succumb to the temptation of helping Him out, she had no intention of koshering Creation, she was satisfied with the whole thing just as it was—though perhaps the training field could be flattened with just a bit more care!—and she felt that the homework the Apostles were assigned was exaggerated or arbitrary, namely, to kindly get moving and make all the peoples of the Earth disciples of the Redeemer, baptize them in the name of the Father, the Son, and the Holy Ghost, teaching them to observe all things whatsoever the Redeemer hath commanded onto them, in which case He would be with them, always, even unto the end of times; it was as if my mother had heard only this last sentence, this was the source of her equanimity and what we might call evangelical indolence: and I shall be with you every day until the end of times), as far as she was concerned, the richness of the world, its abundance and splendor, was concentrated in the rectangle of the soccer field. In my mother's head the world took shape from these rectangles—from an airplane, from above, Beckenbauer had said with the courteous envy of the winner, Holland looks like it was pieced together from football fields; this is what I read somewhere—everywhere she looked, she saw eighteen-yard lines and sidelines, touch flags and offsides. You could tell from her eyes when she was daydreaming. Always. For a long time we went everywhere hand in hand, to Puskás not yet, to Mass, to buy food, and, at first, to school. And now again, whereas statistically arm in arm would be safer, more sensible. And then suddenly, as if a light current were running through the back of her hand, as if a light wind were ruffling some water's surface, she stirs, slips out of my hand and points somewhere, at the plane tree on the corner, the driftwood floating on the Danube, at Aunt Béla (from whom we bought eggs) pushing her handcart, the new chaplain with the ruddy cheeks pedaling his bike toward us, see, son?, if you release the winger now, the time would be ideal, the sideline is the bus lane, of course, the chaplain the center-half, and as such the last man, in which case it is a clear-cut offside, an offside on the governmental level, son, and if you ask who the winger is, who is the winger?, the plane tree, the style rather choppy, no?, lacks smoothness, don't you agree?, with timber toes, not a Garrincha, son, by any stretch of the imagination, but it doesn't drink as much either. We could analyze the world like this ad infinitum, but should the Danube take a step back, provided, of course, that the Northern Connecting Railway Bridge is the center-half and Piroska Rozgonyi (the street, not the girl) runs up to the empty space thus created, then it's checkmate. Whatever you say, mother. Just like chess players who recall positions and moves going back many years, do you remember, colleague, when in thirty-eight Shalyapin, as if he were blind, chess blind, mistook his rook, for crying out loud, not his rook, and not Shalyapin, but Aljehin, and he didn't mistake anything, on the contrary!, there's a touching photograph, Shalyapin and Gorky, two enchanting young men, two Greek gods, and the affectionate way Shalyapin drops his chin on Gorky's head, you could've blown the entire Soviet Union sky high, in short, Aljehin against Bruce in Plymouth, in 1938, Shalyapin was a sick man by then, though he had lungs the size of the Kremlin, they wouldn't take in the air, Shalyapin's lungs went on strike, wouldn't take in anymore O-two, that was how it was, they were playing on New Year's

Day, the rest of humanity was still sleeping off a hangover when they were already making their moves, but not for long, in his seventh move Aljehin made his Ke5 move, it was a vital move, Bruce didn't have a clue and made clumsy attempts to protect one of his bishops, and by the eleventh move they went home, *vodka, shto gramm*, Aljehin hooted, satisfied; or just like the great wine tasters who could retrieve former drinking bouts from the gloomy cellar of their memories, wines, vintages, concrete bottles with admirable precision, it tasted of cork, colleague, of course, but what potential!, that's how my mother knew everything, too, scores going back many years, the way Bamba Deák evened the score at the last moment,* veritably foreshadowing Hurst's much-disputed goal, and thus—as Toussaint so wisely comments—Zidane's penalty kick as well that rebounded from the upper goal post, a Hurst sampler if ever there was one, which reminds me, with the Gál twins' goal posts none of these would have been a goal, son, paltry aluminum goals; not only did she know the illustrious names by heart, and not just the legendary lesser names, from Csabagyöngye to the Gray Taxi† (when the Gray Taxi . . . , I don't remember what happened with the Gray Taxi, but something spectacular, a big surprise that everybody still talks about), and not only the foreign teams, including the South Americans, I gotta tell you, son, like it is, I'm getting old, the final straight of the Argentine champi-

* Ferenc (Bamba) Deák played center forward for the Mighty Magyars. He was capped to play in the Hungarian select team twenty times.

† Many companies had their own football teams. Csabagyöngye produced wine; the Gray Taxi, or Szürke Taxi, was the only cab company during most of the communist era.

onship leaves me cold; she also knew the small neighborhood teams inside and out, what's going on with Kirchmaier, and can they find a sub for Imi Jandász (they can't; another one that died so suddenly, I didn't even have time to cry), and who owns at this point in time de facto and through what cover the well-known—name of no importance—venerable junior sports club. She saw everything . . . in short, she lived her life through football. When she had her big scene—opera-ripe (mirror translation)—with the drunken Party secretary, she didn't simply call him an idiot, she called him an idiot by merely commenting, that's bagatelle, Galambos dear, Mr. Lakat (from the Fradi team*) can drink you under the table any time, but he can't drink so much that he wouldn't be a thousand times smarter than you. Whereas that's the truth, son. My mother was really and truly interested in the game *as such*, the game for its own sake, the beauty inherent in the possibilities, the esthetics of the play in progress, the far too infrequent, coordinated work of the body and the spirit (it's not true, son, that soccer is played with the head, and it's not true that it's played with the feet), in short, in the universal character *of that certain* rectangle, soccer as the smaller version of the Great Narrative, in short, everything that people generally say about soccer, and yet, because she surrounded all this with her own life, her common sense, she never took off toward the metaphor-laden skies of the *bel esprits*, she stood with both feet firmly planted on the ground, in the extension of the eighteen-

* The Ferencváros Torna (Gym) Club was founded in 1899 in the ninth district of Budapest and has one of the best-known football teams in the country with a wide following. Affectionately nicknamed Fradi, it is a formidable rival of other teams nationwide.

yard line, and yet, if I may be so bold, no, son, you may not!, if I may be so bold as to indulge in a kitschy shaft of light—late-night football stadiums are like the sunset, their undeniable beauty, when lit up, carries as little weight as last year's sport doctor's permission: you may not have cancer, and you may not have a cold, but we cannot take that into consideration—a breathtaking, beautiful shaft of light streaming forth from the direction of the above-mentioned skies, she's got both feet firmly planted on the ground, and yet is hovering above it. I estimate the distance at twenty centimeters, give or take an inch. Possibly angels have such dual natures. My mother, I think, is a bit terrifying (*vulgo*: unhinged), but she's good at hiding it.

THE VISIT, CONTINUED

I have something to ask you, Ferenc.

Anything, Lilike, anything!

Neither my mother nor Puskás lied as much in their lives as on this cheap East European morning. My mother played the vamp verbatim as it stands in *Webster's New World Dictionary* (Third College Edition): hoping to seduce and beguile with her feminine charms, a sober, calculating type, while Puskás acted as if there was something in the world besides football that he could take seriously (there wasn't). He helped my mother push the baby carriage up the stairs, an inverted Eisenstein paraphrase, instead of lifting or carrying it, they pushed it. In the office mother took me out of the carriage, for a while held me in front of her like a shield, then set me down. I could walk by then. I stumbled into a paper pellet—for want of anything better to do, Puskás practiced throwing paper pellets into the wastepaper basket even though he was better with his feet, one of his feet at any rate, than with his hands—the little squirt likes to pass, I see. My mother didn't say anything. Stupefied, she was staring at the wall, first at one, then the one opposite, a picture of Rákosi here, a picture of Rákosi there, the same picture twice ("his bald pate gleaming like a cow's tits"). Puskás laughed, you're the first who noticed, Lilike, I hung another one on the opposite wall, go on, boys, entertain each other, what do you think?! You're out of your mind, Ferenc, that's not funny! At which a cloud floated past Puskás's always sunny face, luminous, son, luminous, a light shade of weariness. He waved a hand. The ball, Lilike, the ball, the *ball's* no joke!

Of all the Mighty Magyars, Bozsik was my mother's personal favorite, the "number one" (English in the original), this choice was best suited to her bashful yet mischievous temperament and was, in fact, its consequence; even in the most dismal, damp and rainy, unpleasant autumn weather she could whisper Ná-á-ndi into the night by the Danube's banks as if the sun were out in full force; her mind was most often on Bozsik, but it was Puskás who became her friend. ("Can there be real friendship between a man and a woman, and if so, why not?")* Apart from their so-called mutual sympathy, my mother and Puskás had a lot in common in the nature of their relationship to football, this formed the solid basis of their friendship. Puskás took nothing seriously except the ball, he respected only the game and not life, because—yes!—the game was his life. Out on the pitch he understood the

* A reference to the jocular sentence by the writer and humorist Frigyes Karinthy (1887–1938), "Can there be real friendship between a man and a woman, and if so, why not?," understandably much quoted by Hungarian males.

meaning of dignity, of infinity, of death. In life he played the starring role of "Ferenc Puskás the legend" (in this he resembled Thomas Mann, though off the cuff I can't think of any other traits they may have had in common), not the heroic but the human version, the always facetious friend who can be trusted to take care of everything and help everyone, the guardian of orphans, the savior of the motherland. Puskás talked to the henchmen of the dictatorship as if they were harmless caricatures from a Chaplin film. In the fifties there was no man alive in Hungary who did not break out in a cold sweat at the very mention of the name of Colonel-General Mihály Farkas,* but Puskás jovially referred to him as Chief or Old Man. Sure, Chief, suspend Czibor if you want to, but then you go play left-winger yourself. As a rule, he went to see Farkas about business with Bozsik in tow. They pleaded someone's case as if they were inside a folktale. Farkas had food and drink brought, dig in, boys, you'll need your strength, won't you? Plus brains, Comrade Farkas. Just go eat, it's something you can depend on, once it's down, it's yours. Farkas had a source in Békéscsaba, he had such mouthwatering sausages, salamis, headcheeses, *stiforlder* brought in, the boys couldn't believe their eyes, especially Puskás, who loved meat, he dug in, meat with meat, Bozsik picked at his food as daintily as a lady to the manner born. In a dictatorship, son, everyone lives in fear, whether he's called Puskás or Farkas, whether he's an inside left or a colonel-general. Puskás knew that there was a world outside the soccer pitch, but he pretended he didn't. My

* Between 1948 and 1953 Mihály Farkas was Minister of National Defense and head of the ÁVÓ (the secret police). As such, he was one of the most powerful and most feared men of the Rákosi era.

mother knew it, too, but not unlike Puskás she, too, tried to turn everything into a football field, to excogitate (I'm obviously trying very hard to avoid the word "dream"), this is what animated her, too, not her playful spirit, not her sense of adventure, which was second nature to her, but necessity: it was necessary to do something, because you can't live in fear all your life.

ON FEAR (AUNT EMMA)

I always saw a cutting presence in those beautiful feline eyes, a dull, persistent flash (either flash or dull, either persistent or dull, but still!), the unwavering presence of fear. She feared lest something should happen to us, and she feared especially for my father. I don't think it was the dictatorship as such that frightened her; rather, the implacable yes-no world of the dictatorship opened her eyes to the bloodthirsty nature of the world, and this helped, for it made her understand that if there's trouble, there's trouble, and then she can't help either us or my father anymore, it made her come face-to-face with her helplessness, her vulnerability. I'm not saying that she was a different person on the football field (the whole world), but she was a different person, able to hide her fear, hide it behind her freedom. The being that emerged from her was not a new, unfamiliar being, a butterfly from a caterpillar, though, and I hate to have to say this, fear really does make a person repugnant, even if that person happens to be your mother, as if their palms were always sweating, cold, clammy, but not—detour—my mother's, on the contrary, she used to brag that her feet didn't sweat either, there's no August hot enough, son! The fear is missing from the old photographs. I first discovered it on the big wedding picture (frightened, oh, am I misconstruing something?), as, with the smile arranged especially for the benefit of the photographer, she glances out from under the wide-brimmed hat she wore to visit Puskás: an imploring glance, as if she were saying the usual, stay, moment, don't go yet, not because this is a moment of joy, but so that time should not pass, the story should not begin, because she seems to have intuited something about the likely order of events. Every good wedding picture is about this, the player's anxiety at the moment of the penalty kick. The man with the most freedom at the moment of the penalty kick is the goalie. My mother had been afraid since 1945, when she saw the first (her first) Russian soldier, who staggered into my grandfather's house, he wasn't drunk, which made him even more fearful, and he asked for something to eat. When he started eating, that's when the fear began in earnest. That boy ate as if he'd never eaten before, he was eating for his life—had the word "appetizer" passed anyone's lips just then, he'd have gunned us all down, son—and so my mother understood right away that a new world was coming in which she would be a stranger, whose laws she wouldn't understand, nor would they understand her. They thought the boy was crazy because he was acting against their expectations. It took a bit longer for mother to understand, but then she really understood, that in the eyes of the new world she would be considered the crazy one. Anyway, at one point, the Mongolian boy looked up from my grandmother's legendary green bean soup with sour cream and shot a cross-eyed, oblique glance across the table. If I were to indulge in dramatics, I'd say that my mother had been living in fear since 11:32 a.m., January 12, 1945. They were enjoying their late-morning repast with the Mongolian-Soviet soldier boy, who had just recovered from the two-day-long wakeful stupor into which he was probably propelled by hunger, my mother and her family were feeding him, and he ate, and then when he recovered he looked up, and his glance fell on mother's sister-in-law, Aunt Emma, who later divorced our uncle but lived near us just the same, we saw her regularly, and we loved her regularly, she was a sweet, cheerful aunt, if somewhat more vulgar than the others, or rather, more honest, less restrained, and willing to buy us three scoops of ice cream, whereas we all know that (European? Catholic?) self-restraint will countenance no more than two. At 11:32 a.m. nothing frightened Aunt Emma, at the time still just Emma; my mother's heart, however, skipped a beat when she saw that look, she jumped to her feet, grabbed a bowl from the table for alibi, and dashed out of the room. But where? It would have been even more dangerous outside the apartment; the presence of the young Mongolian officer protected them from the sex-starved soldiers roaming the building who, with eyes glazed over, wanted to play with the children at one moment, at another to sing, at another they wanted a woman. Finally, my mother locked herself inside the wardrobe (can a wardrobe be locked from inside?), the allergy to mothballs that was its direct consequence I have written about, with a little help from my imagination, elsewhere. It was from inside the wardrobe that she heard the whole thing, to wit, that veritably in sync with her disappearance, the young man, always so quiet, at night playing the harmonica, in his own way so polite, even bashfully modest, who tried to engage my grandfather in conversation whereas, to put it mildly, neither's mother tongue was Russian, and so there was no knowing what the conversation was about, but it was a conversation all the same, suddenly, without preamble, chased everyone from the table with a fearful cry, grabbed Emma by the arm, dragged her into the room where the wardrobe stood, and raped her. According to malicious family gossip, Aunt Emma did not resist with the vehemence and alarm one would expect from someone of her social standing. Aunt Emma didn't give a hoot and waved it off as she ate her ice cream, they couldn't really grasp what had happened, that's why they couldn't take it seriously, all they saw was a breach of etiquette, and without a second thought cast me out from where I hadn't been in the first place: from among their ranks. This slightly askew aunt of mine has a special liking for me because she could tell me stories, any story, because though I was bashful, veritably a prude, I was, above all else, curious; even as a child, words couldn't scare me off. Your family is nuts, they think rape is screwing, they had no way of knowing, of course, that the next day we also screwed, he was crying throughout, the tears streaming from his beautiful Mongolian eyes, but not the first day, then he cleaved into me like an ax, splitting me apart like lard, I didn't know where I began and where I ended, I knew only about that huge ax. Your mother behaved decently. When my mother dared to leave the wardrobe with the mothballs, fear had already settled inside her; she has impressive reserves of it to this day. She picked Emma off the floor—there's a wide iron bed, but he had to do it on the hard floor!—washed her down, and tucked her between the sheets.

CONT.

Respect for women, Puskás I think, practiced this on my mother. Being a Hungarian male, it wasn't something that he otherwise bothered his head about. He was in no position to. In keeping with Hungarian national tradition, at whose epicenter stand the homeland and morals, the Hungarian male, son, thinks of his mother with undying gratitude and respect on the one hand, and he is likewise bound by gratitude and respect and a sense of obligation to his beloved wife, the mother of his sons and daughters, to whom he is faithful until death do them part, that's one side of the coin, the other is that he knocks up every woman he can, and even those he can't, in case, as the ancient tradition goes, they should hold the little whatnots (the pretty little chatterboxes) he missed out on against him in the afterlife. The life of the Hungarian male is spent in this sincere and fertile tension, or used to, because by now even this tradition has crumbled into its component parts, the relationship to the roots severed, stuttering memory become its own disfigured image, with nothing consistent in either the respect or the knocking up, or rather there is no consistency in the respect and there is no respect in the knocking up. Puskás was a well-balanced soul, and my mother was part of this balance. Who at the moment was trying to get Puskás to pull some strings so we shouldn't be forcibly resettled in the countryside.* The paper hadn't come yet, but the thunderclouds were gathering overhead, Uncle Sárli and his family, for instance, had already been bundled off to the flatlands of the Hortobágy, where they were living in a sheepfold, several families together; like always, Uncle Sárli took it in

* Soon after Mátyás Rákosi came to power as the chief secretary of the Hungarian Working People's Party in 1949, "class enemies," including former aristocrats, teachers, doctors, lawyers, other professionals, farmers and anyone who had a small business, were "resettled"—deported to the countryside along with their families, where they were quartered with poor peasants.

stride with subdued good humor, while, like always, my mother's younger sister whined and lamented. Not everyone among the deportees appreciated the fact that, before long, Uncle Sárli was regularly playing cards with the police, the entire command post in fact, but the overfastidious verdict was moderated when it came to light that Uncle Sárli simply couldn't lose, he walked home of an evening, a déclassé, smiling to himself and jingling the coins in his pocket. Uncle Sárli always won. Night after night. Which soon turned into such an embarrassment that one day General Galga, who was looked upon as an unofficial head boy of sorts, paid Uncle Sárli a visit and requested that he let the police win now and then, because the mounting tension was bound to explode, and that would not be healthy for their occasional little community. The general was followed by the captain, the police commandant, each with a similar request, which, due to their respective positions, each naturally disguised as a threat, cheating at cards is punishable by incarceration, the commandant said with a double-barreled smile as he left, she sells seashells by the seashore, but they both know he's just bluffing. Uncle Sárli, however, also knew that the commandant was right. (Later he showed us tricks we could never master. In order to cheat at cards, you have to be a wiz.) Puskás shot my mother an adoring glance. Ferenc, Ferenc, don't promise anything you can't deliver. Puskás put his hand over his heart, don't fret, Lilike, the Chief, they say, is also chief of the ÁVÓ and he's crazy about soccer. Which was true. Mihály Farkas sat in the stands at every game and rooted like everybody else. He eats out of our hand. Still, be careful, they're a lot more cunning than they let on. More than me, my dear young lady?, more than me?! I'm married, Ferenc, married. She was already expecting my brother by then, a fact that she—who knows why?—chose not to disclose. There's nobody more cunning than me, Lilike, and everybody knows it. It was now quiet, only I was making noise, Puskás put a finger to his lips, let's change the subject, we might be tapped. Then practically in tune with the gesture he shrugged, as if he were by himself, let them wiretap me, let them wiretap my ass! I bumped, I toddled against the wastepaper basket, we were the same height, I tried to regain my balance, I threw my arms around the basket, the first hug of my life outside of my mother, and instantly the two of us rolled over like a pair of lovers in the hay. Well, will you look at the little squirt!, Puskás cried. When he moved back to Hungary* and we were reacquainted through my younger brother, the soccer player, I reminded him of this, our first meeting, and he said—he wasn't paying attention, greeting people right and left, "working the crowd"—he remembers it very well, but to be perfectly frank, he was intent on my mother. Intent on. . . . A gentleman does not use such language, Ferenc. Puskás laughed wholeheartedly, who said I was a gentleman?! A spieler, Lilike, I'm a spieler and not a gentleman. He crumpled up a piece of paper—he hated sheets, especially sheets with writing on them—and as if aiming for a basketball ring, threw it at the wastepaper basket, but hit me on the forehead instead. The paper ball bounced way off of my forehead, Kocka can't head the ball half as good, Lilike. Make sure the kid gets coaching. Don't make fun, Ferenc, I've come to ask for something, and asking is not easy. Not easy? From a

* In 1958 Puskás emigrated ("defected") to Spain, where he played for Real Madrid. He returned to Hungary to take temporary charge of the national team after the Hungarian government granted him a full pardon in 1991.

friend? You ask and it's as good as done. And it was. We got off being resettled. My mother bundled me back inside the baby carriage. You know, Ferenc, we're not on Earth for a vacation, we all have something to do, you, me, this little man. I don't want to bore you, but life is too mysterious to think only of survival. . . . Well then, should I or shouldn't I talk to the Chief, Lilike? Do so, Ferenc, that's why I'm here, I was speaking generally. As you know, there's no signing an insurance policy with the Lord, if you know what I'm getting at. That's way over my head, Lilike. But one thing I know. The Lord is a spieler, too.

PLUS ONE SPIELER

Shut your trap Twinkle Toes and listen, don't you go playing snow white and the seven dwarfs with me, the goody-goody sugarplum fairy, haven't you heard about the enemy of the people?, haven't you heard about the people languishing, the country languishing, and the gentry living in debauchery?, have you any idea who you're trying to help?, and wipe that grin off your face, damn you and answer me, the devil take you and your cunning Swabian kind!,* do you or don't you know?, I do, Chief, no Chief, Comrade Colonel-General, and stand at attention, what do you think you're doing, poking your nose into the business of your superiors?, go ask your old man who these people are, he'll tell you, you have it too good, you forget where you come from, you forget the taste of poverty, what it's like working your fingers to the bone throughout a lifetime so they can sip their champagne

* Ferenc Puskás (Ferenc Burczeld), was born into a Hungarian-German family who had come from the southern region of Germany known as Swabia.

from crystal goblets, so stop meddling, who do you think you are?, go out on the field and play, play in the name of the people, the nation, play for communism, and leave the enemy of the people to us, understood?!, fuck the little woman if you want to, that's your affair, the people's democracy is behind you on that, what's she like?, willing?, answer me, damn you, cat's got your tongue?, are you deaf?, answer me, I said. Well, what can I say, Comrade Colonel-General? What, Comrade Puskás?, the truth, Comrade Puskás, so: is she or is she not an easy lay, yes or no? Yes or no? All women can be had, Comrade Colonel-General. Right. And now go to the devil, and I don't want to lay eyes on you for a while, understood? Yes, sir, understood. Good. You're a spieler.

6.

It Comes to Light

LUNCH, DETOUR: BOULEVARD

My mother didn't like my football book;* as a matter of fact, she generally disliked books about football to begin with. This came to light as follows. Whenever the opportunity presented itself, I had lunch with her. It's been like this since 1980, three hundred times per year at least, that's twenty-seven times three hundred, and that's eight thousand one hundred lunches, at least two hours at a stretch, that's sixteen thousand two hundred hours, and that's not nothing, and all sorts of other occasions also come up, and also when I just happen to think of her. I could walk over to see her, she lives fifteen minutes away, but I don't. I'd rather look at her picture. It was taken in 1971 by some friends from East Germany, who then had an adventurous escape to the Bundesrepublik in a specially made secret partition in the trunk of a car. The girl Kitty almost died because she passed out and her brain didn't get enough oxygen, they kept her in a Ham-

* A reference to *Journey to the Depth of the Eighteen-Yard Line* (Utazás a tizenhatos mélyére, 2006).

burg hospital for two weeks, she hovered between life and death (when I heard the story, it was always with this expression, and so that's how I tell it); they now live up north around Husum, while the boy served as the model for the soccer coach, the one who back home talks only and exclusively about balls that wind up in the sewer (*Journey to the Depth of the Eighteen-Yard Line*, 2006, p. 31). But their marriage going on the rocks because of it is pure fantasy. It didn't go on the rocks. They'd spend their evenings talking about the balls that ended up in the sewer. In the picture my mother smiles into the camera with the mischievous squint that—if nature had a sense of style—would belong only to light, refined, glittering lives. It is summer, she's leaning an elbow on the arm of a garden chair, her upper arm fleshier than I remember from any other time. The fleshy, lovely, summertime arm of a woman. My first wife is sitting next to her, laughing sweetly at my mother, her tummy a flat silver plate. Taking this picture as my starting point, there is nothing that could stop the flight of fancy.

As I said, my mother lives at the farther end of the boulevard, near the river, not yet on the floodplain, yet with a significant rise in the number of mosquitoes, one floor up, no elevator, which will cause problems, it already has, the two weather forecasters, this is what my mother calls her knees, at such times she can't climb stairs at all, but even when her knees are in a more obliging mood, she can't come down without assistance. We hired a woman from Transylvania, right now it's all the rage, she cooks for her, sees to the shopping, bathes her, and would talk to her, if only mommy dear would let her, "an auntie from Transylvania"—some auntie!, she's twenty years younger than me! My mother insisted on the one floor up, anybody might climb through the window, but who'd bother?, I just told you, anybody. She gave me a look as if I were after her hide. And as a matter of fact, she was tending in the right direction. Back then, more than twenty-five years ago, we fought over everything, what I mean is, almost everything ended up with us at fisticuffs. That's when my mother began to age; at any rate, that's when I first noticed the shadow of old age casting its spell over her, not even a shadow, a mist, a damp, drizzling mist, a clammy, heavy grayness through which I could hardly recognize her. Every movement, everything about her rubbed me the wrong way, even her smell, because she smelled different, as if she'd changed her smell on purpose. And her aches and pains, which I had no doubt were real, were there expressly to annoy me! My leg, son, it's throbbing, you take my word, they'll have to amputate. At which I flew into a rage, though if the truth be told, her feet were alarmingly bluish red. Blue, yellow, scarlet, shiny, and dry flakes on that beautiful instep.

Looking at my instep?

Yes.

Shapely, yes?

Yes.

When she turned seventy, the tension between us let up, she found her way into old age, she found her very own old age; in short, she found her way back into life. I wasn't as uptight either anymore, wondering what new exasperation she was about to spring on me, what new version of herself. Because this remained, and I didn't like it, this unpredictable new that didn't follow from the old, not its exaggerated version, or caricature, or pale shadow, no, but something wholly different. And that's scary. Gradually, gingerly, I had to reacquaint myself with this old woman, my mother, and I liked this very much, this slightly undermined, because capricious, new relationship of ours. (I was sorry to have to part with my beautifully developing mother fixation, but then, you don't get something for nothing. . . .)

The boulevard began with a double row of poplars, then came the middle section, from our house down to the post office, where, in line with the latest trend, there's a robbery every two or three months (Teri something or other, a former schoolmate of mine, mans the cash window, she was the first in our class with breasts, she usually wore dresses with big polka dots, and after a while there was no escaping the fact that the dots were now beginning to round out; her mother came to pick her up every day, whereas the rest of us weren't picked up anymore, also in a polka-dot dress, and she hardly looked older than Teri; their breasts looked alike; she has never been able to give a description because the moment she sees the gun and the plastic bag, because this is what happens every time, and how, gun, plastic bag, in large denominations, please, she doesn't look up but immediately lowers her eyes, because she's afraid that if she looks at the bank robber, he's going to shoot her; the police don't even ask anymore, they can fill out the report without her while Teri stands lethargically by; when we met after so many years I hardly recognized her, but I usually go to the other teller anyway, the one who takes letters, because I pay most of my bills through my bank); in short, the middle section belongs to the chestnut trees, this is the source of my passion for chestnuts, so eminently suited to remembering, next comes the row of plane trees, this is the most eye-catching stretch with infinity spreading before you, a bit as if the Danube were the sea and Fellini's miraculous ocean liner might glide into view at any moment in the back of the gardens. While I was in hospital, they cut down most of the poplars, reputedly for safety reasons, and they mutilated the planes so their own mothers wouldn't recognize them—in the best interest of the planes, of course. I couldn't care less about trees; still, come late spring, it feels good to walk to my mother's under the leafy arbor of their overreaching branches. Some people think of trees as living beings—an interesting idea. A good thing they don't call them Joe.

SO IT GOES

That I can grow old along with my mother I consider a great gift from Heaven. It's as if the Lord God saw fit to reward me. In which case, I must have done something right (after all). This possibly simplified notion of the world led to a certain lack of proportion, and my mother watched my exuberant ontological, historical, phenomenological, and personal exuberance re. growing old, our growing old, with mounting disapproval. And then, son, she said softly one fine day, in which I couldn't yet intuit the omens of the approaching storm, I loved it so much, I loved it more and more when she called me son, I saw nothing objectionable in it, I let it wash through me, like a Krúdy hero* the music of the violoncello before meeting the one and only love of his life (for the day) in the graveyard, I let this son vibrate

* Gyula Krúdy (1878–1933), the "Hungarian Proust," was a writer and journalist whose novels about Budapest were extremely popular between the two world wars.

through my being as, carefully, not bending, disciplined, using my thigh muscles, and not from the waist, I lowered myself next to her on the old family *fauteuil* (wing chair),

THE ONE

in which my grandmother, my mother's mother, used to sit at one time, an exceptionally tall, bony draught horse even in old age, she sat and crocheted and crocheted and crocheted while the chances of her guessing who she was talking to gradually diminished; toward the end I was often Veronka, the former chambermaid from Dunaszerdahely, and how the Slovaks did me a world of good, they taught me humility, and how there's no ambition in me, and she appreciates that, if only I didn't glance quite so brightly at the boys, because they're after just one thing, and then, burping and guffawing, as if she were vomiting and swallowing at the same time, that's how grandmother's bout of laughter erupted, but we women are after the same thing!

SO IT GOES, CONTINUED

I'm aghast, son, time and again I'm aghast how thoroughly you forget, from one day to the next, from one moment to the next, as if you were forgetting on purpose that I'm old, that I've grown old, my cells, I've grown old all over, son, and not just my hand, which you like to hold so much, and don't interrupt, you hold my hand beautifully, gently, like a nestling, and I love you holding it, and I love you kissing it, the aging of my hand doesn't bother me, quite the contrary, my skin is silkier than ever, as if it were covered in light, expensive silk, it has a beautiful sheen to it, really, and you always write about it beautifully, even the increasingly voluminous gnarls of the joints don't bother me, and yet, it's disgusting, these protuberances growing out of me in my old age, and for what?, but let's not talk about that, let's talk about beauty, I'm not working, son, that's why my hands have grown beautiful, but the cells in my heart have grown old, too, and my lungs and my liver, my kidneys, my intestines, your mother has lousy, blighted intestines, son, and lousy, blighted brain cells. So I will say it again while I can: I like it best when nothing happens. When my day is empty. It is a contradiction, but just barely, that I'm happy when I see you. But I am not happy to have to wake up. When I wake up, I pretend, for half an hour at least, that I'm still sleeping, so that Transylvanian woman with the huge ass, to whom I owe nothing but gratitude, shouldn't swoop down on me instantly, that she shouldn't bulldoze me flat with her eagerness to help; in this blessed, lighthearted half hour of idleness I imagine the day up ahead, I see time as if it were a stream, that Einstein of yours, son, leaves me cold, and in this stream I see, like an island or like some trees leaning over the water, the events of the day to come. I have also noticed that I must devote more and more time to this, and in the end I will need the entire day to imagine it *in advance*. If it should come to that, I may ask you about Einstein after all. I'm just joking, dear, by then it will be too late for questions. It is already too late! Kindly get it through your head: a person is in a much worse shape than they look. This is what old age is, this invisible "much worse." And it is the only reality. I'd have to wet my pants all the time for you to see my situation clearly. By the way, just so you know, I know that you know that from time to time I do wet my pants. My muscles have grown tired, all sorts of muscles have grown tired. So it goes, remember?, Kurt Vonnegut Junior. Not wiping the saliva off the chin, letting the body fluids seep, sometimes recognizing one's own child, sometimes not, causing a scandal with words, actions or omissions, standing naked on the loggia on a whim, trying to ignore the mosquitoes, the commies, though, they were good at exterminating them, they're good, and that's all there is to it, they're reliable exterminators, though the non-commies are good at it as well, it's something we're good at, waiting patiently for the boxes opposite to fill up with the audience, then launching into it, like a vermin stuck in a tree trunk, howling how I'm the mother of the illustrious writer, sobbing, the snot dribbling from my nose, so it should be clear to all present, that, though there's no knowing exactly for what, but that you, son, are to blame.

INTERPOLATION ON ETERNITY

I'd give my right arm if at a time like this I wouldn't think of the Camus sentence from *The Stranger* that somehow one can't help feeling a bit guilty, and instead were to seek comfort in Lampedusa's Prince: Nothing can be decently hated except eternity.

LUNCH, DETOUR: THE TRANSYLVANIAN AUNTIE

As I advance through the veil of overhanging branches toward my mother and our Sunday lunch, which is invariably the same, chicken soup, fried chicken with parsley potatoes, about which my mother—and you can depend on it as on the day's (next day's) sunrise, comments that it should properly be served with potato salad, and the following Sunday it's with parsley potatoes again, and she comments again on how this humble yet noble repast should be served, and I will go to my Maker without mustering the courage to ask why in that case we, concretely she, never serves it with potato salad, oh, mother, do tell, why is it so; in short, as I trod the irregular, unregulated chess board of shady and bright spots, I feel that there is no king or queen here, no bastion, no faithful subjects, there is nothing but moves, rules without rules, as if for miles around I were the only living being, or rather, and this goes without saying, my mother and I, there is just the two of us, plus some birds whose identification not only is a burden, but also leaves me incredibly cold, sparrows, crows, indubitably, swallows probably, thrushes maybe. Whatever is not sparrowcrowswallow is a thrush. Or a whooping crane.

Dear Mom is in a spiffy mood today, said the Transylvanian woman as I entered, in whose eyes the spark of recognition was always ignited just a flash before it was ignited in mine. And yet, I had it easier, I could work by exclusion. Who?! Who do you mean?! This, dear mom, my ears couldn't pick it up. She repeated it and I nodded, like my former theology teacher, and just like him, I wasn't indicating the slightest approval of the admittedly unintentional arrogance and humiliating ingratiation inherent in the sentence either—and me, too, what am I shilly-shallying for, why does this large-assed goose think she can talk about my mother like this!—yes, I nodded, I understand what you're saying. At times I was so angry, I couldn't even look at her; on the other hand we were dependent on her. The same old story. The "Transylvanian aunties" came and went; as far as I could tell they respected the Protestant ethic of capitalism, just barely cheating their employer, improving on their equitable (oral) contracts with recourse to clever, petty swindle, and since the discipline of producing receipts was tempered by the humane considerations of the victim, who was at their mercy, this was not particularly difficult, it did not call for direct baseness or large-scale cheating; in the final analysis, it can be put down to the centuries-old Transylvanian imperative to live, or, rather, to survive while just barely brushing up against the Ten Commandments—no more, really, than some *petitesses* not even worthy of mention: the somewhat too liberal handling of the money meant for groceries, the creative redefinition of its use, its redistribution, furtive night calls with respect to the upcoming family christening in Kolozsvár, the re-rationing of the toilet paper for private use, stuff like that. Rallying her impressive inner reserves, my mother did her level best to be irascible; she spared no effort, left no stone unturned, moved heaven and earth to be on bad terms with them; she went looking for faults and she found them, and if she didn't, then whatever she found, that's what she called a fault. Each one thought she was stronger than the other, mutually scorning each other thereby.

Mother had tubes sticking out of her just then, temporarily, something I had to get used to every time, that's how dramatic that complex configuration of tubes from my mother back into my mother seemed to me. She had laid the legendary yellow "butterfly blanket" on her lap. Her body had disappeared as if it were nothing but a talking head; this upset me, I missed her body. My mother didn't greet me either, and as if on purpose to prove the Transylvanian auntie wrong, when I entered she was fractious and grumpy; that woman said, and that's another awful thing, son, there's no remembering their names, this house is like the central station in Kiev, with these Rékas and Kingas and

Kincsős coming and going, move back of the yellow line on track two!, is there such a thing as Zsuzsonna with an *o*?, never mind, this one here is Júlia, I say to her, Júlia my dear, you're getting everything dirty as you clean the house, because, you know what she does?, she takes the garbage out, the vacuum cleaner bag and God knows what else, then drags up the dirt from the yard on her shoes, clumps of soil, whole heaps of soil, vacuum bag out, heaps of soil in, which gets my goat logically, if you know what I mean, son, and what happens?, she gives me a look, shrugs, smiles ever so *sweet*, I'm not blind, I can appreciate it, though let me add that she's not parrying her huge ass in my house, anyway, there she is, grinning like a sack of new potatoes, as they say on the soccer pitch, like a precautious adolescent, well, Lilike, because she finally managed to learn it, it wasn't easy, but she's not momming me anymore, so she says, well, Lilike, *that's fucking life*, that golden tongued, gurgling Transylvanian mountain stream, can you believe it?, nothing like an untainted source, I looked at her aghast, while cool as a cucumber, she picked the dry clods of soil from off the soles of her shoes, you speak English?, no, Your Ladyship, but I watch a lot of TV back home, how do you like that? *That's fucking life*, mother.

She waved it off. By the way, what are you working on, I see you don't want to tell me. Which is one, i.e., one sentence, it's in one, without a question mark, with one intake of breath, come-to-think-of-it-what-are-you-working-on-I-see-you-don't-want-to-tell-me. She instantly curtailed what she hadn't even begun, this was her way, and that guess what?, while she was waiting for me, she tried very hard to think of me—a proper and salutary thing to do, is it not, son?—but a pair of socks came to mind instead, again and again she thought of a pair of socks and not of me, mid-calf, with a Prince Gall pattern given to her in her early teens—my chubby teens!—when the panic broke out on Wall Street and people jumped out the window my mother pulled on her socks, but that's not why she got those socks, they were for skiing, and will these socks replace me in her memory from now on, these undoubtedly high-quality and, above all, warm socks, but still!, and she gave me a searching look. Like maybe shouldn't I be putting up a fight against these socks? Unto the breach, dear son, draw your saber! The area around the eyes is the oldest part of her, her most unfamiliar terrain.

Our lunches always proceeded according to the same schedule. While we waited for the soup my mother always, now, too, whispered to me—this, too, how horrible, son, having to whisper in my own house like a common servant!—the previous week's atrocities, humiliations and betrayals, in short, about the misdemeanors of the Transylvanian auntie of the moment. It took some time before I caught on that my mother, how shall I put it, allows herself certain playful liberties with the truth. She fixes those fabulous grayish blue eyes of hers on mine, or was it hazel?, let it be hazel, fixes her beautiful hazel eyes on mine, the lightning flashes of confidence dovetail, and in this blinding light my mother—lies through her teeth like a pro. If I counter her, she waves an arm, she agrees, of course, you're right, of course, but basically, it's as I said, and she goes on; if I listen without a show of protest, she swoops down, triumphant, you're your mother's son, son, after all, isn't that why you're a writer, to take the cold and incomprehensible and unbearable facts of real life and turn them into the mysterious and the bearable? It is a mistake if, in response, I ask her about my books, but the soup always comes before I can take offense.

I wheeled my mother to the table, took a pillow from under her, is the height alright?, why ask, you know it's alright, with two pillows it's not alright, with one pillow it's alright, when I take her in my arms I have to be careful not to crush her, a little bird, before I know it I practically bump into her shoulder blade as if she had no flesh, with everything shrunken, dried out, except for the bones. That's why we have the repeatedly mentioned hand project. It was safer to hold her hand; all sorts of alterations appeared there, too, more and more striking gnarls, her hand the same elegant item, the protuberances clearly do not belong to it. It feels good saying this, it feels good showering my mother with my love, these don't even belong to your hand, we might as well ignore them. Her bones might be frail, but she is not; she bristled so that I dropped my eyes, what do I mean they don't belong to her, what affectation, and would I kindly tell her, if they don't belong to her, who do they belong to, but most especially, who does the pain belong to, the pain that is her constant companion now, and it's this firm foundation that's ripped wide open when, for instance, she moves her fingers, she can hardly bear to hold the cutlery, if she had her way she'd have someone feed her, except she knows, for instance, how that would upset me, my meticulous insistence on harmony would go off kilter, that famous ontological good cheer, you're just as impossible as that Goethe, son, if only you were as good a writer; so fine, the gnarls may not belong to her, but the gnarls belong to the pain and the pain belongs to her, besides of which, why do I pretend that I know the first thing about football?

Oh. The question came in that tired, resigned and reproachful tone parents reserve for calling upon the fruit of their loins to reel off the list of the country's natural resources without a hitch—alum earth!, for crying out loud, alum earth and not aluminum!—and in fact it sounded a bit threatening, as if neglecting to mention the salt mines were not only the zenith of obtuseness and ignorance, its peak, apex, and epitome, but a sin against ethics into the bargain, low and perfidious. (Seeing my grownup children, this is one of the greatest of reliefs: never again will I have to sound them out like a leery upholder of morals, I'm asking you for the last time!, does the Ukraine have a significant goat breeding program?; good!) This transpired on July 9, 2006, Zidane's day,* as I recall. The comment took me by surprise. My mother's attitude vis-à-vis my books was *tolerably* light (which, as I've already mentioned, was my father's word, by now every word belongs to someone, I could brood with good reason in the clutches of Zeitgeist), provided that my books were a success, she was happy, provided she was happy. Generally, she talked about my books like a Communist Youth secretary with a constructive bent, who wouldn't like to sweep the problems that at this point in time he wouldn't like to specify under the carpet—those days are *gone*, Comrades!—on the contrary, he would like to call for a sincere, concerted effort with respect to lighting on a solution. I never told her this either. But to give her her due, she knew the

* On July 9, 2006, Zinédine Zidane, the French soccer player and famous head-butter, became one of only four footballers (the others were Pelé, Paul Breitner, and Vavá) who achieved the feat of scoring in two different World Cup final matches (he scored twice in the 1998 FIFA World Cup final). However, during the second World Cup final, he received a red card for violent conduct after head-butting the Italian Marco Materazzi, thus also making him the fourth person to have been sent off in a World Cup final. (The game was won by Italy.)

positive reviews by heart—in this respect, quantity sometimes really turned into quality for her, "It's not what they say, but how long it takes them to say it!" (Hanna Honthy);* she especially liked it when my name appeared in capital letters and/or in boldface, and also, if there was an accompanying photograph; she was aware of her primitive attitude and stood by it—pointing out, as if by way of an aside, but with admirable ingenuity, how bagatelle the bad reviews were, sloppy, groundless pseudo-reasonings, pseudo, son!, the slapdash and amateur expositions of pseudos, the provincial wallowing in personal malevolence. I did not protest. And also, prior to 1990, a casual remark about "Moscow hirelings" also characterized the murky critical horizon. When any of my books got on any list at all, she cut out the newspaper article and glued it to the kitchen door, and showed it off to one and sundry. The door creaked like a living thing. She translated my triumphs into the language of football, so she could feel their weight. An unexpected Dorogi† tie; and once she said: this is as if you'd played at Maracana in front of a crowd of twenty thousand with Edson Arantes do Nascimento.‡ Then after a brief pause she added: *behind* Edson Arantes do Nascimento. She wasn't placing me on a lower rung of the ladder, just that she promptly imagined a structure in the mind's eye, a team of the Gilmar–Djalma Santos type, let's say, and proceeded to define my place

* Hanna Honthy (1893–1978) was the legendary diva of Hungarian operetta, who sang onstage till the age of eighty. She is best remembered for her performance in Ferenc (Franz) Lehár's *The Merry Widow*.

† A small town north of Budapest with a football club.

‡ The international football star better known as Pelé.

in it; it would've been ridiculous displacing Tostão, and so on, and in what followed, she concocted bright dreams for this team, and not for my bright novels. I reached the pinnacle of literary fame in her eyes when the German Football Academy awarded my book second honorary mention, and I got to shake hands with Beckenbauer at the Nuremberg gala. My son shook hands with Beckenbauer, she reflected, weighing the situation, which by definition means that I am now the mother of the person who shook hands with Beckenbauer. My mother didn't have a snobbish bone in her body, but she understood the order, the hierarchy in the world of football, her awe was addressed to that. Franz and my son, she sighed blissfully, my hero!, as if she could not reasonably expect a greater boon from life.

Offended, Júlia removed the soup pot; there was no immediate reason for her wounded self-esteem, unless it was the fact that she knew—she knew!—that at this juncture my mother would always snap, to no one in particular: pots do not belong on the table!, I will never get it through her head! But in truth, only one thing got her dander up: the woman's colossal ass. How is it? You'd think the woman had a big ass on her on purpose to annoy my mother—tell me, son, don't Transylvanian women have posteriors instead?, *after all*, you're the great stylist!—and that she must've spent years, nay, decades, among the pines in sweet, far-off Transylvania bent on growing her posterior, and throughout Chau's dictatorship stuffed herself with the most precious jewels of Transylvanian cuisine, its *lavalières!*, son, with perfidious intent, and later, under the new East European freedom, with chips, coke and burgers of all kinds (which, by the way, she calls devil's meat), all of it exclusively to grow her posterior, thereby annoying my dear little mommy.

MY MOTHER DISHES IT OUT (ARIA)

The problem is not that you don't know the first thing about it, that's given, but it doesn't hurt anymore, for a while it hurt, but now it doesn't, but that you talk about football at all. It's one thing watching the game, and another talking about it. The problem is with the words, son, and don't yell and don't throw a fit—if it weren't for you, mommy dear, I'd die an ignoramus—I know I'm right. I'm not saying that the words, the gab, aren't part of the watching, but it's one thing standing by the sidelines and shooting your mouth off, it's not you doing the talking there, the words just happen, they speak themselves, or, as you would say, the pitch is doing the talking. However, I can buy that. I've done the same thing all my life, I stood by the sidelines, you can be a smart-ass, a know-it-all, partial, half-baked, what have you there, or all of it together. You're not the crowd, but neither are you you. You're part of the game. A person like that is free, not just the one playing, but also the one watching. It's in the air, son, you absorb it even if it hangs over you like a canopy of dense fog, you barely see as far as the net, the men, too, grow indistinct, the referee is seriously considering calling off the game, and also when the valley is sparkling in the sunshine, and you can't tell where the field ends, it doesn't, son, you can see infinity with both your eyes, first the foggy goal posts, and now the squinting. But these writings! Memorial poems, short articles, short stories! Short story cycles! Sonnets! Books! The mere sight of those thematic jackets fills me with the sort of irrepressible *ennui* Pascal couldn't begin to imagine. One glance at a green cover like that, because how clever can you get, they're generally green, green like the all-important turf, are they not?, depressingly original, and I can't repress a yawn. I am gripped by a yawning fit, a yawning tsunami, son. Keep that it mind. In the twinkling of an eye everyone's become a soccer pro, but certainly everyone and his brother has stories to tell, maudlin outpourings about the strict but just coach (an Uncle Imre), and also a team that we simply can't do without, but which, also, doesn't exist, a third-class dust-ridden Eldorado overgrown with creeping grass, a lost Golden Age on the drab outskirts of town, a lofty spirit in an emphatically pauperized environment. Don't make me laugh! Tiger Balm as ambrosia. Steer clear of it, son. The petty myths, the superannuated spielers whose bright careers came to naught due to some chance fatality ("my ankle went out, a shame, because Junior said right to my face, hey, kid, you're the ace"), this whole disgusting warming of ourselves by the bonfire lies of lemonade memories, the somniferous, disgustingly mawkish bonfire of lies, that's what I'm talking about!, and also the great myths, a football nation, the Mighty Magyars as the be-all and end-all of Hungarian history, King Matthias and the boys . . . Bern, 1954,* that's no national wound but a quagmire of nostalgia, a morass of sentiment, son, a parody on the death of a nation, affectation, kitsch! And these insider pet names, cleats, a footie, a cubbie, a nutmeg, a two-touch, this stale and putrid cliquishness, like when I sit down in an easy chair after a stranger and am repelled by the heat of his body, this whole shameful religion substitute!

* On July 4, 1954, the legendary Mighty Magyars lost the FIFA World Cup 3–2 against West Germany. The match was played at the Wankdort Stadium in Bern, Switzerland. The legendary lost match put an end to the Hungarian team's long string of wins, during which time they remained unbeaten in 32 games and were reigning Olympic Champions and winners of the Central European International Cup in 1953.

You can't put the ball in God's place, what a ridiculous quasi-solution, either kindly have it out with Heaven, a tough game, good pitch, led by Bircsák, or, as an honest to goodness agnostic, be satisfied with a throw-in. By the way, familiarity with the soccer field in its entirety also has its theoretical limits! Which doesn't preclude a short prayer, son, before a penalty kick, it's alright to pray, no matter what anybody says, you can pray the ball into the net. . . . But where was I? I lost my train of thought. . . . If you don't watch out, these books will end up teaching you the *real* essence of football. Being too clever by half, intellectual pyrotechnics, eggheads. Ridiculous! They're oozing art from every pore! Aging, haven't you noticed, they're all written by aging men, that's why all that whining and whimpering and nostalgia for the sweaty locker rooms, and then I haven't said half. You're aging, too, son. So stop this thing right now! An aging man is not a genre, it carries no weight. An aging man is only about aging, about decline and nothing more. The hysteria of decline. An aging woman has drama, at least, there is something at stake. A man turning gray at the temples, there's something to be said for that. I hope I haven't hurt your feelings.

CONT.

Which is true, she doesn't mean to hurt my feelings, but she doesn't care if she does. What she cares about is the precision of her words. In some measure we all grow tougher with time. My mother, too, became more severe. She loves me, that hasn't changed, and it's what counts, but she doesn't pamper and cuddle me anymore (the way she pampered and cuddled my father until the moment of his death), she's stopped shielding me, yet all the while she keeps me in the status of a child, that's what makes the tough tough. She no longer tells me to take my scarf (or if she does, not like *that*), or to dress in layers. Solve it as best you can, her inert expression says. I'm not your nanny. I believe in you, but don't look to me for strength. I can give you only as much security as I give myself. This is what her expression told me. We focused in on the fried chicken. Place a paper napkin over it, sit on top with a pair of porcelain trousers, starched, with a sharp crease, and if the fried chicken is properly fried, juicy but not oily, it won't leave a mark. The number of times I heard this! And invariably, after it: Of course you don't know what porcelain trousers are anymore. I'm not shouting, but by way of an aside, son, why must I repeatedly ask you, every Sunday, to cut up my meat? Is this what you call discretion? It's not discretion, it's ill breeding. You know, because I know you know that I can't cut it up myself, my hands are shaking, and even if they weren't, they wouldn't have enough strength, and even if they did, I still couldn't cut it up because that lumpish Transylvanian lily of the field never sharpens the knives like she should. Which reminds me. You don't cut either, you hack back and forth. You think I don't know, that I don't know? That I don't know I'm weak? When should I be weak if not *now*? She bowed her head and gazed at the yellow butterfly blanket for some time. Her complexion had retained its former enchanting Creole tone. An Arabian princess, that was one way of seeing my mother. Let's go to the green salon—meaning I should wheel her chair back there and place the extra pillow under her—let's have our coffee there. And that by all odds this Júlia, Turkish coffee is the only kind she might be able to make well, history is a great dictator, son. (To wit, during the sixteenth and seventeenth centuries, Transylvania enjoyed a daily working relationship with the Ottoman Empire—which I mention with reluctance and a certain, if light, bad grace, because the other day I read that the reader has the right to understand the references, etc., found in literary texts. Well . . .) Also, kindly keep in mind that I'm two years younger than Gyuri Tábori! As I maneuvered the pillow back under her small, skinny behind, I imagined my mother and Gyuri Tábori growing up together as children. They use the formal mode of address with each other, always the formal mode of address. And everyone hopelessly in love with everyone else. It was like that with my mother, and it was like that with Gyuri Tábori, always, whenever they met, this being hopelessly in love would burst its bounds. Then they began coscripting Hitchcock's films.

7. Love, Love, Love

ADALBERT TÓTH RINGS MY BELL, 2007

I flexed the muscles of my buttocks, flex, flex, relax, the black Volga drove out of sight at the north end of the boulevard, just like a ship on the horizon, because of the roundness of the Earth, I should think, except ships don't turn off to the road to Szentendre. I didn't want to know, no, wanting had nothing to do with it, my memory was ebbing and flowing too aimlessly for that, I preferred not to know, yet I knew who this Uncle Lajos with the Czeslaw Milosz eyebrows was talking about. It'd only been a couple of months (or weeks?, sitting at my desk, I lose all sense of time, or else keep just enough in reserve so that a question like this, if it were important for the Bench, if the outcome of the investigation depended on it, even then I couldn't answer it, even if I tried) since he rang my bell, then he phoned me a couple of times. Which must've been difficult for him, because it must've been him that kept putting the phone down after the first ring. A bad feeling. Those Eastern European telephones, the calls, the ringing, the old, black, hulking sets, the incessant noise and crackle and silence and echo in the earpiece, the proverbial dead phones, all this carried a meaning beyond itself, real threat and real paranoia. Not an easy habit to break. Hopefully, the cell phones are "clean" and have regained their virginal technical status. A single ring like this is like a signal, but there's no knowing who, why, or for whom. And though it has stopped ringing, you pick up the receiver and say hello. Making a fool of yourself is inevitable. And the anger, too. Later he didn't put it down immediately, but didn't talk into it either. You can feel if there's someone at the other end of the line, I sometimes receive anonymous calls like that (in a dictatorship less often), at such times I go out of my way to be polite, which is simple conceit and presumption, whereas I should send them to hell—a natural reaction—or slam down the phone. It doesn't happen often, but it happens. Not a good feeling. Then after a while he got up the nerve to speak. The first time I denied it's me, no, I'm not home, I hissed at the person holding the receiver (the person holding the receiver?, what an absurd expression!, who picked up the phone?, a question easy enough to answer—the lady cook at the Greasy Spoon—but that's the subject for another story, for another time); the next time I picked it up myself and in answer to his formal and courteous inquiry, is he calling at a bad time, I laughed and said, well, now that you mention it; I'm sorry, he said, and put it down. Disappointed, I stood with the receiver in my hand for some time yet. Then he called again, which was the last time I spoke with him in my life, though I was just pretending that—oh!—I am not I, and masking my voice, I said, wrong number. Wrong number? Yes, sir, like I said. Isn't that you, sonny? Excuse me? There was no shame in me, just impatience. Playing for time. But why? Well, if it's not you, sonny, then I beg your pardon, sir, but if it is you, Petikém, I haven't called you that for so long, then . . . he breathed a deep sigh, and I slammed down the phone. You can't slam these newfangled receivers down properly, you gotta stuff them back in, while you can't stuff something back in briskly, forcefully, with anger. I shrugged. I wonder if he's crying or cursing? I gingerly picked up the receiver again. He was still talking, which annoyed me. All his life he loved to talk, and he always told you why he wanted to talk, and what about. I feel a need for talking like Father Pirrone in *The Leopard, Il gattopardo,* sonny, the great Giuseppi Tomasi di Lampedusa, so as to fix into a pattern of phrases the ideas obscurely milling in my head.

ADALBERT TÓTH HAS HIS SAY (ARIA)

For a time I put up a fight against transience of all kinds; when my first dog died, I cried like a child, as if my mother had died, I mourned at the sight of a withering bouquet of flowers and stroked the back of a dried loaf of bread with a heavy heart; I didn't want to let anyone go, sonny, not because I wanted to own them, or not only because I wanted to own them, but because I am faithful by nature; I wouldn't have wanted to lose anyone I had anything to do with because, when all is said and done, isn't this the essence of the feeling of intimacy?, isn't this web of relationships, however insignificant, but in any case, minor, isn't this what gives shape to the environment in which we then . . . what?, in which we feel safe? But that's an exaggeration. In which we can get our bearings, more or less. We know what we should fear and what not, we recognize the hidden references and recognize the blatant nonsense, too. I yearned for this peace, sonny, oh, how I yearned for it, for my life to attain this sense of balance, except I wasn't up to nurturing these relationships, not even the major ones, I let friendships and loves slip through my fingers, because it seemed to me, and I wish to emphasize this: it seemed to me that they wanted to slip away. I put up a half-hearted fight, but there's no fighting halfheartedly. You're the one exception. Forty years don't count, forty years have come and gone, sonny, even more than forty, and still, I know you as if I'd seen you every day. But not a photo, and not a film. There are two photos of you and me, one is rather embarrassing, when the boys team won a championship, a Hanula photo, you're all striking poses, the photographer clearly asked you to smile, and this didn't work, maybe only Miki Görög looks natural, he's the only one not laughing, just his eyes; on the other photograph you're not laughing either, that's a bona fide picture, you're just coming off the pitch, everything about you says that the team lost, I'm heading toward you, but I'm out of focus, yes, I'm always out of focus, somehow, only I know that that's me, and you knew, because you knew!, the fans turned against the team that time, you boys weren't just playing badly, you were arrogant, you refused to recognize that you were bad because you knew that you were good, something that's bound to happen with good teams from time to time, and if they're really good, they'll keep it in mind, and then it won't happen again for a while, but then eventually it does. I carry you inside me, not a photo, and not a film, a film on the saltpetered wall of memory, what do you say, sonny, a pretty image, that!; what a laugh, me talking to you about words. I read your books, but I'd rather not go into that just now. I should have done it before you wrote them, that would have been the time, you were a quiet, sad little boy, as courteous as any adult, you said good day and not I kiss your hand, you were too withdrawn to be friendly, all tied up in knots, for a while, anyway, though not your movements, even if you did hold your upper body too stiff while running, you liked to think that Albert ran like that, you even raised your hand and elbow like a chicken, it was the thing to do back then, to run like Albert, to want to run like Albert, as if running like Albert without Albert were possible, and of course, it was, even if it was ridiculous, but it was possible to feel what it felt like, and you, too, felt your way to this raising of the hands, even Miki Görög's mother held her hands like that; but your solitude was the most touching of all, and your bones, I carry that inside me, in the form of a hologram, it's important, having the right number of dimensions, the number of dimensions is vital, that you should have bulk, I know you don't like me saying it, that you should have a body.

I didn't want to listen to this anymore and put the phone down. He knew I'd put it down, and also that I'd heard everything. I didn't care. I tried not to think of myself with disgust. Standing on the sidelines of our lives, if that's what it was.

THE RINGING, CONTINUED

They may have called him Adalbert Tóth at the Works only, and even there only at the Party office, but no, there it was more like Comrade Tóth; Uncle Ádi, nuncle, nuncle Ádi, but mostly just Magician, we usually called him Magician. And later: Magician, old man. I'm not sure what his title was in the team, the Farkasvölgy Football Club, or, as they say, the mother club, though you usually say this only when you're playing for someone else already, if you stay put where you were in the first place, there's no mother. These are fragile distinctions, son. Yes, mother. Section head. Or club secretary. In the spirit of two hands drawing each other, an Escher drawing, I might (wittily) say that someone rang the bell, I was working, *I was just at the point that I was just at the point* when, like the lethal whistle of a corrupt referee, the bell shattered the sylvan creative woods.

MY MOTHER, THE SOCCER FAN

A referee who knows how to cheat (who is gifted that way) goes unnoticed, he never blows his whistle when we don't expect it, on the contrary, we feel that he whistles only when he should, his decisions are not in the least outrageous, just possibly interesting, witty, arguable; and there'd be no problem if only our hearts did not grow heavier and heavier and a profound gloom did not weigh on our chest, it's clear that somewhere something bad has taken its start and it will soon be here, it's already here, we know it's here, but we don't want to acknowledge it, it's here, but we don't know what it is, which only makes matters worse, that's what a referee who is an expert at cheating is like, everything is in order, only your heart has grown heavy (like the Gaffiot dictionary, as I wrote somewhere, but that was a different matter of the heart). And, of course, so much for the game!

My mother has a remarkable gift for picking up on the metaphysical decay settling on the field, the team, *our* team. My genteel mother could root like a navvy. My mother's gentility embraced a sense of form, and if that form called for vulgarity, what was there to stand in her way? But more to the point, why should it, son? She was repeatedly led off the field; at such times she exited in a huff, on the borderline of abuse yet still on this side of it, reiterating her arguments, but now, instead of generalities, she zeroed in on the referee, not forgetting to mention his human dimensions, family circumstances, and more especially the questionable morals of that demimondaine mother of his. All told, she evidenced mind-boggling ingenuity in her abuse of the referee and the opposing team. She would revile and vilify them as if they were old friends who had just now let her down, a brilliant move, it would actually create confusion, a defender would stop in his tracks, or just look up and reflect, hold a quick survey of his conscience—and that's all our team needed. Mother made her exit to frenetic applause. The fans didn't just appreciate her boastful spirit and the turmoil; mother's maddened, hoarse screaming—because her tone, unity of form and content!, conformed to the text—spoke for them all; what's more, she veritably took upon herself the burden of the defeat and lack of talent of the team, and she did this so that the entire grandstand heaved a sigh of relief; nobody thought that we'd won, because we'd lost, but my mother reminded them of the great, eternal gift of the born fan, the gift of hope; if not now, then next week. . . . Like all truly great fans, my mother, too, was blind and partial, but her demagogue cogitations were always strictly along professional lines. I held her hand as we walked away to the receding sound of applause.

CONT.

It never fails. In the morning, during working hours, my working hours, the ringing of the bell inflicts a heavy, dull pain on the heart; there I was, building the small, self-parodistic tower of the working ethos with admirable ingenuity, but my "progress" had made me careless and expansive, and I threw a glance at the garden gate without the usual annoyance. I didn't recognize the old man, I hadn't seen him in years, and I hadn't thought of him once, it never even occurred to me that I might see him, he wasn't on my list of those I might have to recognize one day. The sunlight came streaming into the room diagonally, like on some devotional picture, a soft, autumnal glow that doesn't sparkle. it flows, a golden light swimming in a sea of gold. Staying inside on such a day is a questionable occupation, as if life were outside, while inside . . . frankly, there is nothing inside, just me, me and my work, and this, compared to the quiet, near-lethargic frenzy that is the light, this is truly nothing, a Tonio Kröger effect of the lowest possible standard. Still, by the time I reached downstairs, I was preoccupied with trying to guess the identity of the audacious individual whose mid-morning (!) ringing at the gate had just shattered the habitual order of the created universe. I can talk about the nature of writing, the bureaucratic majesty of the daily grind, the inviolate character of one's working hours in a truly graphic manner, enough to make your heart break. I didn't take the key to the garden gate with me, just my pen, which I held up before me like a lance, an old habit. The veil, as they say, fell from my eyes only by degrees.

What can I do for you, I said ungraciously. For some reason I think I manage to hide my bad grace well, but certain signs seem to indicate otherwise.

Well, sonny, here I am. This sonny constituted the falling off of the veil from my eye; my mother always, to this day, calls me son, the Magician always, and now I learned that to this day, calls me sonny. My mother never says sonny, and the Magician never says son. We looked at each other across the wrought iron gate, a curved iron bar was just at eye level, sometimes I moved my head to the side of the curved bar, at others raised myself on tiptoes or bent my knees so I could see his eyes. I had stood just like this with someone years before, and held my heroically grudging pen in the same way, my younger brother, who veritably clapped the gate to his bosom, leaning against it, wracked by sobs, dead, he kept repeating, the little one is dead, their child had died just then—half an hour before—choking on her saliva. I didn't have to seek my brother's eyes partly because it wasn't possible, because he wasn't really there, his eyes looking into nowhere, or inside himself, or straight at the Lord God, accusingly, and partly because he was taller than the fence, had outstripped it, and was looking down from there, down into the void, at me. We never spoke about the dead child, ever; I wouldn't dare write down her name here. The Magician had hardly changed; he always seemed to be rolling; every part of him was round, as if he'd been assembled out of hemispheres (and spheres); I'm not saying that he was sloppily patched together, but the parts are too obviously parts, while the whole looks, first and foremost, as if it were hidden by the parts: the belly innocent, a happy belly, its shape much like Kálmán Mikszáth's (see *Production Novel*, 1979, pp. 321–323), except Mikszáth's has weight, something is at stake, there's a risk there, the defeat inflicted at the hands of time; however, there's nothing of that here, just the innocent sweep of the hemisphere, his buttocks an independent living being, two living beings, twins, his skull an almost perfect sphere, his cheeks, too, but without looking bloated, his nose with two "twists," first a concave, negative sphere, more like a circle, an anchor ring, then convex; his what we might call classical bowlegs, too, describe an arc each; in keeping with my budding interest in mathematics, I had once been wrapped up thinking where the center of this arc might be. Accordingly, I drew—this happened a long time ago—a string between the knee and the base of the thigh as well as the knee and the ankle, and feasted my eye on the perpendicular median. Once, after practice, I told him about this. Oh, my dear, my dear, he repeated over and over again. Because, instead of sonny, he sometimes called me dear. The sphere, my dear, is the ideal shape. The Magician, we chuckled, is ideal, which clearly makes us unideal.

So, then, sonny, here I am.

Yes, I nodded, as always (when I understand something), as if I didn't know who I was addressing, but of course by then I knew. He'd hardly changed, except he'd grown rounder still; only his eyes aged, though they were gleaming, like always, as if they were filled with tears. As if he were about to cry, which wouldn't have been the first time. When you're a child you don't understand; it's more terrifying than ridiculous. I'm dying, he said out of the blue, as if we were fencing and he'd come up with a surprising new (deadly) thrust (the Nevers thrust, right between the eyes!), and don't interrupt. Don't interrupt, this was another frequently used expression of his. I can safely say that it was the first sentence we held "in common." When the boys team won a championship in 1964, the last year that I played (my mother had stopped attending the games by then, she already knew what I refused to concede, that I'd never turn into a soccer player, neither world class nor fourth class, nothing), we have the honor, this is how Uncle Vili, our coach, put it, we have the honor, gentlemen, of having Uncle Ádi from the grownup team bear us company, and he took a deep breath (we didn't understand this honor and we didn't understand this bearing us company either), they got wind of our progress, and Uncle Ádi will make a referral upstairs, if I got this right. You have, Vilikém. It's purely informal, of course, you boys are the future, don't mind me, proceed as usual, no use improving on a good thing! We liked Uncle Vili because he made sure that we should think we're acting of our own free will. We were putty in his hands because we thought that the idea came from us. In return, we didn't pay much heed when he spoke. Or else, we made wisecracks. Just one clown at a time, gentlemen. At which, Uncle Ádi, like the voice of the Lord: Don't interrupt, sonny. Uncle Ádi appeared sweet and grownup at one and the same time. Uncle Vili was Uncle Vili, he'd gotten too long in the tooth to be in the first division the season before, in our eyes he was a sad old man. He dragged his foot just like me before my operation, though I suspect he drank more than I do.

I tried to catch his eye among the wrought iron tendrils; I leaned in, I shuffled in place, I stretched to my full height, as if dancing—how long it's been since I danced! What's this, a death gate, with everybody depositing a dead person at the door?, I grumbled, then shrugged. I won't go inside, I haven't got time, I won't impose on you. Still, he just stood there looking at me. His eyes were bathed in tears, his round face a splash pool. The tears were mixed with sweat. He had grown old, after all. I couldn't have said what rubbed me the wrong way, or rather what grated on my nerves, but something did. I attempted to put on a friendly face, I couldn't help thinking of the forty years as an accomplishment, not seeing someone for forty years, that's not nothing. Neither of us spoke. I brought you your papers, sonny. I raised an eyebrow and instinctively aimed my pen lance. Your football papers. I didn't understand. The old one, the first. I signed you up for the team, sonny, don't you remember? I didn't. And that I should have it now, he said, because of what he'd just said before. He's going around to the boys to give them back their papers, this is his farewell round. He handed me the small book in its blue plastic cover through the iron grating. It was sticky. Without realizing, I immediately opened it and looked at the vaguely familiar little boy's timid smile. It's you, except you weren't as famous, and don't interrupt. I had no intention of interrupting. There we stood.

I'd like to ask you something. Go right ahead, Magician. This time I could distinctly catch the sly-fox politeness in my voice. I'd like to ask you something from the maw of death, and don't interrupt, I say what I want now. Death is written all over me, sonny, don't you think?, and don't interrupt. The doctors are not saying it's terminal, and they're not saying it isn't, but the nurse told me, she said it's terminal, how much longer?, I asked, three months, she said, I see, I said. The nurse is related to Béla Vosnyik, Vosnyik was a goalie with a God-given talent back during Dr. Mike's time; also, he became personal physician to the Abyssinian king, you boys didn't know Béla, his two brothers were with the ÁVÓ, he defected in '56, but those bastards caught up with him and did him in in Australia. His two brothers? Of course not! The ÁVÓ. They got a long reach. I had to stifle a laugh, because it was at that moment that he forced his hand through the bars, as if his hand couldn't reach as far as the ÁVÓ. In line with the spherical conception, his small hand was as chubby as an indolent bishop's. Or more like an angel boy's, a putto's. It was on fire when I pressed it. He kneaded, he shook mine, and wouldn't let go. I was on tiptoes again; we'd just now cemented a contract. I'd like you to make a speech at the funeral, sonny, and don't interrupt, I'll have everything arranged beforehand, paid for *fix und fertig*, and no priest, I'm warning you, a funeral's difficult without a priest, and don't interrupt, without a priest one can't help thinking right away about the clods of earth and the worms that consume the corpse, not the body, the corpse, and then you will give a speech. Promise. What you say is up to you. Say what you like. Take from the current of my life whatever you think appropriate. My dear. I pulled my hand away. Don't go yet, stay a while longer with old Adalbert. And promise. Promise me, for chrissakes! You say whatever you want, you don't have to elaborate, maybe ten minutes? Or five? Yes, five, I muttered without thinking, and now I took his wrist. His wrist was chubby, too, chubby bones. Five, you're right, okay, five will do. I wanted your voice to be the last voice I hear, it wasn't until later I realized that once I'm there I won't be hearing anything at all. But if I could, yours would be the last, and I'd like that. Besides, who else could I ask? Certainly not Józsi Kaszás, heh, sonny?, and he squeezed my hand.

JÓZSI KASZÁS, JUNIOR, INSPECTS THE FIELD

Pleased to meet you, Józsi Kaszás, Junior, this is how he introduced himself, even as a child, and we thought he was making fun, but he never made fun, he played right back and, to use a popular expression, he was as dumb as an ox. He was so dumb, we honestly suspected there must be something behind it, a clever ulterior motive that Józsi Kaszás, Junior, had up his sleeve (I, for one, had lots of things up mine), except we'd never catch on, we're not smart enough. But he had nothing up his sleeve. He was just as dumb on the pitch as off, which is rare. This junior Kaszás has so little affinity for the game, son, he's so much in the dark about what's what, that if I didn't know that everybody counts, I'd say he doesn't count, that it makes no difference whether he's on the field or off. Maybe that's why he made such a fuss about the field, the turf, before a game; he studied it, inspected it, gave it the eye; he strolled down to center line first thing, still wearing his civvies, slowly, gingerly, as if walking on thin ice, and he felt the soil with his shoe or, as he called it, his clods. What the soil was like that day, what mood it was in. Kaszás Senior was not just a shoemaker but a master shoemaker, my old man's an artist, Kaszás Junior would declare defiantly, glaring at us. ("No bargaining. Time is money. No credit. Balázs Unyi, shoemaker," I read in Balassa.) Oh, sure, an artist, we nodded condolingly, shit, Kaszás, haven't you noticed?, all our fathers are artists! We laughed, that's why we liked Kaszás Junior, he made us laugh at him. But I gotta hand it to him, he always wore exceptionally handsome shoes. He came to practice in a different pair every time, and he always explained why the shoe was beautiful or special. Take it. Light as a feather. This light as a feather, he must have heard it from his old man. We passed the shoe around and said, oh, to be sure, to be sure, light as a feather, shit, Kaszás, old boy, this really is light as a feather, until we burst into another fit of laughter. But the shoes were really nothing like what we were used to, except we couldn't apply the concept of beauty to shoes; be that as it may, these light as a feather *objects* certainly stood in sharp contract to Kaszás Junior's conspicuous ugliness. Perhaps his ugliness was made so striking due to his pockmarked skin, the purple patches of various intensity that veritably throbbed on the back of his neck, the dry skin on the back of his hand, the small scales as shiny white as native soda. The back of his hand was in bloom like the alkali soil of the Great Hungarian Plain. In the nineteenth century, the native soda that was swept up was used for washing clothes and was sold and bartered for produce; according to Mór Jókai,* native soda attracts Calvinists. If there was anyone for whom the ground made no difference, its consistency, hard, soft, light, loose, loamy, grassy, specifically: creeping grass, domesticated turf, well, that was him, Józsi Kaszás, Junior, he was your man. Since he grew faster than the rest of us, he was transferred to the youth team, but he continued to grow, or just grow stronger—this despite the hostile ground conditions!—and ended up in the adult team. As if he were the best. He wasn't the worst, but he was the least like a soccer player. His mother had shacked up with Uncle Vili. Uncle Vili limped because once during practice Kaszás tackled him so they nearly called an ambulance. It didn't look like a major foul, as if somebody had taught him, too, about refined, invisible, underhanded fouls, like Gabi Tóth in my novels. Old man Kaszás chased away the blues by working on his shoes. Once a pair of red women's shoes fell out of Kaszás's bag. Shut up, everybody, he burst out, and we did, because the dazzling beauty of those red shoes cast a spell, even over us. They're for my mother. Every month, Kaszás Senior made a pair of shoes for his wife, she took them, but she never went back to the shoe artist.

* Mór Jókai (1825–1904) was a wildly popular Hungarian novelist, short story writer, essayist, and dramatist, called by many the Hungarian Dickens. In the United States and the United Kingdom, he is better known as Maurus Jókai.

CONT.

Are you saying that the Man with the Scythe is coming to get you? Perhaps you shouldn't make the speech droll, but do as you think best, sonny. Though it's not a bad idea, actually, people standing around the grave, chuckling. Still, crying might be better, it seems easier, somehow. See, I'm crying, too, I'm holding your hand and crying. (Thanks, Magician, old man, and goodbye. I never saw him again.)

8.

Would You Like to Be a Great Soccer Player, Son?

YOU BET

"I've hated soccer all my life," this sentence is not as off-key as it may appear initially; I read an interview with a pearl diver the other day, and he says that only a fake real pearl looks unerringly real, when testing a real pearl, an attitude of doubt is the only authentic attitude. (I would love to write, but it's too late now: It is deucedly difficult to dive for pearls when you don't know the truth.)* It is difficult to judge these things, and I wouldn't like to psychologize either, especially since this whole football caboodle appears through a mother-sieve and always did, even when I was a child. Later, I said that the Hungarian language and I enjoy a friendly relationship, that it is generous with me and allows me a lot of leeway, that we're on a first-name basis, that it suits me like a glove. And the ball suits me like a shoe. This became apparent

* "It is deucedly difficult to dive for pearls when you don't know the truth" is a playful reference to the much-quoted first sentence of Péter Esterházy's novel *Celestial Harmonies*: "It is deucedly difficult to tell a lie when you don't know the truth."

early on, I couldn't write yet, but flipping the rubber ball in the air, I knew no bounds! I was short and scrawny (I don't remember why anymore, but this filled me with pride), which made my dexterity with the ball even more conspicuous. Which, on the other hand, did not impress my mother, she knew that dexterity and a good player are not the same thing. Whereas I did everything for your professional development, son. Who would have thought that I'd have a professional development, and me only in first grade? Sometimes I play with the thought, and it doesn't even upset me, that possibly it's the football that my mother loved in me? The thing that's missing from me—except through her? My mother behaved like an undercover coach or manager; she kept a close eye on me, I don't know how she did it, but whenever I was playing, she was always lurking nearby. If we played in front of the house and she came outside, we naturally thought she wanted to order us inside, and so we promptly started begging, she waved us off, go on, play! My classmates gaped first at me, then at my mother; they'd never seen a mother like this.

God only knows why, but coaches insist on football wisdom (clichés), as if they'd come up with it themselves personally. I've never met a coach yet (I asked my brother, and neither has he) who didn't say that this game has to be won on the flanks. Or that you can play badly, but without a heart, never. My mother never said this, but she said things very much like it. You can play badly, but you cannot play without using your head. You must play badly in an *intelligent* way, if that's what is called for. It's easy to learn on the field: practice, practice. . . . Kick with both feet, head the ball fairly (!), be quick, be strong. But really, it's the game you have to learn. To acquaint yourself with it, that's the right expression. You must acquaint yourself with as many faces of the game as possible. You must learn to spot when this face changes, the game is in progress, and then suddenly it changes. A trickling mountain stream into a wide, lazy, rolling river. A tiger into a cat. A sow's ear into a silk purse. But there's no need to do that much thinking. When you run up to head the ball, don't be smart, son, be massive, with the backs bouncing off you. *Back, corner, offside*, that's how my mother talked, like this, in English. When you're off the field, you needn't be strong all the time, that's not natural. Sometimes you're strong, sometimes you're weak, that's natural. Besides, off the field weakness has its uses, and I wouldn't like to bring up your father at this point. You can learn from defeat, too. But not on the field, please, weakness has no value there. Out on the field, don't learn from defeat, learn from victory or, worse comes to worse, from a tie. It's possible to play badly, but it is not possible not to want to win. Out on the field, you should want to die.

When she first whispered this in my ear, it sounded pretty scary. Or silly. Why should I die now, when we're playing offense? It was recess, we were playing in the school yard, I never thought of it as a field. And besides, I'd just managed it, I played that famous feint, back-heeling the ball like Puskás in that 6–3 game in London*—possibly the most shameless gesture in all of football history, son, the way he sent Wright, who had attacked him on the five-yard line, into the needle furze with that devil-may-care,

* Ferenc Puskás played his famous feint during the game against England on November 25, 1953, at the old Wembley Stadium, when the Mighty Magyars beat the English 6–3. Dubbed the "match of the century," one of its highlights came when Puskás, playing against Billy Wright, dragged the ball back with the studs of his left foot and whacked it high into the net.

negligent move that one can afford in a school yard, if that, but even there it is highly irresponsible, "alright, Mister Wright," the witty Hungarian commentators screamed—and then the third-graders said I could join them. It took another year before my mother would take me down to *the field*. I was shorter, weaker, slower than the third-graders, but better than most of them. Get used to the battle conditions, my mother countered whenever I whined that, for instance, the others kept shoving me, but she never said, shove them back. You're a mediocre shover, son, so don't count on it. Be strong, not aggressive. (Later, my mother hardly bothered with my soccer-playing younger brother. He grew like ragweed, first slowly, then quickly, a veritable miracle. My mother bought a notebook and entered all my brother's matches, and later cut out and pasted into it even the briefest news that appeared about him in print. She could relax now: she finally had a soccer player for a son.)

THE RAGWEED ORDEAL

It was deceptive, the way I was advancing along the path my mother had marked out for me; still, the meadow at the Ragweeds' was off-limits. The Ragweed children, I was scared of them, because everybody was scared of them. They lived five houses down the road, three brothers and a breathtakingly beautiful older sister. (Once I sat with her for hours on a large heap of coal. It's interesting sitting on coal: black diamond and soot at the same time. All we did was sit. Actually, I didn't just sit, but concentrated real hard on whether she had panties on. I still think of it today, though she's dead, she fell off the cherry tree and broke her neck. We had larded bread with cherries at their place lots of times.) Nobody said they were gypsies, nobody thought of them as such, I thought they might be that only because the middle boy, Fecó, and the girl were gypsy-brown and they lived like gypsies (the way non-gypsies imagine gypsies live), not in a regular family home on the boulevard, but in a hovel-like shack, and there was no knowing how so many of them could fit in there.

They played on the meadow by the train station every day, attended a separate school (why?), the other boys came from there, too, five on each side, with a small net and no goalie. They played rough, "end-to-end" games, they did a lot more running than we did in the school yard. The first time I told my mother that I'd like to go play on the meadow, it was only natural that I should tell her, not yet, she said, and from then on, she had me running along the Danube every afternoon with the same relentless rigor that real coaches used later on, and which, apparently, seems to be called for. There was no way not to hate this—and I would have, had I not seen the radiance on my mother's face. It kept coming back to me, then, as it does now.

What's up, Count, want to join in? It was the spokesman speaking, the oldest Ragweed, the other two stood by grinning, as if they'd asked themselves and were waiting for my answer. They used count differently than other people. They spoke to me, how shall I put it?, like the unionized ironworkers in the thirties. In short, they looked down on me, just a bit. Which was new to me; it got my goat but, to my surprise, it didn't occur to me that they were unfair, on the contrary, there seemed to be some hidden truth in it which, thanks to the Ragweeds, now surfaced into the light of day.

A-ha.

At which they glanced at each other like the Three Stooges, and launched into a spectacular display, playing for each other's benefit, something I would have never expected of them, they were always so serious, doggedly determined; they never did anything that they didn't think mattered. For instance, they didn't bother with school. Should we stick him in, or have him stick it? Well, Count? What do you say? Should we stick you in, or have you stick it? I see on the old photographs that I had this defiant hamster look in my eye, and now I threw it into the fray, it's as much as I dared, they had a reputation for being quick fisted, I knew some of their victims personally. The youngest had a round head, round eyes, was short of stature but swarthy, his name was Bogyó, he even had a boxer. He might as well, Fecó said with a shrug, we're short a man. When he spoke his lips were always half smiling, as if he were always laughing at the world, at times, unexpectedly, maybe even at himself.

A nightmare. The game took on a different character here, they played as if their lives depended on it, dangerously, yes, grownup-like. I saw no signs of enjoyment (which is what I liked best about the game), just a mad rush that knocked everybody off their feet, especially me. If anybody laughed, it was never an expression of joy but of superiority, power. Practically speaking, I barely knew which net we were playing, sometimes the opposition mowed me down, sometimes "us." Like a flood or a windstorm. It also bothered me that I didn't know their names. I was always just getting up off the ground, it seemed. What's up, Count? Running out of breath? But they didn't really pay me much heed, and made only occasional fun of me. Still, with time they gradually noticed that I was there. They kept lobbing the ball, which in the case of a small goal post is either foolhardy or you really have to know what you're about. Once I "interrupted," instantly kicking the ball back, chest high, into the net; Bogyó, who was always way in the back, stopped in his tracks. His jaw dropped. From then on, they didn't knock me over, only when it was really called for.

There stood my mother, on the edge of the meadow, on this side of the ditch, but no longer on the sidewalk. The Ragweeds saw her, too. When Janó Ragweed knocked me over, he made sure to step on my hand. Are you crazy? What're you doing? I'd never seen anything like it in all my life. The referee didn't see, he said laughing. But there's no referee! That's just it, Your Highness! Whereas I'd been under the opposite impression, namely, that you should cheat only if there's a referee, if there isn't, you must play fair and square, you've got no one to cheat but yourself. With time, though, I gave as good as I got. I even changed the character of the game a bit: the exaggerated intensity remained—that's all they saw, the intensity, the hard work, life is difficult and there's no reprieve, but you gotta trek on—but a bit of calm, even enjoyment, crept in. Practically speaking, there were more goals, for instance, and more time (I never told anyone, but I was convinced I had created it) to enjoy a goal, or, to use a current hidebound expression, there was time for score frenzy.

In the evening I waited for mother to praise me, to say how well I accommodated myself after the initial difficulties, and how intrepidly I gave Janó as good as I got, who took a fall that made even his own team laugh, I didn't dare step on his hand, though I would have liked to. A hill of beans, Golden Boy. At the time I hadn't seen my mother in action yet, screaming from the stands like a madwoman; for a moment I didn't know whose voice I was hearing. A hill of beans. You can't play from fear, you can only play from the gaming spirit. Kicking Janó Ragweed, that's the courage of a coward, a responsible individual doesn't do a thing like that. A responsible individual—from then on, these were the key words of her teaching. A responsible individual, if he can, passes the ball with his instep. A responsible individual doesn't get sent off. The subtle vulgarity of this sentence so unsuited to my mother was like I'd discovered a secret. A responsible individual has no secrets. Come, come, son, only a responsible individual has secrets. As for hiding, we all have something to hide.

THE FIELD

My mother kept an eye on me for another year or so. Then one Sunday morning she led me up to the "bastion." She took my hand and we solemnly made our way up the iron stairs. She pulled me behind her gravely, my head level with her buttocks. I walk up to my study on these stairs every day, there's no buttocks in front of me, there's no one, my head lowered, eyes glued to my shoes, only minding the steps. I'm not saying that of a morning there's no expectation in me, excitement, anxiety, hope, and (a little) fear. Back then, championship games were played on Sunday, and so on Sunday morning my mother would make herself scarce, no later than nine, but if the team played out of town, at a distance, on the outskirts of town, in Rákoskeresztúr, for instance, then at eight. She prepared our food on Saturday, but she was always back in time for lunch (we had lunch when she was back). In the meantime we attended the student Mass. But that day was an exception. My mother wanted to hand me the world on a platter, that's how I like to think of it. The world in the image of a soccer field. We were standing on the roof, with not a howitzer in sight. If the royalist Labanc should attack now, woe our beloved country! I didn't like the looks of it, but I hadn't been informed at the time that our family had had more than its share of Labanc sentiments, and so it couldn't have occurred to me either that, in that case, the Labanc would not launch an attack or, if they did, it wouldn't bring woe to our beloved country. All of which left mother cold. And well . . . me, too. Who're you calling Labanc? (Cf., Who're you calling count? You're precious, etc.) The cemetery lay to the southwest. In years to come I would go there a lot as an altar boy; I liked this cemetery thing because in a cemetery it's easy to think of God, easier than in church, and even if it didn't bring me peace, still, it felt good (I liked it, okay?!) when I managed, managed to pray; and also, I liked doing altar boy duty at the cemetery because there was every hope of receiving a small tip, from the women, temperance!, less, from the men, self-pity!, more; I have described elsewhere that stochastic system of appraisal based on experience, sensitivity and childish knowledge of people which told me with relative certainty the size of the upcoming tip (from two forints, never one, to a hundred, more than a hundred never, the average I'd say, was about fifteen, fifteen forints). To the north the line of (artificially planted!) pines of Farkasvölgy clustered into a forest, and beyond, the quarry marred a yellow scar into the mountainside (for the record, Farkasvölgy—Wolf's Hollow—is a mountain!) which, hesitantly, with a number of start-ups, gradually rose to converge in the shape of a growing series of protuberances—not too high. In front of the first small protuberance, which was gradually being covered by the homes and gardens of the nouveau rich that grew "veritably like mushrooms," off to the side gigantic electric poles made their way toward the mountain's spine like giants, while in front of the protuberance there stood the field, the Farkasvölgy Sport Association's football field. My mother pointed at it with the pride of Alexander the Great, Conqueror of the Known World, and the undaunted optimism and good cheer of Mátyás Rákosi on those harvest posters of the fifties. Would you like to be a great soccer player? she asked in the meanwhile. I knew the right answer, but not what she was getting at. I didn't want to be anything, I had no plans for my future, it never even occurred to me that I should. I was happy to be alive and have kept this dubious, at times irritating, trait of mine intact to this day.

It is good to be alive, I finally said to mother, on the verge of tears.

The field was enveloped in the festive spring fog of early morning. When my mother announced, that's where you shall play, it sounded like that's your homeland. Or that it's the place where, as the poet says, you must live or die.* Or more like at the beginning of *Time Stands Still,* when in '56 the mother looks out the window, her sons by her side, the father already gone, the Russians already come, and she says, with quiet desperation and determination: Fine. In that case, it looks like we're staying (Gothár-Bereményi).† Having learned from her own life, my

* The poet being quoted is Mihály Vörösmarty (1800–1855), the great nineteenth-century Romantic poet. His patriotic *Appeal* (Szózat, 1836), one of whose stanzas ends with the line "here you must live or die," has become Hungary's second national anthem.

† The 1982 movie *Time Stands Still* (Megáll az idő) was coscripted by Péter Gothár and Géza Bereményi and was directed by Gothár.

mother was offering me escape routes, but I had no intention of fleeing, because I didn't know that I should. We stood on the bastion hand in hand. The fog (or mist?) lifted from the field as languidly as from the surface of a lake. But instead of the swans (the obligatory swans, son, what's obligatory?), it was the goal posts that appeared in the distance, and then, in this milky monochrome, unexpectedly, the green turf. The fog (or mist) floated above it only in patches now, the visible breath of a giant. The orange-colored early-morning sunlight trickled over the scene, as if nothing else existed in the world, just this football field at the foot of Farkasvölgy. As if everything were just as my mother had said. For a moment we were lost in thought, and in the meantime the sun retreated and a heavy, gray curtain descended in line with the current social-political situation. Let's go, mother said, insouciant, and like a guardian angel placed a hand on my shoulder. Hand on my shoulder, she's watching over me.

DISTAFF

We had always wanted, we, brothers, four boys basically insensitive to so-called maternal suffering, though possibly because of this, too, by way of compensation as it were, our mother to have an easier life. To the extent, anyway, that a male child will, now and then, evidence a certain inattentive interest in his parents' lives. We were part of her difficulties but clearly were in no position to take that into account. On the other hand, it's not easy (it is, in fact, downright difficult, complicated, complex, convoluted and confusing, circuitous, contorted, confounding, frustrating, perplexing, puzzling, bewildering, doubtful and uncertain and all too subtle by half) inventing an easier life. Like everyone else, we, I, also thought that perhaps *another* life might do the trick, because another life seems lighter to begin with. The question that keeps popping up is whether, theoretically at least, it is possible to know if we're already spinning the spinning wheel of that other life, if indeed spinning is what one does with a spinning wheel. Let's make it a distaff. I am spinning the distaff of my mother's life, it is something I had always wanted to do (but certainly since August 14, 1980).

9.

My Mother's Congenial Time Passes

Time passed. Before he died—because all men are mortal—Bozsik wanted to pay my mother a visit, the Swab and Nándi and me, we'd like to drop in for coffee, Lilike, if you don't mind.

You know I don't mind, Cucu dear.

But are you certain?

Only death is certain, son. I don't mind, you know I don't mind, you know everything, you know this, too. Your friend Ferenc also knows everything, except he doesn't know about everything that he knows.

What about Hidegkuti? Bozsik had never shed his childish joy in mischief.

Oh, Nándi, Nándi, my mother purred and stretched into the phone.

The rock garden was built along with the house years ago by Dr. Aurél Bognár, the father of the millionaire, maybe that's why he also built one next door, an exact replica of ours, of his father's, which really got my mother's dander up. She took it as a personal affront. Thanks to the ingenious landscaping, which involved a series of terraces, a variety of "terrains" came into being, the fern, the flower, the herbal, even a pine court, because my mother had a Douglas pine planted in the middle of the rock garden. It was the same size as me back then but has since outstripped me, though when my mother and I stand in front of it, to nip in the bud my usual onrush of sentiment, she always says, shooting me a look, sizing me up, then the tree, my, my, how the two of you have grown, but in a tone that suggested that either I or the Douglas should reflect whether we did the right thing. The tree had been hauled in by the goal post twins, there's even a pair of pictures, in one they stand on each side of my mother, in the other the pine. And I started whining that it's not right, two people looking alike like that, but the rumpus didn't faze the twins, who waited, unperturbed. As did my mother, who was also curious about further developments. I looked at Nero, I looked at Hector, my tears dried up; as if they'd been waiting expressly for this, Hector Gál came over, see?, and he showed me a birthmark on his earlobe, now you'll always be able to tell us apart.

The most important part of the rock garden, its heart, its agora, was the bay-like recess where my mother placed a small round table and wicker chairs, as if by way of an afterthought, so that you could talk "with anyone about anything at any time" there, a chatting bay. I went into hiding up on the bastion, watching the people below through the turret where the howitzers should have been, aiming at each in turn, my own Smith & Wesson, all in the spirit of good fun. Or better yet, a more serious hunting gun. With a telescopic sight. They were enjoying the sun-drenched afternoon. Bozsik didn't know that he would soon die, Puskás knew that he never would, while Hidegkuti didn't concern himself with said eventuality. They were busy courting my mother, who kept turning from one to the other, laughing.

Now, in early summer—and my mother, where?, where, where, at the far end of the boulevard, that's where!—no matter where I tried to hide, the bastion, the garden, the farthest reaches of our rooms, just so I wouldn't have to hear the neighbor's, Bogi's suffering, her little boy had died, just like that, without warning, and she contracted carcinoma of the skin and also lung cancer, the great pain made her scream; the howl, like some horrible sigh, could be heard issuing from next door, the intermittent moaning penetrated everything, the walls, the brickwork, the down comforters, as if Bogi were lying next to us and we were thus responsible for her unbearable pain, from the pet name it may appear that we were on intimate terms with her, but no, her husband Bognár, the grandson, is a quiet man, a quiet millionaire, which is not a contradiction, his silence is mostly discipline, there are no undisciplined millionaires unless through inheritance, you can inherit in lots of ways, even undisciplined; the woman next door roared with pain, as if we were sleeping in the same bed with her, as if she were relaying her terrible future to our ears, closer, closer, closer still, and we listened, more and more frightened but seeing less and less of her on her accustomed rounds, the grocer's, or the way she toadied up to the butcher, who wouldn't, son?, at the post office where she invariably argued with Terike, locking horns, nor did we see her busying herself in the rock garden, where she used to be on her knees a lot, as if praying, her hands, knees, soiled; on the other hand, and parallel to this, the millionaire could be seen around the neighborhood more and more, mostly walking with his cat, and if in the garden, then with the cat half a yard behind him, faithfully, like a dog, though a cat is stranger to faithfulness, while on the street he would pick her up and carry her in his arms like a child, seriously, responsibly, and a bit taken aback, too; he became softer, shorter, rounder, his strength had somehow left him, whereas all millionaires are strong, and—again somehow—you knew not to talk to him, good morning, neigh . . . , at which point we always clipped the word, we looked at each other, he didn't lower his eye, but we never thought of connecting Bogi's death cries with this, we didn't connect it with anything, not even with Bogi; the millionaire appealed to us more and more because of the cat, we said, what's her name?, I asked him some time before, he shrugged, I don't know, hasn't it got a name?, I already told you, I don't know, and then Bogi couldn't bear the mounting turbulence of her pain and walked down to the nearby quarry lake and waded out, farther and farther out, clutching a small piece of rock in her hand.

The heart of the Mighty Magyars (its essence, pith, substance and quintessence) was chatting with my mother, who was triumphantly serving up her legendary stuffed white bread variations. When the small talk came to a halt—because it would repeatedly come to a halt, the three handsome men would have much rather feasted their eyes on my mother in silence, even the big-talking Puskás, but my mother amused them with anecdotes, the border guards ask Matyi Cseh, what's in the suitcase, birdseed, they open it, it's full of coffee, but this here's no birdseed, Matyi Cseh looks at the coffee, then he looks at the border guards, then shrugs, like it or not, that's what they're gonna get, or she tested the professors of soccer with tricky offside situations, the female forward's breast, is it offside, and don't you dare answer that, boys. Hidegkuti told stories about Fiorentina, Bozsik listened with dignity, Puskás tried to make them believe that once when they were playing against Barcelona, it was so cold that when Gento kicked the ball into the net, but so delicately that it veritably stroked the upper goal post, anyway, it froze to the post, Lilike, somebody brought a hair dryer, we started defrosting it, the Basques weren't paying much heed, the ball came tumbling down, I flicked it in, the referee pointed to center field, and the Basques were madder than hell, that, too, what a name, Basques, it figures, them basking in their national pride that they're so inordinately proud of back home in Basqueland while it's made short shrift of, but all I said to them was, my little Basques, why don't you take a look at the score board and shove . . .

Oh, Ferenc, Ferenc!

My mother was there and back—son, son!—and brought coffee in the patterned (!) Herend cups she kept for special occasions. The three football legends held out their pinkies in an identical manner, like three tiny spears. At other times my mother would have been indignant, or would have contemptuously pretended not to notice, making her contempt all the more obvious thereby. Now her glance flitted playfully from pinky to pinky. You're so cute, boys! The sun gradually retreated behind the poplars in the direction of the mountains and the shadows of goal posts stretched full length over the face of the Earth. Time to roll up your sleeves, gentlemen, my mother announced with a new seriousness in her voice. Puskás, Bozsik, Hidegkuti nodded gravely, for they knew that hard times were now upon them. My mother drew out a pack of cards from a secret pocket and began to deal. Like always, they played one-handed *ulti*. In that case I'm going, and Puskás stopped short, he used the word only in my mother's presence, otherwise never in this fucking life, in that case, Lilike, I'm going to pee. Because one-handed *ulti* is played with three players, if there's a fourth, he's left out, which makes it his turn to pee. The one who goes pee is the odd man out, son, that's what real *ulti* players call him.

The congenial time, it passes.

10.

Love, Love, Love

FIVE SECONDS

I know down to the minute when I first saw you. I mean *really* saw you. Apparently, it takes man, or *Homo sapiens,* five seconds to decide whether he wants the other person, the decision is made within the space of five seconds, the cells decide for you, and you can protest, of course, launch into another story, play for time ad infinitum—and I mention this only in passing, sonny, as a defrocked mathematician you'll know what I mean when I say that man, yes, *Homo sapiens,* basically calls what's very big infinite, which is far from the same thing—in short, it is possible not to launch into your own story, but like it or not, after five seconds, the story's time begins to unfold. Once, your mother dragged you with her into the Works, but that's neither here nor there. She thought she could manage something through me, what it was is no longer of consequence, I couldn't manage it. Your mother thinks everyone is like her; she, if she thought something was right, went and did it. Perhaps she wasn't aware of the danger involved.

♣ THIS IS DEFINITELY NOT TRUE, SON

We were sitting in the dining room at the Works, your mother with son in tow, the tension mounting, financial and political inspection, both, because of the French connection, the comrades conspicuously at a separate table next to ours, picking at Bözsike's Serbian meat with rice. There were no restrictions on smoking back then, your mother puffing away like a chimney, but there was no ashtray at our table, so she asked the adjacent table for one. Oh, Lilike, I whisper, you can't just up and talk to strangers like that. Dear Ádi, dear Comrade Tóth, that's what she called me, dear Ádi, dear Comrade Tóth, anyone with a prick is no stranger. The ashtray tarried in midair, and it looked like it would tarry there for ever. Meaning, for a very, very long time.

♣ THE FIRST MEETING, DETOUR: DR. GRUBER

The first time she took me down to the field, mother seemed uptight, as if she were about to palm off some dubious merchandise, which made the presentation all the more important. The enervated late-morning sunshine streamed over the field on a slant which, as a consequence, was alternately enveloped in a pink, then a lilac veil of mist hiding the functions thereby, the function of the field, its fieldness, in short, its concreteness as well as its limitedness, and this aquarelline uncertainty made what could be seen seem unreal—exactly in line with what a sentimentally imagined "first visit" calls for. That's only true of a grassy field, son, a dirt field is beyond redemption, nothing helps, neither the light nor poetry, neither the fog nor the angels—you didn't use to have quite such a lot of fog and angels in your books before!—a dirt field is so vulgar, so commonplace, there's no raising it to new heights, though that's the good thing about it, this certainty. Certainty is a good thing, son.

The boys' team always played in the back on the practice pitch, the dirt pitch (actually, clay, the nearby brick factory was no accident, and it was no accident, though independent of the clay, that this is where the Jews were dragged in '44 for work, then even farther from here; it is bad playing on a clay pitch, it is either so hard that there's no getting rid of the lumps with either a clod breaker or a roller, or so slippery that . . . in short, very slippery); we kept eyeing the turf for years, but even this was too much for Uncle Gruber, the ever-present kit manager, *nix* Unkel Gruper, Dochtor Gruper to you, gentlemen, I am Dochtor Gruper, and if you so much as lay eyes on that turf again, I'm going to break your back, yes, sir, Uncle Doctor Gruber!, at which he waved an arm, you will never learn to be gentlemen, you are nothing but country bumpkins, gentlemen.

We were happy to learn that we were country bumpkins, and so—with time—we got up the courage to take a secret step or two on the grass, it's turf, son, not grass, on the turf, it felt like walking on silk, a bevy of princesses, we didn't dare put our heels down, we automatically walked on tiptoes, affectatious-like, as if we were in fact princesses. Or sneak thieves. At first, we didn't even risk this much, we just touched our toe to the pitch from outside, from this side of the touchline, as if testing the water in a swimming pool. We were not afraid of Doctor Gruber, still, we obeyed him. He spoke meekly, he didn't order us around, but he didn't ask for anything either—he just announced something, and this was a novelty for us: he announced something, and it came to be. He spoke the same way with the grownup team, he showed respect for each player in keeping with how well he played the game. In short, he was most respectful to Laci Gál, who'd signed back up again from Videoton II. Homeschooled, he kept saying, Lacika Gál is homeschooled, and now he's come back to the roost. On the other hand, Laci Gál didn't speak respectfully to Doctor Gruber, look at those bowlegs, Doc, the spitting image of Garrincha, what did you play?, right mermaid?, they grow legs like that, let's lay a bet, Doc, even a goose could pass between them, a well-fattened Martinmas goose, *dottore*. Who at such times just smiled to himself while tidying the supplies; he was always tidying up, although order *reigned* in his supply room, he tidied up what was already tidy; I'm only good at inflating the ball, Lacika, not kicking it, if you please. That sounds kinda Jewish to me, Doc, say, are you a Jew or a Swab, because there's a heap of a difference. And so there is, Lacika, and so there is, if you please. Let me put it to you this way. If we go by the book, all my ancestors were Swabs—and his relentlessly busy hands stopped for an instant—but you, Lacika, consider me a Jew. Alright, old man, no need to work yourself into a state, I was just asking, can't a man even ask a question?, okay, give me my ball. In the first division each player had his own ball.

As soon as we reached the pitch, various males pulled my mother aside or came over to her, to us, as if in a drawing room. Glancing at me, everyone said the same thing, oh, a new recruit, very good, very good. I stood around pale as a ghost, everybody's looking at me, I thought, with no more basis in fact than the last time when, as luck would have it, I ended up standing between my younger brother, the soccer player, and Puskás in front of the TTVE ground in the third district; Puskás loved my brother very much (he loved everyone, and everyone loved my brother; though possibly the word "love" is not quite the right word in this context?), the two men were conversing over my head, heckling and making fun of each other with great linguistic ingenuity, and when I looked up at the stands, I saw—a joke!—that every eye was riveted on me. Back then, as I stood by my mother's side, my hair was blond and longer than customary, Thomas Mann would probably say that my countenance was pale and gracefully reserved, surrounded by honey-colored locks, and would surely also call attention to the evenly sloped nose, the lovely mouth, the expression of alluring and divine earnestness. I didn't feel good, my mother felt good.

A man shorter than herself rolled over to her, not fat, yet rotund all the same, Lilikém, he said by way of a greeting while he, too, was looking at me, and with a grotesque gesture that was nothing if not ludicrous, he patted his knees, just so you know, we owe Mezőgép a point, you know what that means. Well, I'll be danfangled, my mother nodded, for she could never be persuaded to curse outright. Uncle Ádi also repeated the new recruit sentence, adding, we'll patronize the child. The patronize word filled me with fear and loathing. I'd already let go of my mother's hand by then.

A PÉTER BALASSA SENTENCE (REPETITION)

"'Give me your hand.' So then is this Zerlina or the Commendatore?"

BODY

I know down to the minute, sonny, we were playing an honorable draw against Mezőgép, that's when I first saw you. A scrawny, weedy child, you stuck out of your surroundings. You were the stronger, and I always felt your power over me, and you made sure that I should. From the very beginning. Your solitude, your aloofness, your loosely hanging hand with no one to take it, it was meant for me, I knew. But I never had the courage to take it, only now as I stand at death's door. From that moment on, I was always seeking to be near you. I really should stop this, there's no talking without indelicacy, but I can't stop, nor do I wish to. I knew when you were going off to school and when you were coming back, when you had Bible class, and when practice. You always pretended that you didn't notice anything. Even now. I went looking for you a thousand times, just seeing you filled my heart with joy. Joy and despair. But the most joy and the most despair, they belonged to the first moment, I felt feverish and my knees grew weak, they tremble, people say, but they don't tremble, the bone seems to soften up; I had to touch them repeatedly to make sure I still had them. I knew I would never be alone again, and I also knew . . . that no, because I knew the nos, too, that I couldn't talk to you about this, that I could never be close to you. That you are my hopeless passion, this is how I deluded myself. Miki Görög, that was different, poor little Miki Görög, I'm glad I don't see you now, it was not good seeing you, whereas I was happy to see you standing by the gate, pen in hand, barely younger than myself! Not that it ever made a difference. I never thought of you as a child. That's why I tried to be rude, not in order to be superior, but so that this clearly scandalous equality should be apparent. Bodies are equal. When I'm at home I wear a skirt, and don't interrupt, I know you hear me, a skirt, no panties, because sometimes I need to go to the toilet so quickly, the whole apartment smells of urine. It's the smell of death. And even so, it happens that halfway to the bathroom I can't hold it back, I wash the brown filth from my thighs, my legs, it's like washing myself clean of myself, as if the feces were me turned inside out, me as shit, and all this the harbinger of death. Man is his own harbinger, sonny boy.

I never spoke about you to anyone, not even Lajos. But Uncle Lajos always knows more than he lets on. It's in that KISZ-secretary blood of his. Never mind, it makes no difference now. You're just like him. I was always hoping to lay eyes on you. A ravishingly beautiful love without a body. Exalted beyond imagination. That's the lie I fed myself. But the body is the only thing that I can think of. I lack spiritual dimensions, sonny. To my mind it's the body that's personal, and not one's memories. To live in the body is to die, I read someplace. I live only in my body, that has been my life. And I shall die in my body. I think of the body, mine, yours, and Uncle Lajos's and Miki Görög's dead body, your mother's body, the way I think about nature. Trying to catch a glimpse of you was least risky during practice. I sat on a chair by the sidelines, I took a chair with me from the clubhouse, Gruber frowned, this here's no seaside resort, and I watched the practice. Your Uncle Vili had his suspicions. You stood solitary, away from your people, and very close to me—erect, hands tied in your nape, slowly rocking back and forth on the balls of your feet, and dreaming into the distance, as if the ocean were really spreading out before us, lazily, with awesome calm, as if the small waves were washing over your toes meanwhile. Your honey-colored locks caressed your temples and your nape, the sun illuminated the fluff of your upper spine, the finely drawn ribs, the symmetry of the breasts accentuated by the tight-fitting jerseys, your armpits were still bare as in a statue, the hollows of your knees were shining, and their blue maze of veins made the entire body seem to be fashioned from some translucent substance. It was not your beauty that enthralled me, you were not beautiful enough for that, you were not sufficiently Tadzio and I not sufficiently Aschenbach, and don't interrupt, when my eyes caressed your body, your noble body, if you like, on the sideline of the seemingly bleak yellow and gray practice pitch, not even the blissful rapture could lull me into thinking that my eyes had embraced beauty itself, the divine essence of Form, the one and pure Perfection of the soul, whose near-divine human image and double was just rising in front of me with artless ease. No. On the other hand, it was ecstasy, and I welcomed it joyfully, eagerly, without reservations.

ON REMEMBERING

The ravishing widow of a famous and distinguished sculptor whose huge, celebrated, ample, and exquisite derrière Budapest's appreciative public can admire every day on the statues of the master, and who remained a woman to the last moment of her life, come, come, son, I hope you're not implying she was made of woman, dear, dear, how disgusting!, and who to the last moment of her life was the subject of erotic (as well as sexual, autobiographical interpolation) dreams, told the story that an old friend of the family, a famous and distinguished painter in his own right, who took tea with the widow every Friday, a custom of his old age, once lowered his voice to a whisper and asked, hand on your heart, Erzsikém, was there ever anything *like that* between us? Silly old fool! Wanting revenge, I lied that there wasn't. I saw by the disappointment on his face that I'd hurt his feelings. Which made me happy. I think.

♣ THAT BLESSED SERENITY

I am trying to retrieve my memories of the Magician, but there is nothing to retrieve. Or almost nothing. When I look in the mirror—I don't look in the mirror—I see by the disappointment on my face that this hurts. I was a young boy and innocent. You can feel what's permissible and what is not. Which is not quite the same as telling your mother or not. For instance, Ica Ragweed on the coal heap, that's permissible, but talking about it is not. But ever since I can remember, there is someone watching inside me, I'm not saying an Other, an Other that's me, of course—from Sartre to Imre Kertész the literature is replete with such things. My watchful self—a joke: *nomen est omen!*—kept watching and watching, and saw and accepted of the world only and exclusively what it had seen. In short, it wanted to re-create the world. It wanted to start the history of the world from scratch. Recapture its innocence. And so, by innocence it did not mean the domain stretching from chastity and purity through virginity but, quite simply, freedom. I was not afraid of my childish solitude, but I suffered from it, not very, but persistently. As if there were a perpetual light drizzle, and the damp was penetrating everything, not only the joints—a child, I think, doesn't think about the joints; perhaps when he sprains (dislocates!) his ankle for the first time, then—but the lungs, too, it seeped into your belly, your brain. You can't avoid it. You can feel the damp, and yet it is not tangible. It's there, but where? You can't talk to grownups, they're no good for that, but the Magician was different because he could talk about anything, he had a subscription to *Life and Science,* that's why. That the shark, for instance, hasn't changed in over a hundred and eighty million years, a hundred and eighty million years!, in short, that in its own way, the shark is pretty close to perfection, which just goes to show you that you mustn't look down on anyone, sonny, anyone. His eyes filled with tears. We were sitting on the side bench, as if eating the bitter bread of the reserves, but only I was eating, the Magician had brought me something from the factory, for a while now I'd been coming to the field straight from school, bread with meat loaf or rolls with fried meat, stuff like that. Promise you will never look down on anyone. I didn't know what he meant, I promised. And . . . and now the shark is never going to change anymore? I'll look into it, sonny, I'll definitely look into it and will report back to you, if you please. Reporting is like patronizing. The Magician liked to look into things. The warmth of his palm dried up the dampness. I remember his palm, the slightly chubby fingers, the throbbing, red padding. The touch of a stranger's body, I hadn't thought of that before. I considered mine that, too, the body of a stranger, but now this changed. I swung my legs back and forth as if I were a *very* small child. Anyone watching could see for himself. In the distance, almost on the horizon, Uncle Doctor Gruber was fixing the net to the goal post. I felt the kind of serenity by the Magician's side, a serenity that was a mixture of excitement and fear, too, that I've never felt since. Ever. I thought of the green grass like some generous promise regarding my future. From time to time the sinew between the thumb and the index finger quivered, as if the serenity were the by-product of the conjunction of the green's infinity and this subtle quivering. I'd have liked the practice to be called off, but it never was. (For some time now I've been trying to avoid the following words: through a glass darkly.)

BODY, CONTINUED

When I think of you, sonny, I think of your body, and I am not ashamed to say so. The way you stood there by your mother's side, with the same aloofness masquerading as politeness on your face like the last time by the garden gate, which you honestly believe is politeness, this *distance* was the first thing I noticed about you, and our story was on its way, the five seconds had begun to roll. You didn't deem me worthy of your attention, or anyone else, for that matter, and that held out hope. I saw the hopelessness, too, but I didn't care, and I was right not to. All my life I have thought of you. If there is any compassion in you, and I'm not sure that there is, you'll feel shit hearing this. But that's not why I'm telling you, sonny, I'm indebted to you, I don't want anything, I'm going to die. I even remember the first time you smiled at me. Perhaps the most beautiful six months of my life were when I took over the running of the team from old man Paták, I went along to all the games, counting you boys, tired but proud, as if I were your mother, and bought tram tickets and lemons. I insisted on the lemons, like it or not, during a break, you had to lick it. It was on the Goli field once that this glum, sour-lemon expression turned into that sweet grin that bore no traces of distance. That's you, too, this sweetness. It was generally Miki Görög who said, speaking for the rest of you, something about licking, we might as well lick down to the bone or, shut up everybody, it's the forwards' turn to lick. You made a comment just once, lick it, who knows how much longer you get to lick it, but basically, I was the only one that laughed. I have always tried not to act ambiguously, whereas I am ambiguity itself. I see by looking at you, I've grown old. Andor Földes, when he turned sixty, said: from now on he wants to live without a score sheet. I have always lived without a score sheet, but desperate, terrified, was always trying to light on one. The body has gone out of fashion, I know that. You like talking about God. My own dictionary has a hole there. The age of body worship is gone, too, when they put the body in place of God, whose nonexistence was a proven fact. Not me. I put it in place of the hole. Excuse me, I didn't mean it, but possibly, it's truer like that. Talking dirty as the only path to truth? Ridiculous. Sin, forgiveness, mercy, as far as I'm concerned, these words do not exist. My body is nature itself. This is how it happened that for an entire year, spring, summer, fall, winter, I took a picture of my prick every day. I learned photography so I could develop my prick 365 times in a row. After a while you don't see what it is, only that it's some sort of living creature, it's got its good days, and it's got its bad. Of course, whose day are we looking at on the photograph? The prick and the viewer together, that's the hybrid being the pictures talk about. I didn't dare show you, only Miki Görög. Sometimes the creature we see is strong, at other times feeble, sometimes confident, bursting with life, at other times pathetic, insipid. After a while, I don't see that it's mine. What you see are visual warnings about life, about existence. Or, rather, reminders. Live and don't get lost in the details, and don't ignore the details! You see, sonny? It's the old song again,

I *end* here, for a while I can play for time but then, like it or not, the anthropomorphic thoughts burst to the fore, and before I know it, I come to something positive again with respect to life. As if being a prick were superior to not being a prick. As if what we see on the picture were good by its very nature, a good human being, wise, sober, cooperative. Home assignment: find the baseness, the treachery, the ignominy in the picture below. But I will stop now. I've said what I meant to say. Or else I'd have to go on talking. Vili didn't like me joining in during practice. When I did, I took my shower with the rest of you. I thought I would die every time, it was so good. The suffering too was good. I showered all the way back at the end so I could wind a towel around me right away. I was the most prudish, because I had the filthiest thoughts. Filthy, that's what they say, but it's not that. I pulled on my drawers and sat on the primitive john outside, my body trembling with . . . with relief. My funeral reminds me. I recently read somewhere that horseflies are attracted to black tombstones, and not just dragonflies. They're attracted by the horizontal, polarized light, that's what it said. That's why they land on black cars, and also red cars, too. And guess what? They're going to set up horsefly traps with this in mind. Have you any idea how much blood a horse or a cow loses every day because of horsefly bites? You'll never guess. As much as 200–300 cm^3. I meant to say something about your mother, too, but have forgotten what it was.

11.

Farewell to the Characters and Other Linguistic Units

SENTENCES

Last sentence: What lights? Evening lights, son, evening lights.

Tripe monologue. To come to naught over tripes, gentlemen, the rumen, the vitals, the innards, because that's coming to naught, even if it lacks drama! Vencel Ulrik was the ace in tripes, one could question anything in life, is it alright for us to play with two triangular formations when Jandász and Brigyás are both left-footed, is it true what the Count says, confusing the entire boys' team, that the sum of the three angles of a triangle adds up to a hundred and eighty degrees, meaning *all* triangles, every triangle in the world, the Cegléd triangle, the Peruvian triangle, *shecko yedno, ganz egal*, a hundred and eighty, according to the Count, in short, you could question anything, but that Vencel Ulrik has the most stamina when it comes to eating tripe, is the most ingenious in finding it, is the most passionate about tripe—

Let us posit that a football pitch is triangular, etc.

* * *

I never, ever (ever) stayed alone with him. Once.

Nádas's latest big novel* has more than its share of dead men. Livemen and deadmen. (At times I feel a definite sense of gratification knowing how hopeless it is to translocate something of mine into another language. That this something is incapable of breaking free of the confines of Hungarian. It is not so much a feeling of patriotism as of simple vanity, *hángérien* vanity.)

Isn't it confusing that the hospital nurse and the aunt with the Mongolian features are both called Emma? But if that's what they're called?

You are emotionally unpretentious. (You, dear, are emotionally unpretentious.) Who, me? (Me?)

I got used to the male body early on, regarding the nakedness, finding it beautiful.

Title: *Intrigue, Love, Offside Rule*

During the 1937 fall season, the newcomer Gray Taxi held its trainings on the BVSC field on Szőnyi út, but the field not being suitable for a first division game, it played the championships in various places, just like Budai 11, *pron.*: budayeleven. Instead of the original gray and brown, they changed their colors to

* A reference to Péter Nádas's three-volume novel *Parallel Stories* (Párhuzamos történetek, 2005).

blue and yellow. Though they beat Törekvés 6 to 1 during their first match, during their third, Hungária bulldozed them 7 to 0. Matyi Cseh kicked three goals. And I could go on and on: Aunt Mari, i.e., Géza Takács, chose the Gray Taxi, etc.

Am I never going to die? As if she were asking, will you never leave me in peace? Never. Or the other way around: promise you won't write about me anymore. I can't promise a thing like that. But I can't go on living forever. I know, but I'm not about to take that into consideration.

Sunshine, sunshine, lovely sunshine,
Don't shine on me on the touch: line

Glycerin suppository, sonny (son), my digestion is on hold.

I had to meet Pelé, what can I say, I promised! He was crushed because everybody was making fun of him over the length of his *real* name. But I just said to him, look, love, Pelé *is* your real name, because you are what you are on the pitch, and on the pitch, you're Pelé. I see, said Edson Arantes do Nascimento.

Adalbert Tóth is fifteen years my mother's junior. Don't blush, mommy dear. And twenty years older than you, son. Don't, etc.

There's no time for that now. Hurry, hide behind the door. Who is the hero?

A mother won't do against solitude, sonny, a mother will never do. A pity. A child will not do, etc.

* * *

Disgust, fear, and curiosity; yearning. I yearned for him to be near me. That he should just talk. Or the other way around: I'd have expected endearment and cuddling from life. From you.

Do tell me, you saintly woman, why not with potato salad? And: how thick was the board? And: how come it killed him (my father) when he's alive? And: you talk about my writings as if . . . never mind, think what you like.

You're a piece of shit.

My mother was in love with my father, my father was in love with heaven. Or: if she had her way, my mother would have *preferred* to be happy with my father except, etc.

Due to my person, the game was suspended. And: I'm saying this especially with the forwards in mind: don't go falling off the wrong side of the other horse.

Streifenmaus in German, it's got a black stripe running down its back and two light ones on either side, it's officially known as the Southern birch mouse, *Sicista subtilis trizona* (courtesy of Antal Festetics), but jumping pouch mouse is a better name for it. Can I lean my head on your shoulder, sonny?

From now on, for the rest of my life, whenever I hear the word, I will hear my first wife's nauseating inflections: *footbaaaaaallll.*

* * *

"Listen to me, son, I say to him."

"She will never understand how I hate this son. Why can't she accept, it's ridiculous, calling a man pushing sixty son? She thinks I like it so much, I don't give a hoot about how ridiculous it sounds. But I do, because it doesn't ring true. A role. My mother is playing my mother."

"All his life he's been this high and mighty. Or not high and mighty, just proud. Or something between the two. Full of himself. Vain. Or more like impertinent. Pugnacious. *Na ya.* Why must he always put his two cents' worth in? Why can't he see how beautiful and accept with feeling, yes, feeling, when an old woman says to an old man barely younger than herself, my darling little son. And now he's sniveling. . . . The man's got no dignity!"

His face like an empty football field after practice, after a tough, hard-hitting, difficult (lost) game.

And to himself he said, ". . .

And to myself I answered, ". . .

The former cruelty reared its ugly head.

About the neighbors: they attended parochial school—they lived like brother and sister. They were somewhat taken aback that they had three children.

Does your mother go with you everywhere? Aren't you ever on your own? I'd like to talk to you in private. And: Everyone mentioned dies.

* * *

As for me, I didn't know, and to this day I don't know, that for his part, he was in love with me.

Let me patronize you. This frightened me, yet I pretended I understood: And who is the base of operations? At which he: Or what, don't you think?! At home, I looked in the mirror: the secret object of desire—I couldn't have been serious. And yet I was. And it was as I thought.

I've told you, mother, I don't need your sincerity. And: Kindly leave my room. But son, this is my room. Yes, I see, indeed, in point of fact, fine, surely, indubitably, in which case I should kindly leave the room, and make it snappy!

The kettle turns, not the stew. The liver only at the end, otherwise it crumbles. Lack of illusion, sadness, the beauty of despair, irony.

Heedless of the consequences, I am not about to cling tenaciously to my tenacity.

A mother-shaped void leaned over my bed, then kissed me on the forehead (just like my grandmother). There is a Portuguese sweet, son, it's called angel's chins, Papos de Anjo de Mirandela.

Netzer variation: A novel's hero(ine) by the name of mother now lost forever in the depths of space.

* * *

Scene: Julia Roberts gently strokes the sleeping man lying by her side, then turns away, lowers her head on her pillow, and with the last hope of the despairing stares into space (almost into the camera). (Variations: Roberts: me, the man: Ádi; Roberts: my mother, the man: me, my father, Ádi, Uncle Lajos; Roberts: Ádi, the man: Uncle Lajos; Roberts: Uncle Lajos, the man: the other, the younger man, Grumpy Junior.

UNCLE LAJOS PAYS A VISIT

The cramps in my calf and thigh cramped up more and more, there seemed no end to the cramping up which, however, could not be considered infinite either, not even very very long, the improbabilities lent probability to the feeling that the increasing tension would find release in an explosion, that my body would explode, my calf, my thigh, tattered bits of muscle dangling from the ceiling of the hospital ward, because if something is beyond endurance, if it can't be endured, then it is not possible to have someone who cannot endure it, because then it's so much for that someone, though it is unreasonable to assume that I will die of muscle cramps, that the unadorned tombstone will say: cause of death: muscle cramps; Beethoven has such moments, son, the unbearable character of the intensified motifs, but then he finishes it anyway. My head was spinning from the excruciating pain and uncertainty, how will this end? I was panting, eyes half closed, and the two figures in the door.

I'll take care of it, Uncle Lajos, I wouldn't want Uncle Lajos to soil Uncle Lajos's hands.

Alright, Grumpy, Junior. You're like your father, Grumpy, Grumps, always grumbling, that's why everybody called him

Grumpy, get it?, an unending drone issuing from his direction, a fretting and fuming, like why is it raining, and why is the wind blowing, and why is he playing outfield, and why on the right, and why is the practice on the practice pitch, and why isn't the practice on the practice pitch, and why are we playing in the red jerseys, and if we must, why in the green socks.

Forget the old man, Uncle Lajos, he's dead, the droning's gone. When a man's dead, he's dead.

You're a colossal idiot, son. But a nice guy. And what muscles! There were no muscles like that in the old days. You're a veritable Schwarzenegger.

Thank you very much, Uncle Lajos. Uncle Lajos knows how to talk to people. Other people keep shouting with me or they're so scared, they clam up. Uncle Lajos's words, they're sweet as molasses.

The two men headed for the bed. I'd have loved to wake up. Grumpy, the door. Take it easy, Uncle Lajos, take it easy, like Uncle Lajos's dignity demands, like that. A good thing I realized (stipulated?) at the very beginning that the narrator mustn't be shot. Guess who's come to visit, you little rat, the younger of the two bristled; he must've known that I wanted to cry for help—I'd never cried for help in my life, this was my first chance—and he immediately clapped a hand over my mouth, his hand covering my face, and I was surprised once again how nice he smelled, even though he practically pushed my nose right inside my mouth. Tell him, Uncle Lajos, now you can go tell him. The old man softly sat down on the side of my bed, up against my thigh. Oh, I groaned, my lips barely moving under the hand, as if I were planting a kiss on the padding from underneath, shut your trap, Grumpy growled, and gave his hand a twist as if closing a tap, shut up and listen.

Make me room. I saw only his back. With great effort I moved farther in, with Grumpy Junior pushing me like a snow shovel. Uncle Lajos lay down in the tub-like concavity where my body had been. Contorting his body, arching over him, the other literally shut my trap. Uncle Lajos stared at the ceiling. Dead, he said after a long pause. He turned on his side, his shoes hanging over the side of the bed, but by then he'd got mud on the sheet. He grabbed my pajamas. I loved him and he let me, he said, then released me. What a little prick you are, he whispered at the ceiling. At the same time, with lightning speed, like in the slapsties game, Grumpy Junior swiped me across the face, the slap came to rest on my ear, which, as they say, rang, Ádi would probably know why, the echo of the Eustachian tube?, and next thing, the hand was back over my mouth again. Is that what you had in mind, Uncle Lajos? The silence was complete except for Grumpy Junior's wheezing, plus the *Il silenzio* from my Eustachian tube. I squirmed. The hand redoubled its pressure. Don't squirm. Your wound, Uncle Lajos said abruptly. I started planting little biting kisses on the palm again, shut your trap, well, well, lookee, here, he's got something to say again, pow!, another hard slap, but so quick, I couldn't make a sound, he thinks he can gab whenever the fancy takes him. The old man was watching me from behind the column of the arm holding me down.

The Magician is dead and buried, and where the fuck was I? He knows that I was supposed to deliver the eulogy, but I didn't take our poor friend's last wish for shit. He knows, because he was the last person that talked to him, who else, Count, who else? Don't go thinking you were the last person on his mind. Don't. You're not that important. So okay, so he talked about you. A bunch of nonsense. That you're like the lapis lazuli for the Chinese. Or the Emperor who stands on a rock at night frocked in cobalt blue to learn the will of the Sky and to structure the world accordingly. In short, the Emperor's job is to guarantee the conjoining of the earthly and the celestial harmonies. If he fails, the Emperor is liable to be killed. Just so you know. This is the ridiculous nonsense we talked about last.

There we were, in bed.

From lack of exercise the Magician's blood turned into jelly, but in the twenty-fourth hour they bombard the clot with blood thinners, but he wasn't allowed to sit, and he wasn't advised to stand, and he was warned against lying down, so he didn't sit, he didn't stand, he didn't lie down but went out to the pitch, the field at Farkasvölgy, where he suffered his humiliation, from where he got the boot, and that I know this perfectly well, but I also lay as low as a snake in the grass whereas, if he's got his calculation right, I wasn't even an Academic yet—shut up and listen!—he liked walking in the vicinity of the field, these were their nicest walks, he took his arm, they looked like any other couple, an elderly couple, a quiet afternoon stroll, what could be more natural?, but most of all he liked to walk where he was officially banned, down to the field, he stayed behind by the touchline while Ádi covered the pitch, played defense, offense, signaled the strikes into the goal, from time to time glanced outside, waiting for tactical orders, etcetera; we were playing, Count, playing, if you know what I mean, but only when that asshole of a new groundskeeper wasn't around, a new generation, in on time, out on time, kept to the books, for him the field was a workplace; but that particular day Ádi went for a walk alone, he climbed into the deserted sports ground, and in the process must have cut his head, his temple, on a nail sticking out of a plank—just like my father!, no claptrap, no tickling the palms!—and walked along the halfway line to center field, the boys are now running out to the green turf, he used to say to himself with a smile, in the center circle he turned, he didn't wave, just nodded in the direction of the stands, then made for the eighteen-yard line where the inside right forward would be, nobody plays inside right forward anymore, even the word is gone, surely I'd given this some thought, whether something that has no name can exist, and vice versa, that something can come into being because of a word, as long as the Magician was alive there was such a thing as a right inside forward, because on these walks he'd walk up to the right inside forward's position and move forward, but this time, just before the eighteen-yard line he lay down on the ground, the grass, because he felt tired, the blood was trickling from his temple, but he didn't notice, that's where that stupid fool found him, he even took offense, he saw from a distance that there's a stranger on the field, he saw Ádi's red and black checked overcoat, he, Uncle Lajos, had bought it for him, cashmere, but that's not the point, he liked soft, fine materials, pullovers, scarves, people don't appreciate stuff like that here, if a man pays attention to his attire in this country, if he's got a sense for color, if a lack of taste pains him, they call him a fag, as if our Chieftain Árpád* hadn't dolled himself up in leopard-skin capes

* Árpád was the leader of the Magyar tribal association that led the Magyars into present-day Hungary at the turn of the tenth century, and is thus considered one of the greatest figures of Hungarian history. After his death, his descendants ruled Hungary for four centuries as the House of Árpád.

or what the fuck, the man was sprawled out on the ground, it was clear from the loose limbed, careless posture that he's sleeping, napping, lying around cheerfully, only when the groundsman reached him, shouting, hurling aspersions at the illegal trespasser, the desecrator of the pitch, there was some truth to the latter, and noticed the dark bloodstain spreading out like a shadow, that's when he understood that something was amiss, but, as he later said, that's not what worried him, but the grass, whether the blood would hurt the grass, he had no information on that, on how the grass would react to being soaked in all that blood, because Ádi had lost a great deal of blood, and then, suddenly ducking under the arm stretching over him, Uncle Lajos bounded out of bed, and the other one, as if they'd rehearsed it beforehand, rolled me over and swept me to the floor, I landed with a yelp, use your instep, Grumpy, and aim for the head, we wouldn't want him going lame, but they didn't kick my head but my sides, I was rolling back and forth, then back again, blood's good for the grass, there's gonna be a marvelous little green island there by the right flank, an Adalbert stain, that's how it will be known, the toughest forwards will want to get faulted there because the angle is ideal for a free kick, and the goal kicked from there will be known as an Ádi, and his name shall prevail for ever, for ever, as long as there are goals he too shall prevail, that'll do, Uncle Lajos, that'll do, and don't you use your toes neither, Uncle Lajos, and don't cry, that little prick mustn't see you cry.

One way, then the other.

HUNGARY'S OROGRAPHY AND HYDROGRAPHY

According to the general male mentality there are few things in this world more beautiful (breathtaking)—with the possible exception of the sacred ground of Machu Picchu!—than the triangle of the panties that shows (or, as they generally say, of course, that reveals itself) through the white uniform of a nurse. Let us posit that a soccer pitch is triangular, etc. From now on, nurse Emma said, coming over to my bed, you will administer your evening shot yourself. What are you doing on the floor, and just look at you, have you been at fisticuffs with yourself? I tried to concentrate on the triangle, but it left me cold, my body had left my body. And along with it, all sense of shame. As I slipped an arm around the nurse's neck and she slipped an arm under me to lift me back up on the bed—mind you, being a nurse involves physical exertion, too!—my weenie came dangling out the fly of my pajamas, what in years past I'd have called my fucker, or would have gone looking for a synonym less shocking to the Hungarian public, though I hasten to add that that, too, would have meant my fucker; now only an organ slipped out, more like a small little organ, like the intestines or the liver, but I barely noticed. (Barely: I noticed that I didn't notice.) Me? Into my belly? My own belly? Why? Have you got another? And don't make a fuss, Professor, any man of learning can do it. Not many living creatures walk this earth who'd have been affected by this sentence, but I was promptly seized by the European sense of responsibility. There was no kindness in nurse Emma, but no unkindness, either, her words and gestures were guided by practical considerations, she did what had to be done, and that this *had* was a reality had a calming effect on me. I would be giving myself Heparin, I learned, low-negative-charge Heparin, once is enough, against thrombosis. Meaning, pathological coagulation of the blood. But in that case I could bleed to death! Only if you're out of luck, Professor. You'll have blue and green spots on your belly. According to experts, if you use the needle properly, these blues and green spots will turn into a map showing Hungary's orography and hydrography. According to the same experts, the best medicine against it is a woman's saliva. Kissing is the easiest way of acquiring it. And now I will leave you to fend for yourself, Professor.

Later I got to see Machu Picchu. I was leaping about on the sacred stones with my newly repaired hip like a—admittedly rather staid—rock goat. I had trouble breathing up there. I'm putting all my wheezes into one basket.

DREAMING OF MY MOTHER

I haven't dreamt about her in a long time—dreams don't lie, mother; but when I dreamt about her, I dreamt that she attempted to tough-talk me into the team among the most embarrassing of circumstances, but with the kind of high embarrassment factor that only fathers can attain when they try to ingratiate themselves into the good graces of our schoolteacher (that thirty-year-old hag), or when they tell our schoolmates jokes, who are making faces in the meantime. When, red as a beet, I lowered my head, my mother cut her lecture short, because she was in the habit of giving little lectures, her repertory ranging from shameless pleading through embarrassing self-abasement, but also open threats; look, Uncle Vili, take the child, you won't regret it, if you know what's good for you, you'll take him because that's where he belongs; my mother even liked to stipulate what position I should play, in the school team dream she walked over to Little Huszár (about whom I made up the chestnut story in *Celestial Harmonies*, and him, too, which goes without saying), you must be Little Huszár, and don't bother with an answer, you hand out the brains around here, that's clear, which is *frankó*, it's when I hear *frankó* that I bow my head in shame, don't bow your head in shame, son, because there is a time for humility and there is a time for esteem of self, are you familiar with the expression, boys? esteem of self, a beautiful Hungarian expression, and you're Hungarian, which means you'll end up knowing more about the world, won't you?, *frankó*, that's a complex word, too; if I was lucky, at this point I woke up, okay, how do we send a prepaid letter?, *frankó*, gentlemen, *tuttó*, and why *frankó*, does anyone know?, well?, tut-tut, a good soccer team knows everything, nobody?, never mind, that's why I'm here, well then, the association of the word with "free" comes from old French because as conquerors the Franks were exempt from paying taxes in kind, that's the story with *frankó*, boys, so then Huszi dear, so we got that out of the way, so then, you and my son, the two of you are up front, the rest will take care of itself, *c'est franc, n'est-ce pas?*

The other recurrent dream is a lot more embarrassing, and while with the former after a while I vaguely knew that it's a dream, here, however, there was no questioning its reality, its authenticity, even though I was all too familiar with the plot; I'm sitting in the locker room of the grownup team, having already made the blunder of going for my apparatus to the storeroom, because with us "juniors" that's how it went, while here Uncle Gruber brought it in individually for the boys, I see you got used to playing the servant, Count, Laci Gál said as if by way of an aside, I'm in my uniform already, my shoes tied, I'm sitting on the bench stiffly, I don't know the custom in the locker room, I'm keeping an eye on the others, Kaszás is sitting next to me, the dumb Kaszás, who knows a lot, don't tie it yet, dickie boy, it'll make your feet swell, he whispers so the others shouldn't hear, now comes my mother's grand entrance, I'm all nerves at the prospect, the coach is explaining something at the magnetic board, the union from the Works donated three magnetic boards, which is how they patronized us, get ready, boys, a magnetic assault!, we sniggered, but to our surprise, the coaches took this "state of the art technical assistance" seriously, as if these boards furnished the incontestable proof of their solid football expertise, the coach is holding a sheet in his hand, reading the lineup, I know I'm no greenhorn, never mind, Pepe, you gotta get used to the locker room atmosphere, just sit on the bench and keep your eye on me and I keep an eye on you, agreed?, agreed, that's when my mother flings open the locker room door like an FBI agent who is in cahoots with the KGB and a typhoon; she's in her tight red skirt, red shoes, Kaszás can't take his eyes off of the shoes, a red bag, red hair, coral red, poppy red, how do you do, boys, how do you do, Coach, hello, son, sometimes there was a round of feverish applause, without a word, my mother spins around, her skirt flying in the wind like Marilyn Monroe's, though just a moment ago it clung tightly to her body!, smiling, the coach makes a correction in the lineup, *gnädige Frau*, and with a curtsy bows his head to my mother, I'm counting on you, son, in line with the cliché she pats my face and flits away, the smiles are immediately wiped off the faces, I'm counting on you, son, Laci Gál hisses scornfully, with meticulous display, the coach takes out the indelible pencil again and makes yet another correction on the slip, but at other times the intruder is greeted with a show of resentment, who the fuck is that cooch, Count?, at which I have no choice but to say, my mother, at which the forwards, in a chorus, use full sentences!, but I never know whether "this fuck is my mother" or "this cooch is my mother" is the correct answer, be quiet, son, she says to me, the Comrades are sadly mistaken if they think I can't speak in another fashion, and then Zoli Sulz stands up, he used to be a bodybuilder, his physique well proportioned and handsome, his pubic hair reddish, as if he had it dyed, and I think he also had the largest prick, and that's just my shower-room prick, boys!, he stands up naked in front of my mother, who looks him up and down with genuine interest, I'm about to move, don't, the oafish Kaszás whispers, don't get involved, my mother has clearly forgotten about me, what chest muscles you have, Zolika, those chest muscles belie your age, Zolika, but I don't want to go on from here, my eyes are riveted to Sulz's reddish flaxen pubescence—it goes well with my mother's reds—and overcome with shame I whisper, the world lacks sense, it lacks sense. This is what wakes me, if it wakes me, this lack.

PARAGRAPHS

When he was resettled, Uncle Sárli played cards not only with the police and other organs of the democratic powers of oppression, but also with the peasants. And he didn't just beat (fleece) the former, but the latter as well. And he didn't just cheat there, but here, too. I neglected to mention this before.

* * *

When a person looks inside of themselves, which is one of your favorite occupations, sonny, they will have to accept, without anger or animosity, that their hip joint, and more than likely the hip joint as such, is a so-called enarthrosis. The shape of the head of the bone is the equivalent of two-thirds of a sphere, while the acetabulum, which includes the head, is like a slice of a sphere whose curve is part of a central angle of a hundred and seventy, a hundred and seventy-five degrees. What one knows doesn't frighten one, unless one should be frightened. A person past fifty, like you, can't help wondering about his acetabulum, studying his spherical slice with doubt and pride, in fact, with pride and prejudice, brooding over this a hundred and seventy or so, is it too much, or too little, or just right, and he musters all his resources in order to recall the all-important theorem of central angles, but to no avail.

Do you know what dying of old age is?, it's when your thymus gland shrinks to nothing. It's no joke, sonny, the calf's throat made me think of it. It's a very clever organ, maybe that's one reason I won't eat it, because I respect it so much, tripe yes, calf's throat no, for your information, it's a type of sweetbread. For instance, the T-lymphocytes, that discover infections or foreign material in the body, the policemen of the body, when they're born in the bone marrow, they go to "school" to the thymus gland, where they learn what is native and what is foreign, and no multiculturalism, then they enter the bloodstream to go on patrol. By the way, in AIDS it's these T-lymphocytes that are destroyed, and that's how you become fully susceptible to infection. In short, careful with those T-lymphocytes, my dear.

* * *

Especially when it came to football, my mother would often speak to me like Bridget Jones's mother, our father, as you well know, was a grain merchant, she didn't say Shilton, but the English goalie, Shilton. Sometimes it's advisable to follow this strategy in translation, which is how Pázmány becomes Cardinal Pázmány, it's not much help, the familiarity and complicity is wiped out, but sometimes it helps speed things along, and—as a Peruvian reader at the base of Machu Picchu—I'm not going to think that Shilton is an important baroque cardinal in the Ukraine. Have you ever thought, son, what the English goalie Shilton must have felt like at the 1986 World Cup quarterfinals when El Pibe de Oro, the Golden Boy, i.e., Maradona, i.e., the Hand of God, before he, Shilton, could have reached it, punched the ball into the net? She was sitting on the side of my bed, holding my hand the way I used to hold hers. Think about that and remember Shilton, the world remembers only Maradona. Me, too, I might add, it's a professional question, but you . . . never mind, forget it, I just wanted to say that you, you be good. Be that as it may, the English bookmakers didn't acknowledge the strike and paid accordingly. That's fair play, son, money's no object.

The Magician is dead, my mother announced by way of greeting and plopped down on the side of my bed, there's not even a decent chair to sit on. Be careful of my leg, I just had my operation. (We had a sexy German aunt, or Austrian?, very distant, I think she may have been in love with my father way back, before the angels, I hear the sentence as she said it, *bin frisch operiert*, which was the explanation for why she wouldn't carry her suitcases, why my younger brother and I had to carry them.) I'll be careful, she said carelessly, and stop telling me to be careful.

* * *

Matyi Cseh—the thirties, László Cseh II, MTK—never deprived himself of anything, he organized the first purely Hungarian striptease, Hungarian tits for Hungarian eyes, some Bella or other, Bellácska, and as such nearly an anti-German cultural program. When he was warned against what they called his irresponsible lifestyle, grinning, he said, put on my tombstone, lived thirty years, but what thirty years! Have the same put on mine, son. But you're way past thirty. All the more reason.

The nurse says Sasha Kertész was here, and what a dashing, well-groomed man he is. And rich, may I add. He also played it two ways, like Ádi. You act like you don't remember him, but when you were a child, or, as you like to say, just don't say it anymore, during your football years, it's deucedly difficult for you to lie, son, when I know the truth, and I promise not to say *that* anymore, everyone else is saying it, and she gives me a proud grin, and I nod in response, in short, you saw a lot of each other at one time. Have you nothing to say? If not, not, so be it.

I asked my younger brother (who told me the Matyi Cseh story) whether he missed our mother, at which his eyes filled with tears and he sent me—in high style, I should think, in Hungarian at any rate—back into my mother's. . . . Why? Because of the blasé way you asked (this, too, is my mother's, our mother's word!), as if inquiring about my favorite make in watches. Fine. So what's your favorite make in watches?

Just so you understand, an offside is a bit like the celebrated axiom of parallel lines. I'm not going into detail, you of all people should know how many have tried their hand at it and failed. The great Gauss, he failed even without realizing he'd tried. I wrote it down for you in one simple sentence, son, remember it, no need to flog a dead horse. (An offside is what the referee calls an offside.)

ONE MORE DREAM

I dreamt that the Lord lay down next to me on the hospital bed, he smelled like Uncle Lajos, a pleasant foreign smell. Because of my leg I didn't dare turn properly toward Him, I hugged Him veritably leaning over myself. I hugged him and I sobbed convulsively. Lord, let me start over again, let me start over again. I didn't see His face, I didn't hear His answer, the hug felt good, let me start all over again, Lord.

The trees, covered with hoarfrost, glistened through the window. They were as spectacular, as unrealistically breathtaking as in a Hollywood flick. I like the dramaturgical twist when the satisfying end is in sight, the hero—interior monologue—makes plans for the future involving either revenge or a happy life, and then we, the audience, see a telescopic sight gradually fading into view and casting a shadow over the person whom, just a moment ago, we confidently called the hero.

ON TARGET

I know you'd rather not talk about it, son, but I rather would, because, for one thing, I don't trust your taste, and I don't trust your and your brothers' respect for tradition, and I'm not talking about the death notice, that's always the size of a picture postcard, but about the memorial leaf, I insist on a memorial leaf when I die, the chances of me living forever are slight, and don't make faces, or is that a laugh?, it's the size of a devotional picture, that's the shape, and I want to tell you about the shape, because you and your brothers don't know what it's like anymore, and I wouldn't want you neglecting it or making it too effusive or too eccentric, clever, I wouldn't put it past you, putting Matyi Cseh's sentence on it, it's not a bad idea, I'd like that, but it can't be done, it must be personal and yet keep to form, in short, in the upper right-hand corner a cross, as plain as possible, two straight lines, two sections perpendicularly crossing each other, nothing kitschy, two, and below it, in italics, the beginning of the sentence: *Let us remember her in our prayers*, yes, kindly remember to pray for me, and I'm not interested in your excuses, if you don't know how, learn it again, learn to pray over me again, and don't say a word, not a word! And under the picture, the continuation, to wit, that it's me, that we should remember me in our prayers, I hope there's no need for me to dictate my name, but kindly pay attention to Lili, one *l* and not a *y*, and have it set in Bodoni typeface, bold, for your information, that's a modern serif typeface, there's no typesetting anymore, I should think, just computers, the who typeset me, or who typeset my mother, that's gone, the masterpiece of an acned printer's apprentice; the photo, the devotional picture, should be situated in the complement of the virtual rectangle formed by the text at the top of the cross, initially I had a picture with my turban in mind, this one, the one I'm wearing now that Cucu custom designed for me, but yellow won't show up on a black and white photo, and you're all so conservative, I have four stick in the mud sons, I wouldn't want to *exasperate* you, in short, forget the turban, make it this tailored suit jacket with the fur collar. And under my name, to the right, centered, born October 5, 1916, died, here write what you need to, for the time being I wrote August 14, 1980, and most important, don't neglect the period at the end of the sentence, because, for your information, this happens to be a sentence and not an address, or what have you. It's often left off. Very annoying. And stretching along the bottom, closing off the space, from the Book of Psalms: Be gracious unto me, O Lord, for I languish away! Exclamation mark, languish away, exclamation mark. Stick to that form, son.

12.

Miki Görög. Epilogue, Or: Another Mother

PASCAL

The other day, when I brought potatoes with bay leaves from the nearby take-out place (the cook had muscles on her backside like football players), I made the classical mistake of warmly recommending it to my mother, saying it's as good as if she'd made it herself. I see, she nodded, and refused to say another word for the rest of the meal. She prodded the bay leaves to the edge of her plate in disgust, as if they were dead vermin of indeterminate derivation, from somewhere within the bedbug-toad-duckweed triangle, let's say. If she were my child, I thought, this would be the time to open the lid of the slap box. That was the first time I used this expression. Surely, this bit of joviality was an unconscious attempt to mitigate the very real shock that I could imagine hitting my mother at all. It suddenly seemed inconceivable that anyone would hit their mother. Of course, there are all sorts of mothers. And all sorts of mothers have all sorts of sons. Miki Görög, for instance, once slapped his mother, I took a shy at ma's kisser. He played inside left, he was number 10, like Edson Arantes de Nascimento. When he appeared on the field, a game, practice, it made no difference, the sun came out of hiding. He died six months ago, he drank himself to death, but before drink could finish with him, he got run over by the commuter service train. Commuter service—who did this serve?

He wasn't even drunk this time, and as usual wanted to avoid the underpass (except for me, no one would think of using it, I bet, though the pungent odor of urine that permeates the tunnel would seem to indicate otherwise), but like everyone else, he headed for the train stop over the tracks and his green trench coat got caught on the wire fence put up to prevent trespassing and cut through to allow trespassing, I seem to remember him wearing this green all the time, only socialism could produce such a green (the color of Bohumil Hrabal's tie, son, that's what I call a point of reference!), you could hear the train approaching, the tracks rumbling like an uncurbed heart, Miki tugged at his coat, which got stuck all the more, seaweed, they say, is like that, the more desperately you struggle to free yourself, the more it binds you, for a long time I was under the impression that seaweed was an animal, a sargasso, a kelp, a horrible sea monster that you mustn't put in a state lest it pull you down into the dark depths of the sea, the train appeared round the bend, still far enough for a warning signal to suffice without it having to use its brakes, when Miki Görög skillfully slipped out of his coat—something similar happened to me once, I was terrified, suddenly everything seemed terrifying wherever I looked, the approaching train like a beast of prey, and for an instant the tracks and the track screws like symbols of suicide, I made it over to the other side without a hitch, though, one doesn't die under such banal circumstances, unless, of course, in a novel, son, don't you agree?, and when I got off at Margaret Bridge I walked up to the driver and apologized, he gave me a casual look, shrugged, it'd been your hide, not mine, then he didn't even look, any idea how many forms gotta be filled out *when that happens?*, it's no picnic, and he took off—Miki Görög skillfully slipped out of his coat, because he had the knack, he was good, his cells, his breathing were good, his lungs, everything about him, not like mine used to be, a mere technicality, a faculty, a facility of which there is no knowing yet how it will be used, something, in short, not quite complete in itself, Miki Görög's dexterity lacked nothing, it spoke for the character of his talent, concretely, his relationship to the ball which you could tell was a divine gift, like Ronaldinho's, for instance, in short, there is undoubtedly a spectacular visual element as well, son, or, to put it another way, these boys are brilliant in spite of the spectacular visual element, Zoli Varga was like that, and later Törőcsik, to bring up just two Hungarian examples, this elemental relationship to the ball, son, or our own gardener, about whom you wrote so beautifully, walking in the garden, playing keepy-uppy, he's in love with my mother, but she's just toying with him, won't you have a beer with me, György—my mother and a mug of beer!, and that little beer-foam mustache!, I'm not going into this in detail only because it has been written away from me in the shape of *Cutting It Short**—I'd love to, Lilike, it's just the thing after work, but especially with you, honestly now, György, if you please, could it be that you're paying court to me?, I must go now, Lilike, thank you for the beer, and if you please, Lilike, I don't even notice young women, if you know what I mean, Lilike, a dignified man, his

* The Czech writer Bohumil Hrabal's novel of 1974, made into a movie of the same name by Jiří Menzel in 1976.

body dignified, *a proud-bodied man*, he (Miki Görög) slipped out of his coat and with a *skillful* motion, as if from a coat hanger, quickly freed it of the fence, the train was tooting by then, its breaks screeching, he tried to leap up to the shoulder from the tracks but fell back, his bad knees wouldn't support his weight, they were always bloated, swollen, the strength gone out of them, he should've had surgery, what for, there's nothing wrong with them except for the pain, he kept saying in the pub, he jumped again, and this time he made it, theoretically at the last moment, but somebody got their calculations wrong, because it was the moment after the last, because the train caught the coat and it pulled him back down, and the train bashed into him, flung him back up, tossed him into the air, head-on into the iron lamppost, this was fatal, he lay in a pool of blood, his temple plowed over (like my father's?), nobody dared touch him, did he award it?, he kept asking as the blood came bubbling from his lips, did he award it, nobody knew what he was talking about, only when the ambulance came with Kaszás Junior, the dumbest Hungarian fullback, son, he knew right away, he awarded it, Mikikém, the bastard awarded it, don't you worry about a thing, he saw that there was nothing to be done, they carefully bundled him into the ambulance while Kaszás Junior kept talking to him, his hand to his bleeding temple, he awarded it, old buddy, it was a clear-cut foul and well inside the eighteen-yard line; Miki Görög had stopped attending the games a long time ago, he didn't care about anything or anyone, but he died with the if not happy yet satisfying feeling that during the last moment of his life, when all seemed lost, he managed to wrest a penalty kick, an all-important penalty kick, everything's fine, old man, god damn it to hell, Kaszás Junior said, his voice trembling, Kaszás Junior, whose shoe shop went out of business, and since then he's a paramedic, a paramedic with the handsomest shoes in town.

While he lived, Miki Görög was living proof that civilian thinking and football thinking, intelligence, sensitivity, are not the same thing, during a game we veritably stopped in our tracks and stared wide eyed, he didn't see, he saw only the game, he slipped inside the game, son, his exceptional knowledge was even more apparent during practice, so then, is it tied to him or is it not tied to him, a running joke, because the ball never rolled farther than two spans from his foot, which is possible only if the ball is tied to his ankle like the iron balls to the Count of Monte Cristo's ankles by those chains, he never looked at the ball, son, you'd think they had an agreement between them, as if a deal had been struck with the ball beforehand, and he didn't look at his teammates either, to see where they are, or where they'll be, what they're thinking, he had eyes only for the game, I can't repeat it often enough, son, the game, to see what it wants, what it will allow, I'm talking about him as if he were one of the great players, whereas I know perfectly well that he wasn't, his limits were already apparent in the youth team, still, because for a time he was the best, but he stopped growing, short of stature, weak, he could be easily pushed out of the way, for instance, whereas a couple of years earlier he couldn't, back then even Kaszás Junior ricocheted off him, as if he had a protective shell round him, an army of angels, son, an army of angels with karate skills, then the angels deserted him, and the poor man was left standing there with his impressive faculties to play soccer, son, for the greater glory of God, the good of the homeland and his own enjoyment, in that order, that's the prerequisite of quality, and I couldn't think of anything offhand for which this wasn't true, even if there is no God, and as for the homeland, it leaves me cold, his stupidity off the field wasn't glaring, because he was a very sweet boy (child), and so his teachers couldn't quite believe that total obtuseness, they wanted to mine the hidden treasure out of him, he shook his head and smiled, don't bother passing me the answer, it's not worth it, also, he played the guitar well, we first heard about the Beatles from him, she loves you, yeah, yeah, yeah, he even had his own band, three guitars, a drum, with me he would only talk about God, that He doesn't exist.

He doesn't exist.

I had just read Pascal's startling, veritably outrageous, not to say scandalous arguments based on probability theory, and in the true evangelical spirit, tried to force it down Miki's throat; we were just on our way to practice, the road that now leads to the take-out place that connects the big and small boulevards wasn't paved yet, from time to time an oil sprinkler chortled along it, spraying oil to stop the dust, I guess; we were on our way to practice, and the time it took to get to the field seemed sufficient for the clarification of the seeming (!) uncertainties regarding the Lord; in the spirit of Pascal as I understood it then and there, it wasn't God's existence that I needed to prove to the primary school boy Miklós Görög, merely to shed light on why it makes more sense to believe than not to believe, what it would have taken to prove it he wouldn't have understood anyway, he wouldn't have been up to it, he understood only that something is or it isn't, though with him everything revolved around the isn't, the isn't at home, at school, the isn't in his head, only on the soccer field was there the is, and then the same thing was inside, too, inside his head, and his feet, and suddenly he knew everything, and I do mean everything, son, and everything is an awful lot, he even knew that it's not he who has to play well but the team, because only then can he play well, he saw the team as a whole better than anybody, and he was dignified and tactful, an English lord, he didn't tell Uncle Vili what he should do and how he should do it in front of the others, he didn't even make suggestions, he just asked, look here, Coach, have you thought how Tomi shouldn't tackle, Little Frog should, he'll just have to *swerve* to the right a bit; Uncle Vili loved Miki Görög to distraction until he realized that he'd never be a great player, partly because of his bones, and partly because of all the there isn'ts, the nos, his life was made up of too many nos, he was a good coach and understood right away what his player was talking about, he even intuited the swerve, and he also knew that Miki knew what the consequence, the universal consequence would be, should Tomi not mark his man.

He talked about the nonexistence of God like two and two makes four, if he existed, I'd know about it (if he was around, that's what he said, and I shuddered squeamishly, as if I'd stepped into dog shit), isn't that right?, but I don't know about it, I can't talk to him and he don't talk to me, neither, and I don't know of anybody that does, that's when I cut in with Pascal, but as if I'd just thought of it, to wit, look, pal, it's simple, I'm better off than you because, let's posit that there is no God, in which case I've been attending Sunday Mass for nothing when could've slept till noon, but if God exists after all, you'll be in ep shit because nobody's gonna forgive you for not believing im, nobody likes being ignored, regardless of who they are, f they're God, and that's certainly worth reflection, be- n only risking the time I spend at Mass and maybe Bible in return, oh, so many things, eternal life!, Miki Görög whooped all of a sudden and broke into a run, a sprint, like after delivering the ball into the net, eternal life, shit, man, that ain't nothin'!, and he shot an arm up toward the sky, stopped, waited for me to catch up, how do you know about that, I asked, my mother said; his mother, like an old, unwieldy wardrobe (smelling of mothballs?), they had nothing in common except their walk, and also the way they ran, because once I saw her chase him, she was waiting in front of school, the minute Miki saw her he broke away to the left, more or less between the right back and the center half's classical position, son, concretely, toward the Small Woods, and his mother after him, both of them running, holding themselves like Flórián Albert, upper body slightly stiff, elbows bent and raised; proud as a wading bird, a Johnny Longshanks, while the hands, as if they had a life of their own, and though a chase scene, as if they weren't running at full speed, still, he came to one Bible class, how was it?, I asked, he shrugged, smelled of soap, who?, though I knew he meant our chaplain, he smelled of powder and soap, and he never went again, and I didn't press him, this smell of soap hovered between us like an explanation of sorts, something that, though it may not refute anything, yet it seems to stand in contradiction, however slight, with the existence of God, either-or, there's nothing there except that soapy smell of yours.

BALLROOM

We'd both grown too old for anything to do with soccer when many years later I ran into him on the boulevard. In my overwhelming, real joy I threw my arms around him, and then again, and then I was lost for words. He'd remained the old miracle for me, it was a cinch conjuring up his former figure, basically, he hadn't changed, you could see the furrows of the passing years on his face, the skin stretched taut against the cheeks, his whole body appeared dry, desiccated, but I wallowed in the onrush of sentiment, the nostalgic memories of him and could hardly restrain myself from telling him how lucky I was to have known him, how happy that my soap-smelling God had created a world in which a man like him is possible, and then I hugged him again, a mistake, I felt, but also that I can't do anything wrong, the just lauded quality of Creation is shining its light on me, it makes no difference what I do, what I say, this meeting contains the universe within it, or if not quite the universe, still, *minimo calculo* the past, present and future that our national anthem says we must atone for, but which, in short, we can now celebrate with glee.

After a goal he broke into a sprint, threw up his arms, then grinning, his face radiant, he walked backward, he kept his eyes on us and always thanked us, thanks, boys, I hadn't thought of it till now, back then we didn't even hear it, it made no sense, this is not the face I should have seen but the taut skin, the mummification, and then I wouldn't have fallen all over him with such an easy heart. I remembered his word, the kisser, when did you take a shy at your ma's kisser, old boy?, I wanted to say something, anything, words, once more unto the breach, dear friends, I greet you, Mikikém, this would have done the trick, he freed imself of my embrace, I could have seen, had I seen anything ıll, that he felt uncomfortable in my arms, in the arms of a ger, ma's dead.

ept my heartfelt sympathies.

a colossal prick you are, Count, now he used count like eds, his tone was so dispassionate, it made me wince, accept my heartfelt what?, what good was all that learning when you talk like the movies, I don't even know what heartfelt sympathy means, why must you go say stuff like that, and he waved me off. Instead of shame, I felt arrogant, death is life's answer to the question "Why?," but I didn't say it, he might have let fly at me, too, and I even refrained from saying, and you're a *small* prick, you haven't the vaguest how language works, what clichés are for, so forget it, we didn't know what to do with each other, if only the world were a soccer field, son, and eternity those certain ninety minutes plus what the referee might give, then you wouldn't be facing each other like this, locking horns, tripping over words, your life would gain momentum and you'd be kicking corner kicks on your half of the field with Emil Paták, the Rat, the world's most mediocre player, his brain could never process a radius greater than a yard and a half, but his technique was good, and with the ball passed back to you you'd release that Miki, force him out on the field, the world-field, son, where concepts couldn't worm their way in between perception and sense, the seeing would be conceptual, the mystics talk this way about the world, plus the sensitive-hearted but horse-blanket-rough left backs. There we stood, each wrapped in his own silence, as if we'd peed in our pants, my idiot mother went and died on me, I talked to Rat, he's a big shot at the cemetery now, a cemetery big shot, we should've thought of it, I said to him, you can do it for free, I don't need any extras, no priest, no audience, this ain't no picture show, for crying out loud, she just gotta be stuffed in the ground so the worms can get at her, and cremation costs, too, but he said it's no go, he's gotta pay the men, the digging, I'll dig it out myself, it's the least I can do for that dumb mother of mine, not dig it out for that shit bag?, got any idea, Count, how much a mother shits?, of course, she had the body for it, I could've fit inside her standing up, like in a ballroom, but no, scratch the ballroom, all that burping and farting, where does all that horrendous amount of fart air come from and how does air turn into fart?, well, Count?, that's the sort of thing you like to fret about, a barn, not a ballroom, you know what a barn is?, I do, and I dug it out, fucking rocky soil, the top layer clayey but then below it's all rock, I'm good with a pick and shovel, I placed three bottles of wine and a small bottle of pálinka for chaser on the adjacent grave, cursing my idiot mother, because if she's not so horrendous, there's less work, get me?, if she's not a barn, just a pigsty, right?, that fucking huge body, though by then just half of it, because they kept chopping away at her, first her left foot, so much for that, ma, you can kiss the team good-bye, she didn't think it was funny, though I said it for the sake of the humor, then her right foot, then from her right knee, will you stop, I says, what're you slicing her up for like a cheap stick of 2 penny salami, they don't even know what a 2 penny salami is anymore, look here, sir, because they called me sir, they're even more idiotic than you, Count, look here, me, sir, any other option, that's how the doc put it, and your mother will die, and that's the other thing, shit, the minute she starts dying, in a flash it's mother dear instead of ma, she a mother, me a sir, a good thing I don't have to go kiss her hand just because she farted me into the world.

We all gotta go sometime, I says to Doctor Doctor Bráner, he leered at me as if I were an animal, Miki Görög grinned like when we were kids, I saw in his eye what I'd seen in the eyes of the backs, he was scared, Count, remember when they didn't have a clue about our next move?, for a moment he was the great little player everyone of old stared at round-eyed, we stared, he shrugged, eh, get off it, it's no big deal, and he grinned like Ronaldinho, whereas he hadn't even been born yet, his poor unfortunate Brazilian mother hadn't farted him into the cool early morning sand of the Copacabana. But ma trusted that asshole, they amputated her leg from the left knee, too, at which point they finally let her have a social security wheelchair, have you ever wheeled a mother around on ninety square feet, you first knock everything over, a maternal wheelchair negotiates a turn slow as an ocean liner, a maternal wheelchair needs space, you rearrange the room, make room between the furniture, plus a small square-like space, like the turnabout at the bus station, but nothing's good enough for the maternal wheelchair, she growls and grumbles, won't shut her obscene trap, so you finally make your mind up to take her out on the street, outside the sun's shining, damn it, the trees offer shade, what more do'ya want?, but the old cunt starts screeching, before she was just grumbling but now she's screeching, will you stop, ma, before I take a shy at your kisser, but the maternal wheelchair just shrieks and squeals, everybody's looking, what's your problem?, ain't you seen a white man before?, you quicken your pace, then break into a run, as if you were at practice, a practice sprint with a legless mother, Count, how do you like them hill 'a beans?, and you grin, let 'em think you're running round whooping under the maples 'cause you're so damn full of cheer, she was shrieking like that because she was mortified, while I wheezed and gasped for air, breathing through my ass, I got no stamina left, there's nothing, last time, too, it took me three tries to kick the ball back into the school yard, why don't you use your hands, old man?, who the fuck are you fucking calling an old man?, that scared them, good, then they amputated both legs from the thigh, the wound got infected, the maternal wheelchair was of no use anymore, I cooked for her, mostly potatoes, we both love potatoes, and also chicken soup, and franks and rice with sausage, she hated it, eat, damn you, don't be so particular, have you any idea, Count, how good it feels getting the fuck back at them for fucking up your life when you were a kid, tea for two and two for tea, I sang, but she didn't get her tea, she got French éclairs!, because Little Lajos was made head of the new bakery, remember?, he was an awkward child, son, and not a player but a goalie all gung ho and not a jot of talent in his bones, son, he got the idea that he should be on good terms with the goal posts, he kept painting them, I know every gnarl in them, he'd announce, proud as a peacock, while I couldn't aim for the net without scoring, in the evening, when I looked in at the bakery, he let me have the leftover éclairs, quality first, Mikikém, that was my motto by the net, too!, I know, Lajoskám, while my motto was stuffing ma full of French éclairs, eat or you won't grow tall, at first she just nibbled at the top like a little mouse, and she ended up looking like one, small, mouse, and not just because they chopped off her leg that they threw in the garbage, she shrank, she kept nibbling away at that dry caramel shit, we even had it for breakfast, my tongue cleaving to the roof of my mouth, provided the old bitch was willing to eat, because she wouldn't just to spite me, she had to be fed, I sat on the side of her bed, there was plenty of room, after all, a bed's designed with legs in mind, two legs, more or less, in the morning I dipped the éclairs in milk to soften them, I fed her like an animal, it even occurred to me how she might go and bite me, the wounds healed, but smelled, I never said you stink, I said you smell, ma, but by then she didn't speak, she let me feed her, she let me talk to her, after all, you can't live in silence all the time, silence is a bitch, I talk to myself all the time, I bet you pray to avoid the silence, I think of all sorts of things when there's silence, all sorts, I heard that they brought defectives like ma over from Romania, begging automatons, I even said to her how she should be put out on the corner, too, an old whore is still a whore, they'd pump her with all that money, small change, but still, I even considered which corner, on the weekend maybe the Danube embankment, a short distance from the beer hall so she shouldn't put a blight on the fun but still be within eye-view, and on weekdays the bus stop, that's where the crowds are, and at night I'd shake all those forints outta you. We're gonna strike pay dirt!, in the twenty-fourth hour, ma!, because in the meantime Doctor Doctor Bráner announced that medical science has its limits, too, who the fuck cares about medical science, we've come to see him, not medical science, and he goes chopping bits off of my mother, my mother doesn't have limits, only medical science?, I was doing all the talking for ma by then, voice courtesy of József Láng, sir, will you kindly stop shouting, why should I, wise guy, you got legs, my mother hasn't got legs, you're not being fair, sir, *fayr* is how he said it, he thought I didn't know fair, fair's the way the English used to play way back, they don't go into contortions in the grass, there's no circus, mud from Swan Lake, they spring back up and next thing they give as good as they got, that's what fair is, and as for you, you better come up with something, consult with your fucking medical science, go on slicing into her or what have you, at which point ma spoke up, it was the last sentence she'd ever speak, but my cunt, you can't have my cunt, little fag.

Mehr Licht, or you can't have my cunt, little fag, it amounts to the same thing.

I started digging in the dark, after working hours, for them after, for me before, the Rat insisted, and after the second bottle of wine I was in no rush, I knew I'd be done in plenty of time, this is one thing you can't ruin, you old bitch, this is gonna be done proper, you can go lay there with your worms for company, barn-mother, there's a ball on in the barn, I thought of the worms like my mother's pals, I stopped work and looked down at the pit and imagined ma in there with her blue feather quilt, she was always alone, I inherited that from her, at the pub and the factory, too, she liked the factory, she made those Trapper jeans, indigo dyed and shrink resistant, she used to say, the size alteration's always under three percent, who cares!, she liked her work because she was good at it, I was sitting on the mound of earth, Count, did you know that there are angels?, that filthy bitch, my mother, who had the nerve to go and die on me, she knew, everybody in the city asleep, except for me, and me looking at the sky, shit, you'd think there was a ball being held up there, too, inside ma the worms, up in the sky the stars whirling round and round, then I drank the pálinka, too, my muscles are bad, sitting's no good, standing's no good, lying down by my mother's side is no good, have you thought, Count, how there's a dance on every night, two dances, Rat brought my mother out on a motor-hearse ahead of the others, and also a wooden cross, he wore a suit, the dead deserve respect, Mikikém, sure, Rat, sure, he brought an extra bottle of medicinal pálinka, I didn't think he had it in him, on the other hand, he always played better than he knew how, I wonder why, maybe because he ran so much, he had good lungs, he and I scooped the earth on the coffin together, this thud, that's the worst part, Rat said, in some places they cover the coffin with a blanket, but then it thumps and that's not much better, he worked faster and better than me, I drank most of the bottle on my own, the thud left me cold, if it's gotta thud, it's gotta thud, poor clod, what the heck choice has it got except thud, or maybe thump, then we leveled the ground with the back of our shovels, Mikikém, he said, raising the cross off of the ground, I didn't have anything put on it, I don't even know your dear departed mother's name, dear departed mother, suit, sympathies, what the fuck are you hoping to get out of it, Count?, I don't need a cross, of course you do, Mikikém, even Ronaldinho crosses himself after a strike, I thanked him again, and said how I hadn't kicked a ball in such a long time, I don't even know what a strike is anymore, oh, Mikikém, of course you do, it's when the ball crosses the goal line at its full length, in short, Count, ma got a proper burial, at her full length, and now they're haggling over the details with the one smelling of soap, is that what you wanted to hear?